Never Say Never

Never Say Never

Book Five, The Fangirl Chronicles

by C.M. Kars

Cover design by Indigo Chick Designs

Editing by Aquila Editing

Contents

Never Say Never

FANGIRL CHRONICLES #5

C.M. KARS

OTHER WORKS BY C.M. KARS

The Never Been Series
Never Been Kissed
Never Been Nerdy
Never Been Loved
Never Been Under the Mistletoe
Never Been Boxed Set
Sera & Hunter: A never been collection

The Fangirl Chronicles
Fangirling Over You
To All the Footballers I Loved Before
Bias Wrecked
Pucked Romance
Never Say Never

The Cuffing Season Series
Get Cuffed
Cuffing and Turkey Stuffing
Cuffing and Tree Trimming
Cuffing New Year's Resolutions

WANT TO STAY IN THE KNOW?

----

*S*ign up for my newsletter here for free books, info on my upcoming releases, cover and blurb reveals and to talk about all the things there are to fangirl over.

FREE BOOKS

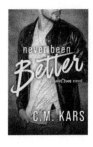  

6

See you there!

AUTHOR'S NOTE

H ello reader,
    If you've been around since the beginning way back when in 2014 when I published *Never Been Kissed*, I know that you've been waiting for this book.

Well, finally, Russia's book is here, and I hope you love it.

Expect cameo appearances from the Never Been gang (honestly, Dean pops up often), and Easter eggs. If you think you've found some, come to my Facebook page here, and let me know what you've found!

Is this the end for (an older) Sera, Hunter and Matty, along with all the rest of the gang?

Wait for it... *I never say never.*

If you want to stay in the know, sign up for my newsletter and you'll see what's coming your way soon!

Happy reading,

C.M. Kars

ONE

As a tattoo artist, I know that nothing is truly ever in black and white. I usually like to live and dream in color—I kinda struggle with the shades of gray in real life, in my drawings and my relationships, wanting bursts of happy color everywhere, making life simpler.

Tattoos and body modification have been around for a long, long time, and I'm just trying to make my mark, like everyone else.

Is it any wonder that I excel in tattooing colorful designs?

Life requires excitement, and body modification is just a small way that you can do that.

Humans in general just like adorning their bodies with jewelry, with tattoos, like we're all searching for something we weren't born with, and it's this that makes me love my job most of the time, love the work, and the creation ninety percent of the time.

But today...today's gonna be a hard day.

"Are you comfortable, Jackie?" I ask, snapping on my gloves, triple-checking my station, giving Jackie that one last minute of privacy to think about what she's doing and what she wants done on her skin permanently.

My own heart's a weighted stone in my chest as I keep my head down and pretend I'm busy setting up. I've thought about placement and pigmentation when tattooing over scar tissue, but in the end, it's still Jackie's choice if she wants to go through with it or not.

Jackie's the canvas, and I'm the conduit and the artist, channeling her wishes into reality.

I've never been more terrified, and I don't want to screw this up.

I keep my eyes pinned to my hands, intertwining my fingers, making sure there's no more air in my gloves, stalling as long as I'm able.

"Yeah, yeah, I am. Thanks. Do...do you think I can get some water first, though? Or do you think I'm going to have to pee really bad halfway through?" Jackie asks.

I turn to finally look at her, this kid who's five years younger than me, who's already had a double mastectomy and who wants to cover up the surgery scars with tattoos.

I smile at her, shrugging.

"We stop anytime you like. I'm here for you today."

"Oh, shit, really?" Jackie's hands go up to her pale face, skin flushing pink all too quickly that I get worried about her. "Now I feel kind of bad."

"Why? We got the back room, and the door's closed for privacy, and you can leave anytime you want, and we can schedule another session, okay? There's no rush here."

"It's just gotten really real, you know?" The kid shakes her head, her hair cut in a cute pixie cut and her eyebrows are drawn on in a wicked Maleficent-esque arch that's pretty awesome if you ask me. "I don't know how I'm going to be with the pain."

I smile at her. "I've had grown men burst into tears in front of me, right at this very bench. Trust me. I've seen it all. There's nothing wrong with tears. Okay?"

It's the middle of the afternoon, and the piece I've traced out for her is sitting in front of me, ready to be placed on her skin where I'll make adjustments if I need to once she's seen it on her body.

I'm nervous.

I haven't been nervous about doing a tattoo in a very long time, like, since my apprenticeship.

Tattoos can be anything really—badges of honor some of the time, or words that we don't ever want to forget that we carry around on patches of skin (hips, ribs, arms, fingers), portraits of loved ones that won't fade with time like a discarded picture or a corrupted file, and sometimes, too, the tattoos hide the ugly, angry parts of ourselves and make them more beautiful.

I have all kinds of tattoos – some were for fun, while others were a way of tricking my brain that I'm more than the sum of my parts.

I shake back the baby hairs that have escaped my ponytail, the long tail of hair hitting my lower back, tickling the dermal piercings I have there through my shirt, making me shiver in reaction.

"Ready, Betty?" I ask, grinning at her when the kid looks at me in confusion. "I know you're Jackie. Come on, hop up on the table and let me just adjust it...perfect. You still want that cup of water?"

Jackie nods, her throat working on a dry swallow. "Yes...yes, please."

I grab her a little cup from the water cooler in the corner, the familiar hum and gurgle getting my mind focused as I get ready to place the stencil on Jackie's chest.

When the kid drops her hands from her chest, I try—really, I try—to stifle my wince of sympathy, of imagined pain while I look at the scarred skin over her chest, where her boobs used to be, the scars still looking angry-pink even though I've been assured they're days under eighteen months old.

The paperwork has been signed, the concerns waived, and honestly, it's not like I'm going to make the scars worse. It's not like I can give her back what she's lost, but I can just make her see something beautiful in the mirror when she looks at herself.

After Jackie gives me the thumb's up on placement and checks herself out in the mirror, I let her lie down again and bring my station of inks and my machine closer. I do one last check that my cohesive wrap is thick enough that it's comfortable for my hand to hold the tattoo grip.

I set up my stool so I'm at a comfortable height, and look at her, Jackie's eyes shining bright as she looks at the ceiling, the fluorescent lighting in here making her pallor even more apparent.

"I'm going to have to touch you now, okay, Jackie?" I ask, making sure one last time that she still wants this.

Jackie swallows, her throat working, making a hurt sound, but she squares back her shoulders, pushing them deeper into the bench we've set up, getting comfortable.

"Make me beautiful again," she whispers, and *shit,* I have to fight back the tears welling in my own eyes.

"Kiddo," I say, and she snorts, knowing that I'm not that much older than her. She's a client referred to me from another client, and honestly, it's not like I'm going to talk bad about Jackie to that client if she doesn't want to do this. People shouldn't do what they don't want to. "You already are."

Jackie sniffs hard, right before the sob is racking her ribs, and she covers herself up with her arms and I back off, tugging up the shirt that she'd discarded on a nearby seat, putting it on top of her. "I'm okay," she says, voice cracking. "I'm okay, *I'mokayi'mokayi'mokay…*"

I make her sit up, adjusting the bench so we're at seated position, and try to calm her down, afraid to touch her without permission.

"Can I…uh, fuck, I wasn't going to do this, I really wasn't, but lying back like that felt like getting rolled into surgery again—" she gasps, fighting for air, fighting her own body's response. "Can you just give me a hug? Please?"

I make sure my station's clear of me so I don't bump into it, and only then do I get up and wind my arms around her, putting us chest to chest, wincing that it might make her feel worse, but not really knowing how else to hug her.

"You're okay, you're good," I murmur, holding her tight to me, this stranger, this kid who's had to go through so much in such a short amount of time. I rock us a little side to side, sniffing hard to try to chase my own tears away.

Last thing you want in a tattoo artist is to have blurry vision right before they start permanently inking your skin.

That would be bad.

"I'm sorry," she moans miserably, still clutching her shirt to her chest when I let her go.

"You don't have to do this, you know? You don't have to do this right now."

"You're, like, the nicest person I've ever met."

I laugh, which makes her laugh, and I'm able to lean back a bit, to let her breathe on her own, to let her hold herself up on her own. "I'm not, not really. I'm exceptionally hard to love, for instance. I've been told so, many times." I wave to all of me.

Let's not got into the fact that I self-sabotage, or the way I've been trying to make myself more palatable for my dates. Nope, not doing it anymore. It's all of me or nothing.

Sounds terrifying, though…

Jackie shakes her head, wiping at her eyes, and then mopping at her face when I shove the tissue box at her. "That can't be true. You're like super put-together and your tattoos are awesome, and I noticed you matched the shade of your nail polish to your lipstick. I feel so boring in comparison. Me and my titless chest."

I snort, the sound coming out louder than intended and there's a second where we both freeze, question our very existence where a sound like that could be made by a human being and the both of us burst into laughter.

"I'm sorry, I don't know why I did that. I'll either laugh or cry when I'm nervous and I don't know what that was, *shit*," I say, flapping my hands around my face, trying to keep the tears (from laughter this time) to stay away from my mascara because I've got somewhere to be after this, and I need mascara runs like I need more eyeshadow palettes to my already massive collection—which is not really.

"No, no, I feel better now, I do. Can we continue?"

We both sober up, and Jackie drinks some more water and then finally lies back down again, looking more *alive* than before, not scared, not worried, just *alive*, present.

I go through the motions again, bringing my station of inks closer, bringing my tattoo machine around and asking again for permission to touch around her chest area while I lean in and am about to start tracing the outline.

"Ready?"

"Yeah, yeah I'm ready. Make me shine brighter."

I nod, that's all I can do.

I don't really wanna go to Katie's new condo.

I'm not feeling up to it after the draining day I had today, after pouring my heart and soul and my intense concentration into Jackie's tattoo, wanting it to be perfect. It took more than a few centering techniques to get my focus back on track instead of thinking what it would be like if our positions were reversed.

It helped that Jackie was a talker—some clients are like that, hoping to distract themselves from the pain. Others stay quiet, keep themselves contained while they fight against it, using everything they have to keep it at bay instead of just *feeling* it, hot and bright and a little sweet along the edges.

Life is pain, in one way or another—that's just the way it is.

And I'm in pain, too.

My back's sore enough that I know that I need a good stretch or an hour yoga sesh to get the tightness out of it, my fingers still feeling the phantom vibration of the tattoo machine, not to mention my chest, being heart-sick over what Jackie lost, of what could have been.

We finished the outline and partial shading in time for me to rush back home to get changed, to wash off the sweat and sadness, even managing to keep my hair under the shower cap.

My eyeshadow's kept intact while I wash the rest of my face, just wanting to wash off the remnants of my foundation and lipstick, my skin ready for re-application as soon as I step out.

I wear my black jeans, pairing them with my sapphire blue blouse that hits me at the waist, showing off my hip tattoo and the belly chain I've got connected around my belly button ring. Half of my wardrobe is strategically figuring out a way to show off my tattoos, my piercings, and all the parts of my body that are bedazzled, bejeweled and art-marked all around.

I fuss with my hair, letting it loose from its tail, fluffing out the waves and half-curls that come from my mom's side, the black roots coming in deeper and deeper, until I'm going to cave and dye it another color instead of keeping it this particular shade of white blonde.

I make sure my eyeliner is just as sharp as it was during the day, nodding at my reflection when I notice that the liner didn't really budge all that much in the first place and there's very little for me to fix.

I can hear that Elena's bustling around in the living room, always waiting for me it seems because I'm perpetually late all the time, just because I'm convinced the space-time continuum doesn't move the same for me as it apparently does for everyone else.

I don't do it intentionally, and Elena knows that, but she can't keep her impatience to herself, and I get yelled at just as I finish putting on another layer of eyeliner in my waterline, smoking it out a little since we're going to dinner, and I want everyone to appreciate the blue halo-eye look I created this morning.

"Okay, okay, I'm ready, sorry," I say, my giant bag packed with dog treats because Katie's got three of the cutest pups in the world and I want to be showered in canine devotion at least as soon as I walk in, and I don't care if I have to bribe them with treats.

"Hey," Elena calls, making me stand up tall after securing my sexy boots (the ones that'll destroy my feet by the end of a workday, but I'll wear them if I'm going to be standing for less than ten minutes), balancing on one foot before going lopsided.

Elena, my best friend in the entire world, who's as opposite to her cousin Katie as a person can be, but I think it only makes her *better*, is perceptive beyond all recognition.

You learn a lot about people when you're quiet, when you listen, and I'd want Elena DiNovro on my team for whatever shit life's gonna throw our way—she's bound to notice something I won't. I smile at her, but it feels forced.

"Are you okay?" she asks, closing and locking the door behind her, a suspicious blush on her cheeks. Looks like Elena was getting up to something behind the closed door and his name is Beckett Donoghue.

"Yeah, I'm good. Let's go eat, yeah?" I'm tired, emotionally exhausted, but I made a promise to my friends that we'd hang out tonight, so that's what we're gonna do. Even if I need a nap, and to get over the fact that I've gotten some really awful comments on the hellfire dating app I'm on.

Some guys have no idea how to talk to a woman, like, at all.

It's infuriating and disheartening.

I'm so used to it that I have no idea what I would do if someone were to actually show *genuine* interest in me as a person, instead of a body.

Elena nods, her careful gaze moving over my features cataloguing, analyzing, and when she's satisfied, I'm able to lead the way back down to my car, and I drive us to Katie's condo building.

I find an empty spot in the visitors' parking section (*yeah, man*) at the building. We head upstairs, my feet already starting to hurt, my stomach yowling from hunger pangs, and the bag of doggy treats is crinkling in my giant bag that holds more of my life in it than I'd care to admit.

"You didn't have to pick me up, I could have met you here," Elena says, knocking on the door as I ruffle the top of my hair, adding some more volume, and fixing the eyelashes I have on, wondering if the glue's finally going to fail me right at this very moment.

While Elena and I used to go to Katie's old place more than twice a month but not quite once a week, the new condo that she and Dean live in now's new to the both of us. Katie's been fussing about the decor, and about making it feel like home for *at least* six months, and we've finally been given the golden ticket to come over and have dinner.

Of course it helps that Katie's boyfriend, Dean, is a chef and makes the best kind of food in whatever cuisine you're feeling at any given time. I think Katie DiNovro won the lottery with that guy, and he seems to love cooking for her, loves feeding her...in more ways than one, hah.

The dogs are whimpering on the other side of the door, little barks of excitement that the both of us can hear in the hall, and I practically vibrate on the other side of the door, shaking with how much I need to *see* the pups, *pet* the pups, *feed* the pups.

"All right, all right, boys, back up, back up. Best boys." Katie's voice floats through the door, and then the lock's being turned and the door's opening, and I have secured the bag of dog treats making sure all of the dogs' attention will be on me, and only on me for the next little while.

I need it, I need to look at good, kind animals that'll look at me like they might think I'm the best person in the world after a hard day at work.

There's three of them: Pongo, Kal and Potter, and they look straight at me, knowing I've got the goods.

"Here, kiddos," I sing-song, moving forward and crouching down while opening my bag, the pups still in their seated positions, like sentinels, waiting for the *okay* to come and smother me with attention and devotion.

"Such good puppies, the best puppies in the world," I baby-talk to them, rifling the bag of treats in my purse, struggling to open the problematic plastic until the bag comes apart with a rattle, and I lose more than a few treats in the cavernous space of my purse.

I dole out treats, one to each of them, when Katie lets them come towards me to accept food, and Elena's saying something in the background, but I'm on cloud nine right now, high above every little worry and stress and the look on Jackie's face when I told her she was already beautiful, curling into herself as if her heart was a black hole and she was collapsing in on herself.

I stare into Pongo's (the Dalmatian) warm brown eyes, getting a flick of his tongue on my nose for my trouble, making me laugh in delight. I place kisses on his white speckled coat, leaving behind some of my chocolate-brown lipstick, rubbing at his coat to make sure it doesn't hurt his skin.

I then get pummeled by the littlest of the trio, Potter, demanding attention by putting his front paws on my thigh, making his tiny frame taller in comparison to either Pongo and Kal. Ah, so *cute!*

Elena's talking above me to Dean, and my stomach gives another growl that has Potter looking down at my torso like he can hear it (of course he can hear it, he's a pup) and then back up at my face, in a canine version of *'what the heck was that?'.*

Potter's tail moves a mile a minute, and then Dean's voice starts to make sense once I stop talking to the dogs, and start paying attention to my surroundings now, smiling up at Katie in a hello.

I mean, I know if I had dogs, I would take zero offense if people visiting my house were to say hello to the dogs first. I mean, I would love that, but Katie sometimes...I just don't know with her. Even after all this time of being friends with her and caught between the two DiNovros that are polar opposites, sometimes I don't know where I stand.

"Okay, okay, boys," Dean says, voice taking on an authoritative tone, his giant Viking ass is coming towards us, and it just makes him bigger, seeing him from this angle.

"It's like I don't even feed you, I swear. Come on, come on. Sophie, please, they're gonna expect it from you now every single time you walk through that door."

I grin, then get up and move to take off my boots, trying to toe them off without squatting back down again, the pain in my back flaring up when I move a little too much to the right, but Dean's already there, holding onto my arm so I can hold myself steady and not faceplant before I've eaten Dean's delicious food.

I look over at a person I don't know, my eyes riveted to his interesting face.

It's not going to be only the four of us here—there seems to be another guest.

A guy I haven't seen before. A guy I *wished* I'd seen before, *oh my God.*

I get attraction, I do, and yeah, there's times when some male clients come in and I have to put on my 'professional' face and tamp down on ogling because in the end we're all just bodies—in all forms and sizes, and I shouldn't prioritize one over the other, but this guy, *this guy?*

Why is the sudden realization that I find this random stranger attractive like a punch to the gut, making me lose my breath?

It could be because you've been on crappy dates, and maybe it's because he hasn't opened his mouth yet...

It could be the way his hair is long on top, dirty blond, shaved all around in an undercut for the ages, and his eyes are the kind of blue that you can see and notice from across the room, too bright and icy.

His nose is a little crooked, leaning on one side more than the other, as if he's gotten punched there at least once. His close-lipped grin is a little cruel around the edges, the kind that you can't tell if he's laughing with you or *at you*, the kind where you don't know where you stand with him.

I reach blindly for Elena's hand, feeling as if I've lost all the feeling in my feet, unsure if I'm standing or sitting or what the hell, but knowing I need Elena there to hold me up, like she's done more often than I can say.

I pull in a deep breath, walking forward without any real input from my brain, stilted walking like I'm a newly converted zombie still trying to figure out its reanimated limbs, reanimated gait.

My hand shoots out ready for a handshake, again without any input from my brain, as if I'm watching myself in a darkened movie theater, throwing popcorn at the screen and cringing at myself in the scene.

"Hi, I'm Sophie."

The guy smiles, and it takes away that cruel edge around his mouth and transforms it, erasing it altogether, the smile inviting you to spend all day with him and hopefully all night, the kind that makes my skin tingle and my breath catch in my throat.

I watch him as he pulls out his hand from his pocket, connecting our hands in a solid handshake, making me jerk at the contact, electrified from head to toe.

Oh, no. Not now.

"Hi," he says, voice melodic with some kind of accent that I can't place, even living in a city like Montreal. "I'm Tommy, but everyone calls me Russia."

TWO

I blink at him, at this stranger, while still holding onto his hand, not wanting to let go. I like the feel of it, the weight of it in my own grip.

"Like...you're named after the whole country?"

Tommy (Russia) laughs, his head bowing back to glance up at the ceiling. Even the column of his throat is ridiculously attractive, all that perfect skin that could be tatted up, and would look beautiful in colorful geometric designs.

My fingers itch to draw something out right here, right now.

There's an explosion of fireworks going off in my brain, bursting with colors and whizzing sounds all around as I keep looking at him.

"Your nickname is based off an entire country? Is that allowed?" I ask, realizing too late how much I sound like an idiot.

But honestly...*Russia*? Who gets a nickname like that?

Is this some sort of willy joke that just went completely over my head? Are guys naming them after whole countries now? Is it supposed to be huge because Russia is the world's largest land mass?

I glance down at the crotch of his jeans, a fleeting movement of my eyes, but I'm pretty sure he catches me looking down and investigating, so there's that, and I'll probably be thinking about this moment, wanting to die of embarrassment, from now until I leave this poor planet behind.

Shit, shit, shit.

"I'm from there," he says, and I drop his hand like a hot potato, rubbing my palm against the thigh of my jeans, wishing I could go out on the balcony for fresh air, but I don't want to seem rude.

Sorry, I'm having some sort of allergic-type reaction to your hotness, and it makes me want to run away! Especially when you're sort of looking at me like you're interested back.

Yeah, that'll go over well.

"Oh, cool, cool, cool."

It's not cool, it's definitely not *cool* enough to say it three times in a row. What the hell?

I'm never tongue-tied, twisted up like this.

He's just attractive! I've found guys attractive before, there's nothing to it! So why is my brain having an epic fart and refusing to *engage* and work at 100%?

"When did you come to Canada?" I ask, and Katie snorts behind me like *she knows* how hard of a time I'm having and having a grand old time at my expense.

"When I was twelve. Cool?" He grins at me, and there's an explosion of butterflies in my belly, and that's it, *that's it*, I'm not doing this again, falling for good looks with nothing to back them up because I'm always being the idiot who wants more.

Nope, this guy is probably Casual City, and I'm not looking for that right now. I've got *shit* to do and banging a hot guy on the side and then questioning what everything means after the fact does not sound like my idea of a good time.

Thanks, but no thanks.

I nod dumbly, then whirl around to Elena. "I forgot something in the car!" I practically yell, needing space, needing to get myself together, because yeah he's hot, and it's been forever, but I'm not going to be a slave to my ovaries, definitely not going to be a slave to my ovaries.

Nope, nope, nope. Not me. *Definitely not me.*

"Yeah, yeah," Elena says, champion friend that she is, hustling me out the door too quickly that we both realize I don't have my boots on, and I'm staring down at my own feet like they've betrayed me.

I press my back against the hallway wall, taking in deep, even and measured breaths, trying to ignore the heat pooling in my belly, appalled at myself that a single look from Russia (Jesus Christ, his name is Tommy. *Tommy, Tommy, Tommy!*), has made my stupid knees go weak.

This kind of stuff doesn't happen in real life—it only gets talked about with those dumb idiots who believe in love at first sight. As if. Yeah, right. In the words of Elena DiNovro, 'no way, no how'.

"I can't go back in there," I say, clutching at Elena's shoulders, fingernails digging in. I shake my head. "It's been a hell of a day, and I sounded so dumb, and he's so hot, what the hell? Why is that allowed? I wasn't mentally prepared for any of this!" I groan, dropping my hands from Elena's shoulders and bending at the waist, because apparently the air down at this level is a bit better than the air when I'm completely vertical. I haven't been a teenager in a long time, I'm not prone to these kinds of moments anymore.

What the hell is this!?

"Are you okay? You're super flushed." Elena's voice sounds suspiciously like she's laughing at me, but I'm not lifting my head to confirm. I need to keep breathing down here until I'm back to normal.

"Yeah, yeah, my skin's about to melt off. What about it?" I say, smacking my hands against my face, the temperature difference between my cold hands and face startling me, even if it feels *amazing*.

"Are you flustered because of that guy...Russia? I can't believe they call him Russia," Elena says, and the surprise in her voice has me looking up at her. Elena's shaking her head at the idea of calling Russia *Russia*.

"But I guess it makes sense. It'd be like if we moved somewhere else and they'd call us Canada, or Maple Syrup, or something. I don't know." Elena shrugs, and I know she's just babbling to try and calm me down, but it's not working.

It's not working!

"I'm...I'm having a crisis, here, Elena. You know me, right? You know who I am, how I am when it comes to guys. And yes, while I have dabbled out and about with many a date, I have never felt this kind of reaction to a guy I just met. I usually get like this *after* I've talked to them for *at least* an hour and figured out if the date in question is a jerk or not."

I shake my head from side to side.

"What's the matter with me? *I want to marry him*, and you know how I am about marriage! And I want to tattoo every single inch of his skin. He'd make the *perfect* canvas. Did you see him? Did you see how perfect he would look, even better than he is now? I'd pass out for sure," I whisper-yell between gulping down breaths.

I chuck off my coat, letting it hang down my arms while I start to fan myself rather ineffectually, feeling sticky and hot.

"Am I dying?! Elena, *am I dying!?*"

Elena DiNovro, best friend since 2011, is *laughing* at me in my most crucial time of need and I want to punch her, but I can't go around hurting my hands like that when I need them to do my job.

So maybe I'll settle for kicking her hard or stomping hard on her foot, let her hobble around for a bit because I'm having a meltdown

There's no other reason for me to be acting like this, *no reason at all*.

"Can you relax? You're not dying, you're just about ten years too late to the fangirling game. Jesus, I never thought I would see the day where Sophie Kincaid is losing it over a hot guy. Wow, only you. You've got *all* these feelings and you don't know what to do with them, right?"

I nod weakly because she's making a lot of sense, either that or she's psychic, and I think as her best friend, she would have told me if she was.

"So your fandom isn't the Habs, or some show, or soccer team or whatever, hell, even a celebrity would make sense right now. Nope, you had to go and make it complicated. Your fandom..." Elena says, knighting me from one shoulder, then pulling her arm up and over my head to land on my other shoulder with an invisible sword, and honestly, who died and made her queen of the land?

"...Is now Russia, I don't even know his last name, population: one Sophie Kincaid."

"Why are you grinning at me like that? What did I ever do to you, huh? Huh?" I slap at her placating *there, there* gesture on my shoulder when I really want to hit something, or hell, *draw* it out, anything to make me forget about this moment. I want to leave, really.

I don't want to face my weird reaction to the guy, having a meltdown outside like some dumb kid unable to be adult enough to wrangle her feelings, deaden the sharp brightness of them so that I can last through the night with my sanity intact.

Maybe this time will be different, huh?

I strangle that tiny, little beacon of hope. I don't believe in any of this. There has to be something wrong with him, and he'll end up disappointing me like all the crummy dates I've had in the past.

I'll get over this weird initial reaction.

I pull in a deep breath through my nose, exhale through my mouth, square my shoulders and head back towards Katie's front door, Elena blocking my way.

I can turn off this reaction, I can. I do it all the time at work. Hot guys come in all the time for tattoos, and you don't see me losing it all the freaking time like this. What makes Tommy so different? I'm not going home, though.

I'm going to go straight inside and confront my fears in the form of a man nicknamed after a country. So he knows I find him ridiculously attractive. So what?

Besides, I'm hungry, but I'm also the nervous kind of nauseous and I don't know if I can eat.

What a dilemma. "Nothing, Sophie, it's just that you get it now. You totally get it about having these intense feelings for someone you never met before, and I'm going to sit here and watch it all with a big, fat grin on my face, waiting for the prime moment to say *I told you so* when the time comes."

I slap at her shoulder. "Rude. The rudest. Help me get back inside." I hold up a finger. "Wait, if anyone asks, I'll say I forgot my phone charger, and it ended up being in my coat pocket. No one has to know about this, okay? Okay, Elena?"

Elena takes an extra second to nod slowly, grinning all the while, like she's got me.

And yup she does.

I take a few deep breaths, the emotional whiplash from this afternoon with tattooing Jackie and now standing here like a horn dog from Horndog City is enough to give me a headache or make me doubt everything and everyone.

Is this *The Matrix?* Is it glitching?

Can someone fix it so I can go back to normal, please?

We walk back into Katie's apartment, Elena leading the way, because yeah, I need a few more seconds to compose myself in front of Russia (even his nickname is making me feel tingly, what the hell?) before I take off my coat completely, and Katie lets out a whistle.

I am not embarrassed of my body, I am not.

I love the way it moves and works, the way it keeps my brain and thoughts and feelings swimming around in my skull while the rest of me gets to move around. I like how it bends and twists when I need it to, and I love the way I'm able to make art with what I've been given.

I have nothing to be ashamed of.

But I still get shy.

I'm as loud as can be in what I put on my body, both art and clothing, and sometimes that gives people the wrong impression. I've been working hard on it being a 'them' problem and not a 'me' problem.

If it were just Elena, Katie and Dean, I wouldn't mind so much wearing this blouse, showing off my artwork since Dean's *always* curious about getting his next tattoo, Katie sighing good-naturedly (I think, it's hard to tell sometimes), and he's always got a million questions that I'm excited to answer.

And while I don't mind my body jewelry being shown off, or my tattoos, I still get looks sometimes, usually from people older than me sure, but still get quite a few from people my own age, looking at me up and down like I'm seconds away from ruining their lives.

Image still matters, what we look like still matters, even if I'm just a white girl with tattoos. That's what people see first, and that's what Tommy sees, too.

Dean clears his throat, then claps his hands together, the sound like a crack of lightning in the living room, making me jump.

"Baby, what the hell was that?" Katie says, and I glance over at her, the look on her face affronted and confused. "We're right here, right here."

"Yup, yup, yup," Dean says, continuing to rub his hands together like he hurt himself after clapping them so hard. Damn it, I love Dean Carter, I really do.

Obviously not in that way or Katie would skin me alive.

Thanks, but I'll be skipping the whole being flogged alive torture thing.

"Russia, come and help me in the kitchen," Dean says, clamping down onto one of Russia's shoulders and dragging him into the kitchen like a puppy that's been caught by the back of the neck. Russia goes without much fuss, his eyes travelling over me in a way that makes everything in my body (and brain) go *yes, yes, yes* and not *no, no, no.*

Huh.

"Wow," Katie says, crossing her arms over her chest. "Could you two keep your longing looks to a minimum, yeah? I've got to eat in front of you two."

"Shut up, shut up! He can hear you!" I try to bring my hands over Katie's mouth, that blood-red lipstick that I need to ask the shade of later about to get smeared, but she growls at me, and I resign myself to letting her speak in her own damn house.

"No, he can't. Dean's making enough noise for people in Melbourne, Australia to hear. You're good. Really, though, Sophie—Russia?" Katie notches her thumb over her shoulder, as if I don't know that Russia is in the kitchen, a half-room away with the way the walls are in this place, maybe even lurking just around the corner.

Another bang comes out of the kitchen and a muffled "*sorry*" before there's more banging and I wonder how Katie's neighbours don't charge her front door and demand answers for the noise Dean makes all by himself.

"I swear, that man, he drives me crazy," Katie sighs, looking up at the ceiling. "Wouldn't want to live without him, though." She knuckles her forehead, as if coming to this realization *again* after so many years, and then looking at me, eyes narrowed. Her eyeliner is bomb today, too, the kind of matte black I've been looking for but don't want to spend a fortune on.

Well, I guess I'm going to have to buy whatever Katie tells me to buy.

"How have you two not met before? I'm sure you've met before," Katie says, tapping at her lips with her black-lacquered fingernail, and I'm awed to find that there's no patchiness to her lipstick, nothing flaking off.

Yup, totally need that shade and brand. Give it to me!

Elena steps up to plate. "Yeah, they did, a couple of years ago, at Sera's surprise birthday bash you had at your old place. I brought Sophie with me, and we all hung out. It was nice. It was before...yeah, it was fun." Elena fishes out her phone from her back pocket, looking down at the message or whatever, smiling down at her phone like it's the most precious thing.

A spike of jealousy rises in me, clogging my throat at the sight of my best friend, *my best friend*—who has been through so much in the past couple of years with her stupid family, those *assholes*—being besotted with her boyfriend, Beckett. It took a while to get there, but it's soft and sweet, and I want it, too. *I want it, too.*

Aaah.

"Sorry, sorry." Elena glances up to me watching her, tilting her head at me in silent question. "What? What's up?"

"You're happy?" I ask, and Elena blushes, and it's adorable, and I will kill anyone else who makes her sad, even if it's Beckett.

I have friends, colleagues I work with who *know* things, or have watched one too many episodes of *Criminal Minds* and fancy themselves as amateur profilers.

I mean, sure, but they know things, and in turn, I know things, and fact of the matter is it wouldn't be that hard to hide a body.

I don't think.

"Yeah. I am. You?" Elena nods, like she's expecting a positive answer from me, too.

"I'm pretty good today. Did a tattoo on this kid—she's not that little, she's like twenty-one, she had to get a double mastectomy, and she wanted me to tattoo over the scars. Wanna see what I came up with?" I ask, turning to get my phone out of my coat pocket, bringing up my sketch that only had minor alterations to it once it was on her skin, taking into account the slopes of her body, the muscle tone underneath.

"Oh, shit, that's beautiful, Sophie. Holy shit, no, really, that's amazing. Aaah, if I wasn't so chicken-shit I'd get one done, too."

I snatch my phone back from Elena. "Nope. I am not tattooing the Habs logo on you. Not happening. You gotta pick something else."

Elena shakes her head. "But then I won't be able to get a discount from you and be able to afford it!"

"You can't have a tattoo!" I crow, batting at her when she tries to reach for my phone again. "You're a first-grade schoolteacher! You have to sort out your priorities!"

"You idiots," Katie says, voice a little on the harsh side, but that just means that she loves us more than anything, and I can get behind that, sure can. "Come on, I need a drink, and I need to figure out a way where I can't see you and Russia looking at each other like *that*. This is my house, what I say goes."

"Oh come on, I can control myself."

Katie's eyebrows go up and up in a *'can you?'* gesture that has me swallowing hard, already doubting myself.

"I don't know what I've done to deserve this kind of treatment," I say, grabbing the pumpkin beer she hands me because it is delicious and one of my favorites in the whole entire world.

"I'm your friend, you shouldn't be treating me this way. You should be trying to get us together so that if we have children, we name them after you and Dean."

Katie chokes on her sip of white wine, coughing and hacking hard enough that Dean comes barrelling out of the kitchen, a baby pink apron on that says *Kiss the Cook (that's me!)* on it, and two oven mitts that look like they're crammed onto his big hands.

It's freaking adorable is what it is, and it makes me feel all gooey on the inside, like my heart's a chocolate lava cake and I need to spill out my own affection on anyone who's readily available.

Russia, Russia, pick Russia!!!

"You okay, kitten?" Dean asks, and Katie waves him off, not before he dives in and kisses her on the cheek after he's made sure her airway is clear and she's stopped coughing, looking more embarrassed than anything.

Dean heads back into the kitchen, walking backwards to keep all three of us in his sight, his eyes tracking over Katie, Elena and me, his eyes lingering on Katie before he turns around and gets back to work on finishing up a fabulous dinner for us.

See? Nothing's going to come between me and my supper. No one. Not even Russia with his mega-hotness.

Not even that.

I smell some meat braising (I think that's the word I'm supposed to use), the scent of wine and rosemary coming together to make me start drooling, just like the pups sitting on the couch in the living room, watching all of us intently, even if they're all lying down and looking like they won't become streaks of lightning if even a *scrap* of food falls onto the floor.

We're seated so that I'm sitting to Russia's right, and my whole left side tingles at his proximity, the guy feeling like a furnace against my heat-cooled exposed skin. Dean's on his other side, keeping up the conversation about a rugby game of all things, a topic I know nothing about, and a conversation I can't even *pretend* to contribute to.

It's when I'm finishing off my beer before the wine has been poured that Russia—God, *Russia*—looks over at me, his blue eyes like lasers, and I feel like he can read every thought I've had about him since I sat down next to him.

"So, Sophie," he says, and my belly clenches and swoops and does a roll, and it's hard to look at him this close, noticing the imperfections in his skin, his face, the way there's an area around his chin that has a couple of white hairs in his stubble that just makes me want to kiss that little section first out of everywhere else on his face, and honestly, that's not allowed.

I've never felt so dumb in my entire life.

What is this, *what is this?*

I make some sort of questioning sound, afraid to open my mouth in case I say something really embarrassing and get banned from seeing the dogs (and Katie and Dean, of course, *of course*) forever and ever.

"I was thinking about getting a tattoo..." he says.

I look over at Katie and Elena, the pair of them seated across the table. I drop my knife and fork from nerveless fingers, mouth popping open in shock. I pull in a deep breath through my nose, ignoring the sudden pounding of my heart that's more concerning than my ears ringing and my hearing going in and out.

"Let me do you," I say. "I wanna do you."

Elena and Katie burst out laughing and I want to *die*.

THREE

E lena meets me at the shop after school—well, after school for her, not for me. She's got plans with Beckett for supper, but she's stopping off to meet me first, to give me the pep talk of the century, a pep talk I desperately need.

I'm wearing my regular work clothes—my comfiest pencil skirt and the star-patterned thigh-highs underneath it, my black Doc Martens on my feet, and a dark purple turtleneck that I'm currently sweating through and it's not like the heat in here is turned up to a hundred and four Celsius.

"So, on a scale of one to ten, how nervous are you?" Elena asks, blowing on her cup of Tim Hortons, the scent of hot chocolate wafting to me.

We're sitting in the back room where I'll eat my lunch (or dinner, depending on the time of day), take my break, and read some smut on my phone, or something, since I've been loving police procedurals lately, too.

"I don't know, I don't want to talk about it." I can't sit still, like I've gotta go to the bathroom but I've peed at least five times in the last hour and I know at this point it's just because I am...nervous, that is.

Elena grins over her paper cup, then winces as she takes a sip when the liquid's still too hot to drink but she swallows it down anyway. "Ah, that hurt. Shit, shit, shit. Okay, we're good. Are you good?" Elena asks, huffing her breath out like a panting dog, trying to cool down her mouth.

I shake my head, digging my nails into my palms, clenching my fists tight.

"No, I'm not. Not really. I don't think I've ever been this nervous in my entire life. And I did that tattoo for that kid the other week. This is somehow worse, and I'm not sure why."

"Not even when we first became roommates, not even then?"

I snort, thinking back to that fateful day. "Please, I knew we were gonna be best friends." I've always had a good feeling about people, about reading them, and I've learned to trust my instincts.

I could tell, back then, that Elena was hurting. Even when I let her move in as a favor to Katie when I was at a place in my life when I needed the money and work wasn't as steady as it is now, I remember just getting the best kind of feeling, like I found the perfect shoes I wasn't even *looking* for.

Elena tilts her head, taking another pained sip of her hot chocolate because apparently, she's masochistic. "Pretty sure I just burned my taste buds right off. It's fine, totally fine." She blows on the cup, the cap making a kind of whistling sound. "I'm glad you thought that, I didn't know what to think when I first met you."

"Yeah, I know. The tattoos and piercings were a lot, huh?" I say, mentioning it first. I've tattooed a part of my ear and have maybe close to thirty tattoos all over my body. I project a certain kind of image. I get that. It's not *all* I am though.

I'm more than just a good time.

Elena nods slowly. "I wanted to be brave enough like you to do things like that to my body. Speaking of which…"

I sit up straighter in my chair, ready for the next question. "What? You wanna get some ink on your skin? Pierced? Oh my God, you're blushing—where do you want it?" I clap my hands together like a seal, and I'm glad we're talking about this, glad that I'm not looking at the clock and doing the mental countdown until Russia—Jesus Christ, *Russia*—comes into the shop and starts to get tattooed, by *me*.

In the words of Elena DiNovro—I'm fine, totally *fiiiiineee*.

"I kinda want to get nipple piercings, actually, but I'm kinda being super shy about it."

"*Whhhaaatttt?*" I yell, clapping my hands again, a seal begging for a treat. "Holy shit, that's awesome. You should totally get them if you want. Mine always make me feel extra beautiful, especially when I change out the jewelry."

Elena gapes, setting her hot chocolate down on the table. "You have nipple piercings? How did I not know this? We've lived together for two years, isn't this something I should know?"

"Buddy, pal, it's not like I've been flashing you or anything." I mime lifting up my shirt.

"No, but you know, we hit our chests on things, like, all the time. I would've noticed if you were wincing in pain. Wow, way to be unobservant, Elena."

I shrug.

I don't tell her that sometimes the apartment felt better when she wasn't around, that her sadness didn't cling to the walls and the furniture, that being that heartbroken was an actual presence when she was around. I didn't expect her to notice me, and especially during the first year, we weren't that close, Elena going through her own shit, me going through mine.

But then we both stayed in the living room one night, watching *Forgetting Sarah Marshall*, the both of us going to pieces at the Paul Rudd cameo, and it's like it opened all the floodgates, and we talked for hours that night, and now she's my best friend.

I don't even know what life was really like before her, honestly.

"It's fine. Don't worry about it. I never really liked the way my boobs looked, you know, my left one's smaller, and I always felt lopsided, but ever since I got them, I just admire them now, they never looked so pretty." I nod to myself.

Some people go to the gym to make themselves feel better about looking in the mirror, the power trip of lifting heavier and heavier things, of running an extra mile, of running faster than they ever have, and I get it, I do.

Some of us just take the canvas of skin we've been given and adorn it with things we love (and some we fall out of love with, too), making our bodies more beautiful in our eyes, just like that kid, Jackie, wanted.

I wonder what Russia's going to want inked on his skin? What does he want to enhance, or change? I can't wait to ask why.

Will it be something I specialize in, or not—blackwork? Script? Or should I send him over to Jonas who specializes in portraiture even though I'm trying to get better at it?

So many questions, waiting to be asked.

"Huh. Something to think about. Maybe after the holidays. I don't know if I'm going to try to go home, or not," she says, looking down at her hot chocolate, not making eye contact, so I treat the situation as if I'm approaching a ticking time bomb—*very carefully.*

"Yeah?" I ask, leaning forward to grab her hand. "You're more than welcome to come home with me, you know that."

Elena nods, glancing away. I would punch her parents if I could, I so definitely would. Punch them right in the throat, the both of them, at the *same time* if I were ambidextrous.

"If Katie's there, it's not going to be so bad. I just don't know what her plans are, so. And I'd bring Beckett, but they're gonna be jerks to him because he's not Frankie, so, yeah. Maybe I'll just skip it, or maybe I'll hang out with Beckett at night after he sees his family. I don't know, it doesn't really matter. I'm used to not going home for Christmas these days, I'm an old pro at it."

I nod, because I'm not sure what else I should do, what else I can do.

"Feeling better?" she asks, and the nerves come back, the butterflies eating at my stomach lining as I glance down at my phone in my lap, checking the time, the reminder on my calendar app flashing at me.

"Now I'm not."

"What's the big deal, though? You're gonna get to touch him, ink him. That's special, isn't it? Like the connection you get with your waxing lady, that's an unbreakable bond." Elena lifts her cup in a mock salute, and I have to mash my lips together to keep from laughing.

I roll my eyes, cough a little.. "I don't want to be his waxing lady, Elena. I mean, I don't even know the guy other than from what we talked about at Katie's. Do you know he mixes up his analogies in English? It's so freaking cute, I want to cuddle him so very hard. Plus, he didn't look at me like he was afraid of me, or like I'm a slot machine ready for the next play, you know?" I shrug, embarrassed.

I can't look Elena in the eye, not when she has everything I want in a relationship, but it's hard to keep hoping for something that refuses to enter my life.

Maybe it'll be different with Russia?

Knowing my luck, he'll turn out to be horrible, and then I can just give up and buy a mansion in a small town and become the village witch. That doesn't sound too bad, if a little lonely.

"I'm not asking for that much, I'm not. He looks perfect, could he *be* perfect? I'll die if he's actually a nice person. Oh, no, what if he's an asshole?" I lift my head, one of my eyelashes going wonky before I press it back into place.

"Elena, *what if he's an asshole?* I can't fall in love with any more assholes. I'll jump out of the window right now." I shake my head from side to side.

Honestly, though, Soph, what are you going to do if he's interested in you right back, and he's not one of those jerks?

Elena's eyebrows high five her hairline. "I mean, we're in the basement, so have at it." She jerks her thumb over her shoulder at the teeny, tiny, barred window at the top of the wall. Yeah, my hips would never let me make it out of there alive; I'd just be sad and stuck forever.

"I didn't ask you to bring the laws of physics into this conversation. I don't want logic hanging around when I'm trying to be dramatic. No, seriously, though, how can I have this kind of reaction if he's a giant dick?"

Elena snickers. "I mean, he could *have* a giant dick, so there's that."

I gasp. "What's in this hot chocolate? Bourbon? Vodka? Actually, that sounds disgusting, let's not talk about it." I flick her paper cup, and the thing almost topples over but Elena catches it, her reflexes honed by hanging around accident-prone first graders all day long.

"Commiserate with me. *Commiserate.*"

"Just...be yourself," Elena says, trying to keep a straight face, shrugging.

I just glare at her and take my time blinking at her to make her realize what she's done.

"Excuse me? That's all you gotta say to me? I need more of a pep talk, please. More pep, all the pep. Give me the pep." I gently smack my hand against the table.

"You're such an interesting person, though. Just say whatever pops into your head. Maybe not that you wanna get married to him and that you're thinking about the house you guys are gonna buy together, but just...be yourself. I think you're an incredibly amazing person, and he will, too. And if he doesn't then you have the answer, yeah?"

"I hate it when you're right. I really, really do. I hate it the *most.*" Even my own conscience sounds like Elena now, exactly like the voice of reason.

Elena smiles, drinking some more of her hot chocolate. "I gotta go meet Beckett at the restaurant. Want me to bring you back some supper?"

I shake my head. "Nah, I'll be good until I get home."

Elena narrows her eyes at me, and I squint back at her, and then she nods and gets up to leave. "You're going to be great. It's actually really refreshing that you're so nervous, just like the rest of us."

"Elena, I don't know what lies you've been told, but I definitely don't have my life together, and I honestly think I've regressed back to my high school crushes phase when I was entranced by a beautiful face. Don't get me started on his accent. *Yes, please!*" I hold up my hand, all '*I volunteer as tribute*' without any of the consequences attached to it.

Well, I still don't know if there will be consequences or not.

Time will tell.

"I've...I've never been in love, not really. Not that this is love, but it could be, you know?" I shrug it off, stopping my brain in the middle of those tracks. I can't be thinking about this right now when I'm going to do nothing but *tattoo* him.

"I just...I'd like to be in a happy, healthy, committed relationship. I'd like to be in love with my boyfriend. Is that too much to ask?"

Elena nods and smiles at me, holds out her arms, and I get up from my seat and rush her for a hug, nearly getting hot chocolate all over me. Honestly, it would've been worth it, *worth it*.

"Just...see how it goes? And call me at any time, or tell me when I see you at home, okay?"

"Yeah, yeah, you bet. Say hi to Beckett for me." I wave goodbye to her as she takes the stairs up and out of the back room, and I steel myself, trying to keep the last five minutes before I have to head back upstairs (my break finally over) and deal with Russia.

I take one last deep breath, ignoring the flutter of nerves, the way I can't seem to stop sweating, the way even the weight of my fake eyelashes is bothering me, and I usually forget about them as soon as I put them on.

I stomp up the stairs and head to the front of the shop, hanging out by the reception desk, practically loaded down with binders of our portfolios, along with drawings lining the walls in different styles of art, meaning all of the same thing in the end.

I glance up when the bell over the door rings, and Russia (gah, *Russia-*), looking just as handsome as he did two weeks ago when we all were at Katie's house for supper, where I thoroughly embarrassed myself by practically fawning all over him like some obsessed teenager—or like a fangirl, exactly how Elena had described me. I tell myself to quash it down, the butterflies chewing on my stomach lining, the nerves that make my fingertips cold and trembly, my lungs ignoring the command to fill up and let in air.

I watch him walk into The Red Seal, looking like he's ready for a photoshoot, the swirlies of snow following him inside, like a Hallmark romance movie scene where the two love interests see each other for the first time. "Hi," Russia says, glancing at me as he walks up to the reception desk. His smile is bigger than a house, his blue eyes practically glowing, and my heart thumps *hard*. "We have an appointment."

I nod, because that's what you do when another person talks to you, and you need to respond in the affirmative. "We do." I fall back on training, making my vision fuzz out so I don't have to really see the semi-perfection of his face, the way it's so freaking pleasing to my eye.

"What did you have in mind?" I ask, keeping our distance from one another.

I mean, we're friendlier now because I've met him before, and we talked and everything, but we're at my place of work, and I can't flirt more than I normally do.

I don't want to give him that impression of me right now. I want to appear serious and professional, even if I'm dying on the inside, just a little.

"I brought something with me, and you can draw it up?" he asks, fishing for his phone in his coat pocket. I notice the cut of it, the material *looking* expensive, but I thrift almost everything, so I really have no idea about anything fashion oriented.

"Let's have a look," I say, holding out my hand for his phone, leaning closer to the reception desk, ignoring the youngest in our shop—Daisy (yup, like the flower) —come skipping to the front of the reception desk, being too chirpy while I'm dying inside as I look at the picture.

It's a symbol, looks like something Nordic, but I'm not too sure. "I can draw this as is, tattoo it as is, or were you thinking something more stylized?"

Russia's looking down at his phone, cradled in my hand, and this close, he's truly breathtaking. I'm an artist, and I can admire symmetry – except for that bump on his nose. I want to ask about it so bad, but maybe today's session won't be a good idea. I want to make a good enough impression that he'll want to come back.

He points to the picture on his phone after unzipping his coat. "As long as the overall symbols are there so the symbol keeps its meaning. You can add your own style to it, and I would like it to be in color, looking something like molten gold."

I nod, glancing down at the picture. "Here, I'm going to send this to our printer in the back so I can have a hard copy to draw out. Where were you thinking of putting this?"

"The inside of my left arm." Russia points to it, the skin still covered by his coat.

My professionalism is nothing but a thin veneer right now, standing this close to him, close enough to see the bluer-than-blue flecks in his eyes.

I nod, clear my throat, force myself to *focus*.

"Can you show me where you were thinking of putting it? Just so I can picture how big I should draw it."

He nods, chucking off this coat to reveal a plain white t-shirt underneath, bringing his left inner forearm up, spanning the width of it with his fingers. I let my mind and vision go fuzzy until I can *see* the tattoo there, my artwork on his body for however long he decides to keep it.

"Yeah, okay, got it." I nod, looking up at him, those wicked blue eyes peering through me instead of looking at me. I suppress a shiver—because of the cold and nothing else, really—and nod again, heart beating too fast just for me to be standing still.

"Let me draw something up. You're welcome to sit here and go through these binders. Yeah, these two here have some metallic-themed tattoos in them, so you let me know about the coloring and shading. I'm gonna go draw it up, and then we'll see how it looks on your skin once the stencil's done, yeah?" I fake the enthusiasm and the confidence I don't feel.

I know once I get my gloves on and my mind homed in on drawing the tattoo on his skin that I'll be able to forget about how attractive I find him, but right now I'm a drowning woman.

Russia nods, throat working with it, and I wonder if he's nervous, and what kind of client he's going to be getting the needle and me pumping ink into his skin, tracing out my artwork.

Is there really a bigger ego boost, having someone else walk around with my mark on their skin? If there is, I haven't really found it yet.

I spend forty-five minutes drawing up two versions, one with the harsh edges around the symbol, the *vegvisir*, which is a Nordic symbol—I had to look it up. The other version I draw up is softer, more whimsical, more magical looking and in complete juxtaposition to the harsh edges, the deep cuts that I'll shade in and make more three-dimensional once I get it on his skin.

Satisfied, I truck over my stencils to the front, where Russia's sitting on the couches.

He's got the binder I showed him before open, his hand covering the page, glancing up at me when I call out his name (well, his nickname), smiling at me with that smile that gives me the warm tingles straight down to my toes.

"Found something you like?" I ask, peering down at the binder, taking a seat next to him in our makeshift waiting room area, the smell of his laundry detergent (something with lavender and vanilla, I think) hitting my nose as I sit close to him and lean in, looking down at his lap—where the binder is.

"Ah, yeah, I can do that, no problem. You like this melted gold look?"

Russia nods when I look up at him and I'm praying to whatever deity exists that my eyelashes do not look crooked right now. Nothing like making a crap impression when your damn eyelashes aren't even.

"So, you've got two options, or a mixture of both, I guess, if you want. It's up to you." I hand him over the two drawings, the harsher-looking one on the left, the softer-looking one on the right. "What do you think?"

Russia nods, and I hate it when people nod right off the bat like they have no opinion.

"Honestly, tell me what you like and don't like. This is going on your skin. Tell me what you think about them," I prompt, wanting him to be happy with it, wanting him to keep it on his skin, so that he doesn't try to find some other artist to cover it up because he didn't have the guts to speak up when I wanted him to, when I *asked* him to.

"I love them both actually. Can you do an alternating style of both with the spokes of the symbol?"

I nod slowly, thinking about it, looking down at my drawings. "Yeah, of course. That'd look amazing." A fizzing excitement settles in my belly and sucks up my heart to my throat while I grab the sketches back and look down at them, grinning.

With the molten gold look on top of them. Shit, it's gonna look *beautiful*.

A beautiful tattoo for a beautiful man.

And I'm getting paid to do this.

I honestly love my job. *I love my job!*

"All right, come on back, and we'll get you started," I say, getting to my feet, almost, *almost* holding out my hand to him, like I'm going to drag him back to my workstation where I've gone and set up my inks, my machine, sanitized the bench, all of my pre-packaged needles waiting to be opened in front of him.

Russia says something—probably in Russian since I don't recognize it as either English or French—and my knees wobble at the sound. I keep my stiff-backed gait all the way back to where I've set everything up to get to work, the area smelling faintly astringent.

I guide Russia to lie down how I want him to on the bench, rearranging myself and my tools so that his left arm is lying flat, the expanse of pale skin ready to be transformed by whatever I decide to leave behind there in the shape of the *vegvisir*.

I can't help but snicker because it looks like I already got Russia horizontal without having to do much work.

This is what I call a win-win situation.

"Ready?" I ask, my gloves on, my stool pulled in close.

I watch his throat work in a nervous swallow, but his smile is *all* excitement, and if I wasn't who I was, it would affect me worse than it already has.

But even though I'm insanely attracted to him for no particular reason other than I like the look of his face, his smile is something else.

"Ready. Are you?"

I don't answer the question, glancing away from his almost-symmetrical face, and get to work.

I've got a tattoo to do.

FOUR

T he bench is adjusted so Russia's seated in a reclined position, his left
    arm stretched out in front of him on a placeholder. The stencil's been
placed, adjusted, and I look up at him from my seated position, eyebrow
raised.

"You finally good to go?" I ask, licking at my bottom lip, and *I don't want
to talk about* how my entire body feels engulfed in flames when he watches
my mouth for a second too long, my attention span and focus taking a
critical hit.

It's honestly warm in here, the back of my neck getting damp enough
that I have to shake out my hair like a dog, from side to side, to build up a
breeze back there, trying to cool myself down.

We've got the radio station on the Top 40 hits, all songs I can hum and
bop along to as I get my mind in gear for preparing for the tattoo, preparing
to touch him.

I don't care what anyone says, putting a tattoo on someone, a complete
stranger, it's intimate for me. And while I won't get into the metaphysical
stuff or whatever, I'm putting something of myself onto him, and that
might make some people uncomfortable, if they really let themselves think
about it. I'm basically putting a part of myself, my heart, my *art*, my skill
and talent, on someone else's body so they can carry it around with them
wherever they go, regardless of the person's sexual orientation or gender
identity, irrelevant to how they move throughout space and time.

This is a human thing, from person to person.

And while I usually love this part of my job, I can't help but feel hesitant to touch Russia, not when I'm so insanely attracted to him.

Like, *what is that?* And why is it happening right now?

I'm turning twenty-seven this year, so aren't I too old for this sudden infatuation with an actual stranger? *Or is it just the idea of a man who can fall in love with all of me, and allow me to shine as brightly as I already do?*

I guess this crush is going to inevitably fade in a couple of weeks, and after I've completed his tattoo, I won't be seeing him ever again (unless Katie gets involved, and I don't know if she wants to do some chaotic good in her life and help me bag this guy or not, so I'll leave that up to Fate).

"Yeah, I'm good," Russia whispers, almost not loud enough to hear over some new song by Ariana Grande that I don't know the words to but can hum along to like a champ. He nods at me, a small, careful smile on his face, even as his throat works on a hard swallow.

"We stop whenever you want to stop," I say, cheeks catching fire at the mere *insinuation* of what I just said, even if the words I used make the statement no less true.

"If you're in pain, if you don't want to continue, just let me know, all right?"

Russia nods, glancing down at his forearm, the naked skin exposed, one of my gloved hands placed there where I can feel his pulse ratcheting up against his wrist.

"I don't have the highest pain tolerance," he says, licking at his dry lips, pupils dilated as he looks at me.

I try to *not* focus on the fact that he licked his lips, or the white strands in his beard mixed in with the dirty-blond that I find super appealing for some freaking reason.

I instead look down at the pale expanse of his inner forearm, a tiny silver scar closer to his wrist than his elbow, a mark left over after all this time. His skin's pale enough that I can see the green and blue of his veins snaking up his inner forearm, like the branches of a tree reaching out and out, even though human anatomy doesn't really work that way.

"That's okay," I reassure him, patting his arm with my free hand absentmindedly, all *there, there.* "Everybody has different pain thresholds. And honestly, we can talk only if you want to. If you want to sit quietly and think about something else, put your ear buds in and listen to some other music to distract you, I really don't mind." I nod at him, and those blue-blue eyes flick up to me from looking down at his arm, making my breath catch in the middle of my throat.

I'm afraid if I start moving again, I'm going to cough hard enough to hack up a lung.

Thanks, but no thanks.

"All right, I'm going to start now," I say, voice almost trembling until I clear the weird animal lodged in my vocal cords right on out of there. Yeah, he's hot, and I'm attracted.

So what? *So what?*

I wipe down the skin with isopropyl alcohol and a paper towel, then shave any hair that's sitting there, getting his arm ready to go, tossing the used razor after using it.

I glance back at my tray, making one last mental calculation if I have everything I need (which I've already triple-checked, but this guy has got me off my game): my ink caps all perfectly sized to fit in the needles I'm going to be using, my vitamin ointment, my stack of paper towels. My machine's been barrier filmed, I've got my nitrile gloves on, my power's set to the right voltage I need before I press my foot pedal.

Yup, good to go. Stop being so nervous, you've done this a thousand times before...

I pull in one last deep breath.

I start my tattoo machine, pressing the needle into his skin after filling it with ink, tracing the outline in a deep bronze color for now, the image already holding its shape in my mind, me just trying to make the theoretical into reality, the intangible into the tangible so he has a wicked tattoo.

I obviously want Russia to have a good experience, like I'd want any client to have a good experience.

There's just added pressure with him since there's maybe the teeniest, tiniest part of me that wants him to fall in love me, head over heels after he sees what I can create.

Would that be so wrong?

I'm tired with all the jerks I've been dating who look down on me 'cause we don't match *aesthetics*, as if any of that's relevant to what's inside a person. I can't believe it's almost the second decade of the twentieth century and I still have to deal with this shit.

When I glance up at Russia to make sure he's still breathing normally and not holding his breath or going ghost-pale looking like he's about to pass out, I see him looking down at my own arms, his gaze still skittering over to where the ink's being injected to his own skin.

I notice his breathing changes whenever he does focus too long on his forearm, his chest and ribs moving oddly, like his brain's finally making the connection between the deposit of the ink and pain, between tattoo and movement.

It's exactly like the time it takes for your brain to realize you've been hurt, only to have the pain signal flare like a lost SOS when you look down at a bleeding wound, the *snap* of the connection clicking into place.

"You okay there?" I ask, keeping my eyes down, wiping away the ink from the skin with a paper towel, tracing along as I go, feeling his arm tighten up underneath my touch as I get towards the more sensitive skin of his inner elbow.

"Yeah, yeah." His voice sounds a little hoarse, but it's not like I'm going to mention it.

I had tears in my eyes for most of the time I got some of my tattoos, it's really not that big of a deal—unless he's one of those emotionally constipated types that'll make me question my sanity more often than not if he *is* in actual pain.

Again, Soph, you're here to do a job, not get a date, yeah?

Why can't I do both?

"I got distracted by your tattoos," Russia says, and I stop the buzzing of my machine to look up at him, trying to keep my face impassive. I've *heard* that kind of tone before—and I don't like it. I don't like it at all. "You have a lot of them, almost too many."

I mash my lips together. Here he is, already disappointing me.

"And yet, you're here, asking for a tattoo from yours truly. I'd rather like to think it means I'm experienced."

Russia shakes his head, his blue eyes going half-mast that has something inside me *clenching* hard. He tilts his head back against the seat, closing his eyes once and for all, too bad it does nothing for his mouth, though. "And piercings. So many piercings, too."

I clench my teeth, clamping my jaw shut.

If Russia walks out of here, I don't make money, and I *want to* make money, want to buy a chocolate cake for myself tonight while Elena tells me all the sweet stuff that Beckett does for her, and then I'll go cry during a hot shower after a long day so I can pretend that my tears aren't really tears, just shower water, all of it rinsing down the drain.

But I've been down that road before, and I'm not standing for an asshole who's going to judge my body and what *I've* chosen to adorn it with (be it clothes, piercings, tattoos) and make a fuss about it.

"Yeah. You noticed," I say through clenched teeth, starting up the machine again and getting back to work, getting a sort of vicious glee when he flinches when I put the needle back in him.

I trace along the edges of the design, the *vegvisir*, a compass of sorts that apparently has a bunch of meanings to it in each spoke of the pseudo-wheel.

Why is it that every guy I'm attracted to turns out to be an asshole?

Here he is, confirming my worst fears. Russia isn't who I though he'd be.
"It's just a lot. For seemingly no reason." His eyes track over my eyebrow piercing, the plugs in my ears, the upper helix on both ears covered in studs and hoops, the lobes just the same.

I laugh, biting down on my tongue so I don't say something stupid. "Again, you're here, letting me tattoo you, so." I leave it at that, cutting the non-conversation off at the knees, closing it down before it even gets fully started.

I continue tracing the spokes, making sure my lines are as straight as can be, accounting for the curvature of muscle and bone underneath the skin I'm currently tattooing.

"Yeah, and if this turns out good, I'll have more work for you."

I don't like the way he says *work*, the way he throws it out there like I'm about to go clean his toilet, looking down at me when he's the one who should be embarrassed about leaving shit stains in the bowl, not the other way around.

"I don't know," I say, even though I do know. Work is work; money is money.

You meet losers in every line of work—from retail, or working in the food industry, to a hedge fund manager. It's just the way it is. "Let's see if you like this one first."

"I will," he says with an air of finality that has me glancing up at him, checking to make sure he's not trying to pull one over on me. There's a half-sneer on his face, the kind that makes my abs clench at the need to tamp it all down and *not* say something that'll jeopardize future work.

Money is money is money. I'm not exactly that hard up, but did I really need those extra five eyeshadow palettes?

So I'm paying for it now, needing the work since we're getting close to the end of the month, and December and January is a slowish season in Montreal, cold enough and dark enough outside that nobody really wants to be out—unless it's for the necessities. We usually only get repeat customers, not new clients bringing fresh blood into the shop, or so management complains to me about it.

"What else are you thinking of getting?" I ask, looking down at my work, getting lost in the rhythm now, even as I try to keep up a conversation. "A butterfly?"

I don't mean it to sound condescending, because butterflies personally freak me out (they start out as caterpillars and then become goo in the cocoon and then became a butterfly! What the hell is that?) but it comes out that way, my feathers ruffled already at the prospect that Russia isn't everything that I thought him to be, that I *want* him to be.

This guy's a bad idea, even if your ovaries haven't noticed a hot guy in a while. That's not a superpower or a reason to keep talking to him, yeah?

I've been through this before, and I refuse to feel bad about myself ever again—I'm the only idiot that gets hurt.

So, nope, not for me, thanks.

See ya!

"I wanted something to do with Slavic folklore, actually for the next one," he says. I watch him lick his lips for a split second.

"*Baba Yaga*?" I say the Russian words for the bogeyman, the only real thing I know about Slavic folklore. "*John Wick* is my favorite movie." I shrug, by way of explanation.

Russia snorts and then laughs, closing his eyes as I remove my machine from his arm, not wanting to be jostled all over the place since that's a permanent kind of mistake, the same kind you do at the dentist when you jerk in that torture device, they call a chair and poke at your teeth and gums, and no one's ever really happy.

"*John Wick*?" he asks, his warm blue eyes on me.

I nod, bristling. "*John Wick* is a *great* movie. A *great* movie. The story, Keanu Reeves, the assassin society, the guy who played the guy in the other show getting killed in a classic revenge plot. It's awesome. Don't knock it if you haven't ever seen it."

Russia shakes his head, turning his head towards me, his eyes at half-mast again, like he's seconds away from falling asleep, but he still wants to see me one last time before he sets off for the dreamworld.

I have zero reaction to that, *zero* reaction other than wanting forty-four glasses of ice water to cool me down from the inside out.

"You sound like a friend of mine," he says, and that *friend* sounds like someone...important to him. I can already tell just by the way he's talking about that person.

I raise an eyebrow, resuming my work, not looking at him. Those eyes have sorcerer's magic, I'm convinced.

"Yeah? Maybe your friend sounds like me, you ever think of that?" I'm grinning down at his arm, and freeze for a second, realizing that I'm flirting. I'm not flirting *well*, but it's getting there, since I always need a warm-up period before I get the creative juices flowing when it comes to a would-be relationship with a guy for me.

My brain's always pre-occupied by the palette of colors people wear, the way people *are*—that I don't fully engage the verbal part of my brain all of the time unless I'm describing a tattoo, a piercing, or something that I'm passionate about—whatever it happens to be.

But even here, Russia doesn't want to *hear* what I have to say about John Wick, especially since I haven't watched the sequels yet. The original was so good, I don't want anything to ruin it by watching the sequels, answering questions I didn't want answered in the first place.

"Pretty sure you're younger than me and therefore younger than her." His voice sounds wistful, and there's really no reason why a surge of jealousy burns inside my chest.

Russia isn't anything to me—other than eye candy right now—and the more he keeps talking, the more I keep getting turned off.

I nod along, because sure, that makes sense. If he's friends with Katie and I make the logical assumption that *they're* the same age then yeah, this guy's three or four years older than me. Okay. That's not a big deal, that's like negligible, not even a thing.

We're not thinking about him like that, remember?

I hum to myself as I keep working, satisfied with the final outline. "Outline's done. How are you feeling? Want to keep going?"

"How long has it been, half an hour? We can keep going. I'm all right." Russia nods down to his arm, settling his head back against the seat, closing his eyes again, and immediately I feel safer, feeling like I can *breathe*.

It's not fair that he's this hot and doesn't know how to talk to me. I don't find that endearing, not one bit.

"What made you want to get this?" I ask, wanting to push and prod like he's already done to me.

It's an explicit kind of question that'll make him sputter and blush, and most of the time, clients *want* to talk about why they get what they get—it could be a memorial, a client's favorite artwork that they want to dedicate their bodies to—just anything. There could be no reason at all, but those usually end up getting covered within the next five years with something more meaningful, in my experience.

So I'm more than surprised when he starts talking, since I made the erroneous judgment that he's the kind of emotionally constipated guy that's going to keep it all close to the vest, as if there's always going to be someone looking over his shoulder and demanding to know what he's got, what he's made of.

Real life isn't at all like that. *Much.*

"I'm looking for...direction in my life," he says, accent getting thicker over some of the words. It's weird. I can detect it some of the time, and other times I don't, like he's actively trying to kill it, which seems kind of sad to me.

"And the compass...the compass is a way to remind myself of whatever direction I'm going in, I'm supposed to be where I am, that I just need to keep looking for the next step, the next one and the next." He opens his eyes, and we make eye contact.

I lift my hand away from his arm, waiting to discard old needles for new ones, so I can start putting in more of the colors now, adding more depth and dimension to the tattoo.

"That's interesting..." I say, going with the words I've used before, tried and true. No one wants to hear that an apple pie tattoo seems kind of dumb, especially if I'm the one doing the tattooing. It's literally none of my business, but it does make me intrigued, makes me want to know more, which is unfortunate.

And if he wants another piece done by yours truly? What are you going to do about that?

I pull in a deep, deep breath, swallowing hard. "Tell me about it," I invite, letting his words drift over me.

I learn that each spoke of the compass represents a part of the journey that every person goes through, his voice lulling me, and I find it soothing, comforting, which is also dangerous.

It's like this guy is the perfect apex predator and I'm the only kind of prey he eats, he's got every single advantage and I can't hope to win against him.

"What does that tattoo mean? The one by your collarbone?" he asks, his blue eyes rooting me to the spot that I just freeze there, foot off the pedal.

I glance down, even though I know what's there—a crescent moon. "It's for the moon. Obviously."

His eyes flicker down to my exposed collarbone again, one of my dermal piercings twinkling inside the crescent. "It's beautiful," he says, and shit, it sounds like he means it. *Huh.*

That doesn't mean anything, that doesn't mean anything!

It doesn't, I know it doesn't, but it could, though.

It *could.*

I get back to finishing up the tattoo, being diligent and careful, wanting him to sing my praises, make him proud to wear my work.

I'm so into it that I don't even hear my name being called or Russia talking to me until I'm lifting my head, dazed, glancing around to see Katie standing there, across the bench, pointing down at Russia's arm, as if he's been scalded with poison.

"What the hell, you actually got one? Because Sera dared you to? Holy shit!"

I frown at Katie and then look at Russia, his eyes darting away from me, looking guilty.

And my mind sticks to that name, sticks and clicks, and I'll be thinking and wondering what this Sera has that I do not that can put that kind of look on Russia's face.

The very look that looks like he's loved and lost but is still keeping the torch alive.

Why couldn't that be me?

FIVE

I tried to straddle the line between looking effortlessly put together and putting too much effort into it, as you do. Whatever, though, just...*whatever*.

Russia walks into the shop, wearing the same coat, a darker wash of jeans, and a smile for me like we've known each other for much longer than we actually have.

Three weeks have passed since I finished up the *vegvisir* on his inner forearm, and November is coming to a close, but there's *still* freezing rain forecasted for tonight and the walk to my car is going to make me want to strap on some skates instead of changing into my chunky (and super warm) boots and braving the outside.

The shop feels hot now, the air dry enough that we try to combat it with at least forty-two humidifiers around the place, trying to keep our skin and nasal passages moist.

I nearly knock over a little humidifier in the shape of a Christmas tree of all things, the star on top shoving the steam in my face, and it very nearly goes flying

Russia walks towards me with a smile on his face, like he's ready for a photo shoot, and I dumbly look around for the crazed photographers trying to snap some pictures.

I shake myself out of it and I give him what I hope is a reassuring smile, even though I know where I stand.

No man has that kind of look on his face, that look of utter fondness, if it isn't for someone he loves, and Russia? He *loves* Sera, and that means there's no room for me in his life. Which is fine, totally fine.

I got some details from Katie over the past weekend when all three of us girls hung out with the dogs. Dean went out with his own buddies, and there was a lot of wine, a lot of questions asked, trying to glean everything Katie's ever known about Russia so she can pass it on to me and I can make an informed decision.

And even though Katie didn't come out and say it, it turns out that Russia was—*is?*—in love with someone else, and I've got an icicle's chance in a raging inferno of getting him to potentially fall in love with me.

I was doomed from the very beginning and now I just have to come to terms with it.

I'm just his tattoo artist, that's it, that's all.

Maybe in another universe Russia and I could have been possible, but here and now?

No, it's better not to think about that.

"Hey," I say, waving at him, the intense attraction I have for him now levelling down from a rolling boil to a barely there simmer.

It's nice and a lot better for me now that I know where I stand, even if my heart gives a woebegone pang, and I feel an ache of loneliness when I look at him, wanting him, *someone*, to look at me the way he looked when Sera's name was mentioned.

That's special, so special.

And I want it for myself, too.

Just...not with him, it can't be with him. If only I could extinguish my attraction to him as easy as turning off a switch—I need an *off* mode, fast.

"Hey," Russia says, head dipping down just a little before stopping himself, and my whole body jolts with an electric shock. Was he going to kiss me? Or is it that a European thing that some of the clients do here?

I don't know, but it's weird, but also, it'd be nice to see what his beard feels like against my cheeks if we do the *bises*, the kiss on either cheek in greeting. "How are you doing?"

Well, Jesus, it's like he cares, instead of just making small talk, and I'm loving it. It's always nice to be asked—always, always.

"Good. Do you know what you want today?" I ask, glancing down at his hands as if there's a drawing there that's going to magically appear. Spoiler alert: it does not. "Something Nordic again?"

Russia just nods before heading over to our coat rack, fishing out his wallet and stuffing it in the back of his jeans and then putting his coat on top of everyone else's, tugging on his shirt collar when the heat starts to get to him. "I'll show you what I have in mind."

We do the same routine as last time, where I ask the common questions and just blink at him when he tells me he wants the piece across the expanse of his upper back, even though Russia looks like the kinda guy that has virgin skin *all over*.

"Can you do something like this, with a lot of depth?"

Depth. I'll show you depth.

I nod again, glancing at the picture that is his inspiration for today's session and sending a copy to our printer in the back, asking him to wait for me to draw something up on the stencil, to figure out how I'm going to leave my mark behind but keeping it true to the picture.

That's the thing with tattoos—and everything else, really—you don't really know what the final outcome's going to be until it's actually done.

Oh, you can talk about color theory and curvature of the body and skin texture depending on scarring or not, you can talk until you can't anymore about how you *want* it to look like, how you *want* it to be, but most of the time you get a different outcome.

Not that I'm going to draw whatever I want on his skin, but what I see and what Russia sees are two very different things.

And that's the way it goes.

I situate him on the bench where I'm working at today, lowering it down so I'm half-hunched over his body once we've talked about placement and I've secured the stencil on there, the image of the tattoo pinned on the inside of my forehead right between my eyes. I'm trusting my hands and my talent to make something beautiful out of this harsh creature that hurts some to draw, to tattoo.

"Again, we stop anytime you want to. This big of a piece, it's going to take at least a couple of sessions, depending on how it goes, all right?" I look down at the expanse of his unmarked skin.

"You're a virgin here, too," I blurt out, donning my gloves and getting my stool rolled even closer to the bench where he's lying down.

Again, I have him horizontal and I can't really do anything about it.

"Excuse me?" Russia asks, turning his head towards my direction, eyebrows raised, one eye glaring at me from this angle.

I laugh. "Your skin. Other than your forearm, that is. I'm ready to take your skin virginity." I grin at him, patting at the skin on his back. "Ready?"

He pulls in a deep breath, his back expanding with it, centering himself for the upcoming pain.

"Try and relax. We stop when you need to, yeah?" Again, it sounds like I'm talking about something *else*, something even more intimate than what I'm doing now.

I start up my machine, getting closer to the bench, shaking away the baby hairs that have escaped my topknot, my undercut fresh enough that I feel the cold wafting in from the humidifier next to me, getting tingles all along my scalp as I try to suppress a shiver.

The last thing you want is a tattoo artist with shaky hands.

Russia hums when the needle goes into his skin for the first time, and I start like I always do, with the tracing of the piece, making sure everything's even, taking my time, trying to fall into a rhythm with his own breathing pattern, trying to be in sync while his muscles go tight under my hands.

I keep reminding him to relax so I can see how the tattoo will look when the skin's at rest instead of bunched, tightened over muscle and bone.

"What made you want to get this one?" I ask, wanting him to forget about the pain for a little while, his body tensing underneath my hands. I keep pressing down into his skin as a reminder to relax, to breathe normally. His skin reddens up quickly as I continue my tracing, letting the drone of the tattoo machine be the whirring background noise of this non-conversation.

"Was it another bet this time around?" I ask, wiping down his skin, smudging some of the ink everywhere, and continue working. I lick at my teeth, ignoring the way my lips are getting dry from this liquid lipstick from hell, and I can bet Elena's ass that I'll never buy from this brand again, I don't care how affordable it is.

Russia snorts, then winces, apologizing to me for moving. "Can I just get a couple of minutes?" he asks, and I nod, turning off the machine, sliding my stool back to give him room.

I head over to our water cooler, grab a Styrofoam cup to fill up and bring it back to him, watching his fingers tremble as he accepts it with a small smile, sucking it back.

Pain makes you thirsty.

"Sorry," he apologizes again, and I just shrug.

"I'm used to it, you know. Everyone has different pain thresholds, it's not a big deal."

"It's like when you gave me the option to take a break, that's all I fixated on, and the pain seemed heightened somehow? I'm not too sure if that's the case or if my mind is playing tricks on me. Thank you for the water," he says, sitting up fully now, hunching his shoulders in, as if he doesn't want me to see his body.

I'm a tattoo artist and I also used to pierce people in the oddest places. I'm used to the human body, probably just as much as a nurse or a doctor would be. I've *seen* everything.

"You're welcome. Like I said, you decide how many sessions you want. I've got another hour and a half on my slot right now, and I wasn't going to go further than that. I've got a few repeat customers today, and they're coming in after you, so we can schedule something else soon, if you feel like you need a longer break?"

If this is the way it's going to go, I'm going to see Russia more often than not, if he can't take the pain.

It's nothing to be ashamed of, really, but I can't help smiling at him, like he gave me the perfect gift on Christmas morning.

"I can do another fifteen minutes, maybe," he says, nodding to the left and right, thinking about it. I'm annoyed at how cute I find that little gesture, how my heart whines at not having someone like Russia to coo over, to want to cuddle and cover his face with a veritable rainstorm of kisses.

I want the boring everyday stuff and sprinkle some adventures in between with my future boyfriend. I want all of that.

But not here, not now.

Thank you, next!

Russia blinks at me, eyes narrowing, and it takes me a split second to double-check with my brain if I actually said any of that out loud, which would be mortifying and I'm never going to be able to come into work ever again, and I really don't want to do that.

If things keep going as they are, I expect Elena to move in with Beckett by next Christmas and I'm going to be left holding the bag. I *need* to keep working here for the foreseeable future.

Maybe if you stop buying lipsticks in every forsaken undertone and color, you'd be able to not sweat rent every month! What about that?

I can always go to makeup school, get a student loan from the government and learn "cosmetology," even if most people know what to do based on YouTube beauty gurus, even if it won't necessarily work for them.

It's not looking like a really promising plan B, huh?

"What's wrong?" Russia asks, and I let out a pained wheeze, like I've been sucker punched in the gut and I'm trying to decide whether to throw up or spill my lunch all over the floor in an emergency evacuation.

Did I actually say anything out loud? Did I really do that?!

I shake my head, waving it all off, even as he continues to look at me, and my heart thumps hard in my chest, wanting what I see in his face to be true, for it to be the *interest* that I'm perceiving on my end.

But I'm not going to do that to myself, not again.

"Nothing. I'm good. Are you...are you good?" Jesus Christ, I sound like a high schooler finally getting that conversation with her long-time crush, elated and terrified in a dizzy torrent, swinging back and forth between the two.

Russia smiles, still holding onto the cup I gave him, swinging it back and finishing up the water, once and for all. "You're very talented," he says, and I nearly go and swallow my tongue.

I love when I get compliments, *love it*.

I smile at him, teeth and all. "Good. I'm glad you liked what we did for your arm. I think it really came out beautiful. It looks like it's healing up pretty good, too. Just keep following my instructions and you should be good to go."

Russia nods, chest still caving in, like I'm going to hold him up and compare him to the buff gym rats that always come in to try to prove something but end up crying more often than not. It takes a lot of effort to hold pain at bay, and it usually ends in tears.

But Russia...Russia's calmer, steadier, like a tree planted against a howling wind, swaying in a storm, but ultimately keeping its place—-bending without breaking.

But then again, I don't know everything about him, don't know much about him—yet. I guess I'm just seeing what I want to see, too.

"I showed some of my friends, actually. Sang your praises."

Compliments. Keep them coming, please!

My cheeks are on fire, and if I'm not careful, I'm going to have to change gloves from trying to hide my face behind my hands, even if I'm trying to keep from being wasteful.

"Yeah?" I ask, my voice not sounding like it belongs to me at all.

Russia nods, catching wind of what's going on, I'm sure of it. "You should expect to get some more clients your way. My friend just had a kid, and he wants an imprint of the baby's feet on his bicep." Russia glances up at the ceiling, chasing a memory.

"Yeah, I think that's what Alex said. And Josh will probably get something to do with *The Legend of Zelda*."

"Oh, I know that game!" I say, because I've heard of it, yeah, just never played it.

We end up grinning at each other, reading between the lines.

"I'd love to give Katie a tattoo, something really beautiful—watercolor maybe, but of something hard and unyielding," I say, stopping myself just in time, afraid of what he's going to see in me when I talk about my friend like that.

"She's strong, you know?" I say, nodding at him, as if I'm trying to get him to believe me, to agree with me in the way that two strangers might. "But delicate, like if you look at her from the right angle, she's just this thin wisp, changing and moulding herself to a given situation." I stop myself, appalled at what I've just said, at how easily it came out.

"Well, uh, don't tell her I said that. Or I don't know, go ahead if you want. I'll say it to her face any day."

Russia glances away, shivering for a split second, but I know his body heat's going to skyrocket when I get back to tracing his tattoo on his back again. "You have an interesting way of looking at people," he says, voice going a little gruff.

I shrug again. "I can't help it. I try to think about the tattoos that people would get if they had the chance, the money, the golden opportunity where no one is inebriated, and in sound body and mind. My favorite is trying to figure out what people who look like my grandparents would get."

"How come?"

I squint at him. This is usually where I lose my first dates, but then again, they never really take me seriously because I look the way that I do, as if tattoos and piercings somehow negatively affect my IQ.

"You sure you don't want to get back to it?" I point back to the bench, and Russia's mouth twists.

He hands me back the cup, which I toss (and recycle, I'm not a monster), and I get back on my stool, twisting at the waist until something pops, making me sigh in satisfaction.

"I'm sorry if I was being too..." Russia says, gesturing with a hand, his arms hanging over the sides as he might when he's dead tired after a long week, a long *year*, and face-planting into bed, too exhausted to bring his arm back onto the mattress.

Why do I find that cute? Why?

"You weren't being anything *too*," I say, snapping on another pair of gloves for cleanliness purposes and sliding my stool closer to the bench. I give him a countdown to mentally (and physically) prepare himself for the next bit of tracing of his tattoo, and I try to move faster now while still trying to be diligent, knowing that if I can finish the overall outline, then we'd be good to go for the next couple of sessions.

"Sometimes I wish I could get all of my tattoos removed and start over. I'd get better art, choose better shops and artists instead of just walking in on a whim one day," I say, and feel him relax under my hand, as if not answering him bothered him. "It would be cool but hurt like a bitch."

"How many do you have?"

I know the answer, I've counted them many times. It's one of the first questions that most people ask, after *do they mean anything?* "I've got one for every year I've been alive," I say, just to make him guess. "I'm twenty-six, and I need to get one more before the end of March. Well, I guess after my birthday."

"Yeah?"

I nod, even though his face is turned towards me, he can't really see me. His eyes are closed, voice going a little tight, a little strained. I stop talking and keep on working, asking him to relax every once in a while, trying to keep him calm.

Eventually I ask him about his friends, learning about them in such detail that it's starting to feel like I know them.

I don't mention Sera, and Russia doesn't either, which I guess, yeah, it makes sense that he wouldn't want to talk about her, not after the look I saw when Katie talked about her.

I also know that sometimes you don't *stop* loving someone, knowing the way they impacted your heart, the way they changed *you* as a person just by being close to them.

But you do stop being *in* love with someone, or so they tell me.

I wonder which one it is for Russia.

But I'm not going to ask. I'm not a monster.

The only monster that lives inside me is the one that constantly demands I buy new makeup releases.

But that's another story.

SIX

E lena's doing a little dance in the middle of the shop, and it's giving me a headache, but also warming me up inside so I feel like the Grinch whose heart has expanded three times too fast with it getting crushed against my ribs.

"What do you call that? Dancing?!" I call as I finish up one of my drawings, one of the sketches I've been working on for one of Russia's friends, Alex—the one who came to me explaining about his son and the health issues he was born with.

It was a bad day yesterday, the kind that constantly made my throat close up on the verge of tears, thinking about the love the guy has for his kid, where he told me, a stranger (easier than it should be most of the time) about his hopes and fears, wanting to hold on to his son while getting a tattoo of his tiny feet.

·♥·♥·♥·♥·♥·

"Do you think that's sick? That I want his feet tattooed on my body when I'm not sure if he's going to live or not?" Alex asked me and his dark brown eyes had glittered with unshed tears. It was even more heartbreaking when his voice cracked, and he rubbed his hands over his face, struggling to keep himself together.

I didn't know what to do, should I have held him tight, even if we don't know each other, give him platitudes?

I gave him the answer he wanted, the answer that he needed. "I think it's beautiful that you want to freeze a moment in time, his tiny feet on your skin forever. I've done a few of those tattoos since I've worked here. I can do that for you, Alex, I can do that for you. Can you get me a print of his footprints? Send it to my email?"

I blindly searched for a business card, handed it over to him, a picture of my face on the business card with my business email right there.

"But again, you don't have to do this if you don't want to. I can't give you the right answer. I just know I can do it for you, but you have to show up."

Alex had nodded, had breathed deeply through his nose, and had scratched at his trimmed beard, ran a hand through his thick, dark hair. I noticed the wrinkles around his eyes, bracketing his mouth, as if he'd been holding back tears since the kid was born two months ago, still in the NICU at the Montreal Children's Hospital.

·♥·♥·♥·♥·♥·

I can't even imagine the worry the guy is going through, but I hope giving him what he wants will provide him a small, *tiny* measure of comfort.

So I'm drawing up the feet, trying to provide Alex some options with how big he wants them to be, trying to keep the scaling right by eye alone.

"Let's go grab something to eat, yeah? I'm starving. I want hot dogs. And poutine. So much poutine. I want the cheese pulls to *end* all cheese pulls." Elena's voice jars me from trying to scale the feet, deciding to make another couple of versions, wishing I got a better look at Alex's arm to figure out what would look best and where.

I flick up my head towards Elena, keeping my eyes pinned to the drawing, finishing up the shading of the little feetsies, wondering if I'm going to have to end up writing the birth and death dates underneath, lifting my pencil off the sketch, not even wanting to jinx it.

Life isn't fair most of the time, but some of the time it *sucks,* and it sucks *hard.*

For now, I can't do anything but sate my hunger.

I pin my hair back, a not-so-corkscrew curl getting loose from my bun at the top of my head, and scratch at my undercut.

I flick my finger over my upper helix piercings, letting the jewelry tinkle against one another.

"Almost done!" I yell, finishing up the drawing and stowing it in a folder, my hands smudging the pencil a little, getting on the curl of my hand. I go to my small locker where I keep my paperwork, along with my coat, my boots, on top of my giant bag that's big enough to hold the sketchpad I always have on me, and the small pencil case where I keep my drawings pencils.

"Oh," I say, stamping my feet so they're super comfortable in my boots, almost tripping on the carpet runner we've set up from the entrance door that runs all the way up to the reception desk, like every (potential) client coming in would feel like they're walking on *the* red carpet.

"Hi, Russia," I say, waving a hello, freezing for a second since I'm *pretty* sure, *pretty sure* that we weren't scheduled for an appointment today, and I'm currently off the clock.

"We didn't have an appointment today, did we? Or is there something wrong with your tattoo?" I ask, thinking back to his previous tattoo of the Nordic compass, how nicely that one's healing up as it's kept moisturized and hydrated, especially during the cold-as-hell winter months.

Russia waves back, that smile still hovering around his mouth, not sure if it's going to be a sneer, a snicker, or a genuine, soft and warm smile that I want pressed up against my own mouth, for *reasons*.

That has to be my favorite moment in movies, the moment where the couple is kissing and pressing their smiles against one another.

It looks *awesome*, and I miss having that, don't know if I ever had that. My high school boyfriend lasted a couple of months before he got a scholarship to the States and I never saw him again, and while I was heartbroken, yeah, it wasn't that all-encompassing kinda love that I see that Elena has, falling head over heels over with Beckett.

"No, no, I actually just came by…I don't live too far from here, actually." He jerks his thumb over his shoulder, pointing to the wet pavement of the stairs and sidewalk outside of the shop.

I can see through the window that the snow is swirling in that snow-globe kind of way that looks pretty from in here where it's nice and warm. Russia looks like a painting, a still-life, his dark coat dotted with white snowflakes, his cheeks pink against his pale skin, his blue eyes practically glowing.

Did he have to be in love with somebody else? And why won't this crush die?

I nod at him to continue, while Elena glances between the both of us in the kind of way that annoying friend of yours did back in high school, making it *super obvious* that you're talking to your crush, and your crush knows it, too, when all of this was meant to be kept a *secret*. "We're just about to go get something to eat, actually. You're more than welcome to join," Elena pipes up, stepping into Russia's line of vision, forcing him to make eye contact with her, pulling his attention away from me.

Was he looking at me that intently? Was he?

Nah, no way.

Right?! *Right?!*

I glance at her, and she looks at me, and I swear we're having a telepathic conversation where I yell at her for forcing the guy to come with us and not giving me a chance to know why he showed up (in a professional capacity, of course).

I definitely *don't* hear Elena yelling at me from her own head that apparently based on this sole reason Russia apparently *likes* me and he showed up for no reason, no reason at all, other than to see me.

Why else come see your tattoo artist if there's nothing wrong with your current tattoo and you *aren't* currently getting tattooed?

Why else, why else?

"Do you guys do that a lot?" Russia asks, pointing between Elena and me.

"Rude," I say. "You don't just point out a nonverbal communication, Russia. But yeah, you hungry?" I ignore the rapid beat of my heart, and the burn in my cheeks is *actually* because I'm burning up from being wrapped up in my winter coat that's supposed to combat forty-below Canadian winters, and for that reason *alone*.

Russia nods, his glance moving from Elena to me.

Elena's already leading the way out of the shop.

I call out to Bekah, manning the desk all by her lonesome in the evening, asking last-minute if she wants something to eat. She's eighteen years old, manning the reception desk, and learning payroll from Jake, her older cousin, and they both wave us off.

I salute my boss and leave the shop, heading up the semi-icy stairs to get to street level, finding Russia and Elena waiting for me.

We head to Lafleur's where you get the best steamed hot dogs in Montreal, and we each give our orders. Elena and I decide to share ten steamies and a giant poutine with the greasiest of fries I can't wait to devour.

Elena always balks when I put mayo and ketchup on my hot dogs, so I always make sure to eat it extra gross, hoping to put her off her food and steal some of her steamies, but my plan doesn't work.

Elena sits next to me, Russia across from us in the weirdest third-wheel date I've ever been on, Russia clearly being the outsider.

The funny thing is? He takes his hot dogs the same way I do.

See? It's destined, fated!

Oh, shut up.

"I thought Sophie was the only one who eats them like that," Elena says, looking queasy. She clearly doesn't mind having onion breath with her hot dogs loaded with them, coleslaw slathered on top, and that nearly puts me off my food. There shouldn't be that many green things on a hot dog, it's a crime against nature, honestly.

Russia polishes off his four hot dogs while slowly picking at his single fry, the grease dotting the paper bag it's in, slurping up his orange Crush, like we're little kids again, getting the most sugary soft drinks available to us at the time. My teeth ache just remembering the taste alone.

I munch happily on my food, and Russia keeps staring at me, flickers of glances that I don't catch all the way.

Elena is the bridge of the conversation, both Russia and I merely passing on top of it, connected only through my best friend babbling her way out of everything. It helps that she knows Russia's friends by virtue of being Katie's younger cousin and being outside of the family circle enough that Katie would want to hang out outside of birthdays and the holidays, friends and all.

"Yeah, I saw Sera and her son the other day," Elena says, and Russia nods, his face closed off, his eyes downcast and on his food instead of on either of us.

It's not hard to see that he's closed himself off, put himself behind an invisible wall that we can see through, yeah, but can't reach him behind it.

Even the way he eats becomes stilted, his jaw clenching underneath that glorious beard, the white strands tucked into the corner of his mouth.

"Matty, right? He's usually not around when we all hang out," Elena continues, and I just stop eating altogether.

I already knew that Sera is married and has her kid; I already knew that. But being confronted with that knowledge while sitting opposite Russia is another thing altogether.

Russia nods again. "Yeah, Matty, that's his name. He's almost nine now or should be." His eyes flicker over to me, the blue-blue roving over my face as if looking for something, the most important piece to the puzzle, the very last one, only to realize it's gone and disappeared.

I blink at him, waiting for him to talk, to say something, but it's not like I'm expecting him to lay out his heart here in the middle of a restaurant that has sticky vinyl seats but the best hot dogs in the world, hands down.

Russia doesn't *need* to explain anything to me.

I'm only the tattoo artist. Still just a passing acquaintance, even if I know some things about him now in the way that people babble to strangers, especially when they're in physical pain.

"He's super cute," Elena says, bridging the gap again, connecting two distant points that Russia and I are pinned to. "And Sera looked good. She was taking him to school, so I didn't get a chance to talk with her much. She lives in our building, Sophie."

Of course. Of course she lives in our building. Montreal has almost two million people, and Sera just happens to live in the same building that I do.

Russia nods along, clearing his throat as if he wants to move the conversation along, talk about something else, *anything else*, but Elena doesn't get the memo.

"Ah, shit, sorry, Sophie, can you move? I wanna take this call," Elena says, pushing on my arm and shoulder while I almost choke around my hot dog, which is stupid funny to me since hot dogs are a choking hazard anyway. Ha.

"Is it Beckett?" I say around my mouthful, forcing myself to eat since I'm hungry, covering up my mouth and teeth in case I've got a mixture of mayo and ketchup all over my face, and I don't need to look to know that it's incredibly unattractive.

"It's Beckett. I know it's Beckett. Look at your eyeballs."

"How am I supposed to look at my own eyeballs?" Elena asks, grinning down at her phone and swiping her thumb across the screen. "Hello? Hey! Just give me a second, okay?" Elena swivels her phone so her voice isn't pitched against it directly, and glares at me. "You better move."

"Or what? Hi, Beckett!" I yell, and I can hear the *"hi, Sophie"* from her phone, making me grin. I slide my ass out of the vinyl booth, watching Elena head towards the bathrooms, talking into the phone all the while.

I take my seat again, feeling the silence press down on my shoulders, on the top of my head, while I try to continue eating, all while having Russia seemingly hewn out of marble or stone, whichever one is more beautiful, because *obviously*.

Talk about something, anything, Soph!

"Hey, Russia?" I ask, swallowing down my food, wiping my mouth with the swath of napkins I stole from the dispenser. I don't make eye contact as I stab my fork into the poutine, getting the most epic cheese pull even though Elena's not around to witness it and will call me out as a cheater because she didn't see it with her own two eyes.

He looks at me, waiting for the question, and even though the silence stretches between us it doesn't feel as awkward as it did a second ago, doesn't make my skin itch and burn with the need to insert any sort of word vomit.

"Why did you come to the shop today?"

Russia's eyes flutter closed for a second, and then he looks at me, *really looks* at me, in the way I haven't been looked at in a long time by a man, as if I'm truly being seen, underneath all the piercings, the hair, and the tattoos. I'm just Sophie.

Maybe I'm reading too much into it, like I've done in the past, but maybe I'm not.

Maybe I'm not.

Russia clears his throat, coughs into his fist, looks at me, his face almost serene if I had to put a word to it. "I'm glad that you're the one tattooing me, inking my skin," he says, his voice a little thicker now, the accent just that bit stronger. "Thank you, for treating Alex the way you did."

I shrug, shoulders hiking up to my ears. "Ah, well, he seems like a really nice person. And I can't wait to do his tattoo, honestly. It's going to make him feel better, and I'm happy to be a part of that." I nod, more to myself than anything else.

"I would like to thank you somehow, if I could," he stares at me, licks his lips.

I wipe at my mouth again, frowning at the remnants of foundation that have come off my skin. *Long-wear foundation, my ass.*

"You're already paying me for my time while I do your tattoo. And you brought me a new client. Trust me, that's enough." *More than enough. I get to see you every week for two hours at a time. It's more than enough, Russia.*

"And you get the pleasure of my company, so, it's a win-win situation." I give him an awkward thumbs up, right before the poutine on my fork plops down and makes a splatter of gravy and cheese. I'm just sad I lost a delicious mouthful, less so that I got some food on myself.

Just another strike against me being Russia's potential girlfriend one day (ha!).

He's, of course, immaculate, always taking care of his clothing, his hair and beard, and while I like it, obviously I do, it feels like he's holding himself together instead of just adding to what's already there. The difference between a canvas, and a botched cover-up job.

Maybe he's a secret slob or something. I wouldn't know, and it's not like I'm going to get the opportunity to ask and find out.

And that sucks, too.

I've got three two-hour sessions left with Russia—maybe one more if his pain threshold utterly collapses and he can't bear it (which has happened before with other clients, not gonna lie), and then we'll both go our different ways, like two ships passing each other by at night, unaware of the other.

But don't they have radar?

Shut up, shut up!

"Still, though. Do you think I can take you out to dinner sometime?"

I frown at him, my eyebrows pinching together. "For drawing a tattoo up for your friend for which I will get paid for?" I ask, the disbelief making my voice rise up an entire octave. "That doesn't make a lot of sense."

Russia grins then, and I feel whatever tension I'd been holding in my own body finally ease at the sight of it on his face. Didn't know I would miss seeing it so much, and now he's right across from me, giving me a full-on view.

"I would still like to, though, if you're okay with that."

"What if you learn something about me and decide that you don't want me to tattoo you anymore?" I ask, knowing it could happen, as it has happened to some of my coworkers before. Shit gets tangled, and you're out of a tattoo, giving a chance to some other artist to disturb the vision you had for the original work.

But those are the apples, and all I can do is bake some pie.

"That won't happen." Russia states it like a fact when it never really works out that way. At least, not for me.

"Of course it could," I say, adamant. "I already know you don't really like the way I eat, but I'm not going to apologize for that. You've been glaring at the stain on my shirt instead of making eye contact with me for the past two minutes and my shirt is *not* that interesting, Russia."

His face goes scarlet, and his eyes jump to mine, the bright blue ringed with navy. I would love to tattoo the image of his eyes, the colors, the depth, all of it.

"I was looking at the rest of the tattoos peeking through at your collarbone. I apologize," he says, ducking his head down, and losing eye contact with me.

My heart beats hard and fast, and everything feels extra sharp along the edges.

"Oh. Okay, then," I say, shrugging it off as best as I can. I've never had a guy apologize for only *looking* before.

"Besides, we still have another three weeks together. Buy me a coffee. Oh, no, buy me a donut, the chocolate-stuffed ones that just came out at Tim's," I say, flickering my fingers at him, my version of grabby hands.

"Yeah? Donuts?"

"What? Have you never had a donut before? That explains so much, *so much.*"

He laughs, the sound louder than expected, and several people a couple of booths away turn to look, each with a smile on their faces as they hear him laugh.

And I did that, *I* made him laugh, the exact opposite to Russia's preppy look, me all disheveled, my hair coming out of its bun, my makeup barely making it past eight hours of wear time (when it promised me more)—- Russia's the prince and I'm the pauper.

And that's just the way it is, even if I wish it could be different.

I'm used to it, though.

I know from his previous comments that I look nothing like Sera, probably *am* nothing like Sera, and while that seems like an obvious *duh*, I know without a fact that I am not what—who—he really wants, so why even try by pretending to thank me with dinner?

Nah, a donut is a better bet, because when he leaves, I'll still have a delicious donut.

And donuts have never broken my heart.

SEVEN

I 've sort of gotten used to the explosion of butterflies whenever I'm
supposed to meet with Russia for an appointment—the first of our
next three sessions together.

He's at the end of my schedule today, the last couple of hours right after
supper time, and I'm finishing up eating an apple.

I check out the state of my lipstick on my phone, a satin formula that I
usually don't wear since I want my lipstick to stay where I put it, but *shit* is it
moisturizing, candy apple red to go with the graphic green winged eyeliner
I have on today.

I'm feeling festive even if the holidays have past us by.

I wash my hands with some antibacterial wipe, fussing with my lipstick
through my own reflection in my phone, counting down the minutes until
Russia shows up.

And counting the minutes *past* when he was supposed to show up.

Five minutes.

Then ten minutes.

Then fifteen.

At twenty minutes I head over to my station, start fussing with the
organization of my inks, the placement of the bench, making sure it's
perfectly wiped down even if I did it before he was supposed to show up.

At thirty minutes I give him the benefit of the doubt.

We had more freezing rain last night, and the radio's been all about
doctors calling in and telling people to stay home if they can, since

the emergency departments are getting bombarded with people with ice-related injuries: broken bones, severe sprains, and concussions.

At forty-five minutes I convince myself to let it go, hoping he's all right, checking with the front desk to make sure he didn't call to say he was late or that he wants to reschedule. When Bekah shakes her head at me, I glance over at her, and the kid's cheeks darken, her curly hair bouncing in a bun at the top of her head as she glances away quickly.

"What? Do I have something in my teeth?" I run my tongue over them, making sure I didn't leave any apple behind, but don't find anything.

"What?" I ask again, more than irritated now at myself since I've been swaying from a crushing kind of worry (that Russia doesn't really merit since I don't know him that well even if I am his tattoo artist) to a simmering annoyance that's about to start boiling over at the disrespect and disregard for my time.

I hate it when people do that without contacting me first, just waltzing in an hour later. Pisses me off to the moon and back.

Russia comes in an hour late, limping (which makes my annoyance flare hotly into guilt), his face all red and splotchy, his hair disheveled, coat hanging loose and open.

"I'm sorry, I'm sorry for being late," he apologizes, looking like he wants to prostrate himself, head bowed down, not looking me in the eye where I've been hanging out with the kid at the desk, straightening out piles of paperwork that have already straightened.

I had made it into a game of sorts, where I adjust minutely Bekah's immaculately organized desk, one of her ear buds in her ears, listening to something other than the Top 40 on the radio.

I raise an eyebrow at the way he's not putting his full weight down on his right foot and get even more annoyed with myself.

"What happened?" I ask, steepling my fingers together, placing my chin on top, waiting to hear some bullshit reason but also ignoring that flare of hope that he couldn't come for an actual, legitimate reason.

"I fell down the stairs, slipped so hard my feet went over my head." His face is still red, his breath coming out in pained gasps, and I want to leap into action, save him from himself when the damage has already been done.

Shit. He really *did* get hurt.

"My phone got destroyed in the fall, so I couldn't call you."

I find myself standing up, leaning over the desk to look down at his foot, then back up at him.

"Did you hit your head? Should I get you an Uber to drive you to the hospital up the hill?"

There's no way he can make the walk up the icy and slippery hill towards Mount Royal with one good foot.

No matter how much salt the city dumps, it never seems to be enough, and if luck isn't on your side, you'll find that exposed piece of ice no problem and fall all the way down the hill like a very sad, real-life version of snakes and ladders.

Russia shakes his head. "I went home to get changed and wrap up my ankle. It's not broken, I don't think."

"You don't *think*?" I say, turning and rounding the desk to come and stand in front of him. "You don't *think* it's broken? Are you a medical professional, Russia? Did you get your M.D. license in the time it takes between appointments? Because I don't believing it."

"I don't want to wait in the emergency room," he says, and the way the radio's been touting the emergency departments filling up and being overloaded all day, I wouldn't want to wait for hours in the waiting room either, but still.

It infuriates me an irrational amount that he doesn't want to even *try*, and I know some private clinics around here that'll do X-rays for a fee.

I roll my eyes, crossing my arms over my chest so I don't start pummeling him for his stupidity. "You could have a hairline fracture, though. Plus, you're not even putting any weight on your foot right now. You *need* X-rays, at the very least."

Russia sighs, his form sagging, wincing when he settles his full weight onto both feet instead of making his left compensate for all of his weight. "I know, I know. I just came here to tell you what happened, and I'm sorry that you had to lose out on your time."

"Huh," is all I can say, the sound almost forced out of me. I didn't expect him to come all the way here, *injured*, possibly on a broken foot, sprained ankle, or combination of the two to tell me *why* he didn't call me and give me notice.

I don't expect a lot from people, and I certainly didn't expect Russia to come in here to let me know about his current situation and how it would affect *me*.

Bonus move—you can extend your sessions together!

Ugh, stop, just stop.

Russia's eyebrows pole vault to his hairline, furrowing his forehead, making him look like those wrinkly puppies that are the cutest things on the planet. Why, why, why?

I pull in a deep breath through my nose, glance at the old-timey clock that ticks away the seconds hanging on the wall above the reception desk, and see I've got only twenty minutes left on my shift, but Jake likes me so. There's also the bonus fact that I'm sure no one's going to be coming in for a tattoo or a piercing if the radio's telling people to stay inside.

I get it, I do.

"Bekah, I'm leaving early."

"Ah," she says, standing up, too, glancing between the two of us with panicked eyes, hair practically swinging with the movement in each direction. "Ah, I don't know..."

I pull out my phone from my skirt pocket (the greatest invention of all *time,* putting pockets in skirts) and call up Jake, letting him know that I'm leaving a little early and that Bekah's manning the desk until we close at nine tonight. "Yeah, your cousin's already on his way, he should be here soon, okay? I think he's trying to find parking on the street."

Bekah nods, sighing with relief, flopping back onto her chair and swinging it from side to side until an unfortunate sound comes out of it and makes all three of hiss in pain.

"Sorry! Sorry! I'll see you tomorrow, Sophie! Bye!" The kid waves with a manic smile on her face and I don't know what Jake's told her, but I'm sure none of it is true. The kid constantly looks at me like I'm going to bite her head off for existing alone, and I'm not that kind of person.

I'm not.

"All right, let's go," I say to Russia, grabbing my purse I'd pre-emptively stowed underneath the reception desk, hoping I'd get to leave early, especially since the weather's absolute shit.

I put on my coat. I'm fluffing my hair back, pulling up my massive hood, hike my bag over the wrong shoulder, and I put my feet into my winter boots stacked near the door, going on ahead of him and opening it.

Russia struggles to keep up with my pace, making me wince, and I get him to hold onto the railing for the stairs on one side, and wrap my arm around his waist, sacrificing myself as the human crutch to help him navigate the stairs, his weight mostly all on my side, supporting him as much as I can.

I grunt with the added weight, and once we're at street level, he tries to get away, to get vertical by himself, to move by himself, but I'm not letting that happen.

I take off my hood 'cause I can't hear anything when I have it on, the sleet somehow getting on the back of my neck and sliding all the way down my spine, which makes me shiver and dance on the spot, still clutching tight to Russia on the sidewalk.

I point ahead of us.

"There's a private clinic up there. All they do is blood tests and scans and stuff. It's going to cost some money, but it's better than waiting for hours at the emergency if it's as crowded as they're saying."

I glance up at the inky dark sky, the sleet falling down and smacking me right in the middle of the forehead, as if trying to make me come to my senses. If I fall and hurt myself, Russia's going to fall right on top of me, and not in a sexy kind of way, either.

Russia's breath comes pluming out in the air on an exhausted sigh. "Yeah, I can make it."

"It's two blocks away. Are you sure?"

Russia looks down at me, his face paled out from the watery light of the streetlight. "It's not like I can get a taxi or an Uber to drive me two blocks. This is all there is. I might crush you though."

And what a way to go!

I snicker at my own joke, then sober up when he looks at me, a thousand and four questions in his eyes.

"Okay, let's go. They're open until nine on Thursdays for some odd reason, so we have plenty of time to make it." I know the business hours 'cause I go there to do all my blood tests every year, and I'd rather not go wait at the hospital to get it done.

We make it the two blocks, Russia taking a breather every half block. "My left leg is killing me, shit," he says, huffing and puffing. "How far are we?"

"Just around the corner," I say, panting myself.

It's hard trying to keep the combined balance for the both of us, a three-legged race on ice without the luxury of skates, and a haphazard toss of salt here and there, like it's some sort of booby trap maze out of *Indiana Jones*, moving from patch to patch with someone who's injured like he is.

I wait with him in the waiting room after Russia pays the fee to get an X-ray. My eyes hurt from the overhead lights, and I'm suddenly tired from lugging him around.

"Can't believe you walked all the way to the shop on a potentially broken ankle and/or foot to let me know that you wouldn't be coming to the appointment. Who the hell does that?" I tell him, unzipping my coat from all the sweating I'd been doing, running a hand over my wet hair, wondering if my waterproof mascara actually holds up to its name.

Russia gives me a pained smile, the sweat along his hairline beading and tracking down his temples. He turns to look at me, his leg splayed out in front of him, waiting to be called behind the magic curtain.

"I didn't have a way to call you. It was the only option open to me at the time. I didn't want you to think badly of me."

"I know," I say, like I understand, when I really, really don't. "But that's so weird. I don't know anyone who would walk on an injured foot to come and see me and tell me *why* they were late for an appointment." I shake my head. "It's so weird. *So weird*."

"I didn't want to do that to you, to make you question. Your time is just as important as mine is. I didn't want to leave you hanging."

I squint at him, leaning back a little to get him all in one visual sweep. "Yeah?"

Russia nods, swiping the back of his hand along his forehead. "Yeah. I didn't want to do that."

"Okay. I'd be lying if I said I was expecting that. Huh." I glance at him, up and down again, just to repeat, as if he's a newfound species of animal and my brain's trying to put all the pieces together for easier recognition.

Russia's eyebrows spike. "Do I not seem like a courteous sort of person?"

I shrug, working my shoulders, rustling my coat. "I don't know. I don't really know you that well other than that your pain threshold's not that high."

"Are you calling me weak, Sophie?" he asks, incredulous.

I smile sweetly. "If the shoe fits, yeah," I joke, and Russia moves his foot along the flooring on a pained wince, looking at me as if *I'm* the new discovery.

"Tomas Ivanov?" a nurse calls, clad in scrubs, a clipboard in her hand even if Russia and I are the only two people in the waiting room.

I help Russia get upright, being the human crutch until I get him to the partition where the nurse takes over my job, making a spike of jealousy tingle its way through my chest, a simmering burn that can turn into a wildfire the longer I think about her arm around Russia's waist when she's literally just doing her job.

I honestly need to get a grip, an actual grip on reality.

I unfortunately have got nothing to do but wait, holding onto Russia's phone and wallet and coat—like I'm his girlfriend, a pseudo-pack mule while he's in the back getting a scan and/or X-ray, not even sure what he's opted for since it was none of my business. I have zero opinion on the matter other than wanting to see him healthy and whole for him to come to the shop so I can finish his tattoo.

How did I even get here, and we haven't even been on a date yet?

Well, he sort of asked you out already, yeah? Why don't you take him up on it?

I might, I just might. Maybe he'll talk about Sera the whole time and this crush can finally die, once and for all.

Russia ends up having a bad sprain and there are no broken bones in either ankle or foot, which is pretty amazing news.

Russia leaves with a couple of lightweight aluminum crutches, adjusting them to his height and size, sighing in relief when he lets his weight sag onto them, supporting his left (good) leg.

"Ready to go?" he asks after I hand him back his things, Russia smiling at me all the while like he's Lois Lane and I'm Superman and I've just saved his actual life. It does my head in, not gonna lie, just a little bit.

"Are you going to be okay to get home?" I ask. I start looking around the street once we get outside, condo buildings on either side of us, retail spaces at street level and ground level, trying to figure out which one belongs to Russia, if he said that he lives close to the shop.

"I'm starving," he says, swinging his head towards me, trying to get the crutches to stick against the icy sidewalk, trying to stay upright. "Want to get something to eat?"

I blink at him, my mouth hanging open.

But Russia's looking at me like he means it, and well, it's been a while since I've shared a meal with a guy I found super attractive enough to lose my head over.

Butterflies erupt in my belly, and I nervously start tugging my helix piercings. I'm failing at acting cool, totally.

I cough and clear my throat. "Uh, yeah, yeah. I could eat."

Russia smiles, his teeth showing in the winter dark. "Let's go, anywhere you want."

I glance around our current location, restaurants abounding, but I'm looking for a place where we can sit instead of going in and out. I'm looking for a place that's warm, cozy, especially after walking him back and forth from the clinic and the shop.

"Let's go there," I say, pointing across the street, glancing back and forth to either side, making sure that there are no cars and that we won't die crossing the street, especially since we're going to be slow snails doing so.

Why did Sophie and Russia cross the road? To go and eat something and escape the crappy weather.

Before long we're seated inside a cozy pasta place, the Pasta Emporium, getting a booth by the window, which makes it doubly comfier since I can watch the people outside deal with the shitty weather while Russia and I are inside, getting all cozy and warm and I'm about to eat my body weight in tortellini or gnocchi.

"Thank you for helping me," Russia says, handing me a menu, adjusting his weight on the booth so our knees end up bumping underneath the table. "I really appreciate it."

I nod, glancing down at my own menu, trying to figure out exactly what I want to eat, which type of pasta *and* the sauce I want, enough to give me the pasta loafs and not move for the rest of the night.

"You're welcome," I mumble, glancing up at him. Shit, did he have to be so damn attractive? Did *I* have to find him so attractive? It just doesn't seem fair.

Russia's blue eyes are bright, and he's giving me all of his attention.

He could have easily called it a night, left me behind at the shop, but he didn't. In a way, I'm pretty sure this meal is going to be a 'thank you' of sorts.

I mean, who busts their ankle and *walks* to an appointment to let them know they're not showing up?

Hell, I don't even know if *I* would do that.

That Russia did definitely says something about him; it says something about me, too.

"Again, you didn't have to walk to the shop, and I hope you can get your phone fixed soon."

Russia pulls out said cracked phone, a whole chunk missing on the upper corner, flung into the abyss that is the Montreal weather forecast.

"It's unfortunate that it broke, but I didn't want you to think that I cancelled or was going to someone else to finish up your work on my back."

Russia looks at me after stowing away his broken phone.

"Why?" I tilt my head at him, having a hard time swallowing. "Like, thanks for telling me and all, but people *do* do that all the time, it's just the way it is." It would suck never to see him again, though, right? It would suck, but maybe this crush will die a thousand fiery deaths and I'll never see him again, and I can *move on*.

That would be good for me.

That would be the *best* for me.

Russia runs his hand through his hair, dislodging some sleet, then moving his hand to the back of his neck, clutching at the back of it like there's a myriad of shivers there.

"I want you to finish it. I want you to be the one to finish the piece on my back."

I squint at him, scratching over my left ear, my undercut making a satisfying sound and prickling against my fingertips. "How come? I'm not anyone special."

"But you are. You are special." Russia says it, those blue-blue eyes rooting me to the spot, making me hold my breath while I'm held, stuck under the weight of his gaze.

What is happening right now? Is he saying what I think he's saying?

My jaw practically unhinges, and I'm looking at him with my mouth hanging open, letting a draft in. "What? What?"

"You're incredibly talented. I admire your skill and your work." Russia says this like I don't already know.

I nod, because yeah, I know. I can always be better, sure, but I know I love my art, and by virtue of working hard on it, it's going to come out good, even if I've never been completely a hundred percent satisfied with it.

"Thanks," I mumble, struggling not to squirm in my seat, struggling to not extrapolate and make would-be connections as to *why* he's talking to me this way, what he wants from me.

My heart pounds, and my ears start to ring as his mouth starts to move, so it takes me a second to realize what he's saying.

"I'm sorry, what?" I say, leaning forward a little, watching his mouth, paying *all* the attention to his mouth. "I didn't hear you."

"Nothing, nothing at all. What are you going to get?"

I feel like I missed something, embarrassed him somehow, even while I spaced out.

"No, no, say what you were gonna say!"

Russia sighs, sheepish, glancing up from the menu, those blue eyes making me shiver, they're just such an interesting color.

"Would you like to come with me to Alex's house this weekend? Their son's coming home from the hospital and I think you should be there."

I blink at him, stuck, my brain repeating the information but not synthesizing and *understanding* what it actually means.

Russia wants me to do what now?

Russia wants me to meet his friends...this weekend?

Russia wants to take me to meet his friends this weekend...with him?

What the what?

EIGHT

"You want me. *Me*. To come with *ou*? To your *friend's* house?" I emphasize the words, pointing between my chest and then jabbing the air in front of him, just so that we're both clear on what Russia's proposing.

Russia does nothing but nods, eats some poutine like his whole proposal isn't ludicrous, as if we're both crystal clear on what he's asking me to do.

"But why?" I ask, slumping a little in my seat. Is he playing with me, is this a joke? Does he know how much I'm attracted to him? Is that allowed to use my attraction to him in this way?

What happened to toning that attraction down, huh?

We both know it doesn't ever work that way...

Russia stops mid-chew, narrowing his eyes at me, like I'm the one who's not getting it.

I blink back, waiting for him to explain himself as he dabs at his face carefully. He wipes everything off his face and beard, running his tongue over his teeth, checking for stray bits, taking his time in a way that's going to make me lose my mind, killing me with the patience I need but don't actually possess.

"Because I want you to be there with me, if you're willing to come."

I scoff. "Hold on a second, hold on a second. You want me to be there? Why do you do that, constantly qualifying your questions?" I sigh, waving at him.

Russia doesn't sigh, but it looks like he wants to.

I push myself back against the booth, putting space between us, as much as I'm able to by the constraints of the booth we're sitting in.

"Because I learned not only to ask for what I want, but to take into account what the other person wants, too. I used to have my head up my ass, and I'd like to think I've gotten better, gotten easier to be around, but I don't know." He shrugs, looking uncomfortable now, eyes skittering away, only to come back like I'm the magnet and he's the spinning dial in a compass, pointing to true north.

"The compass," I say, notching my chin towards the forearm he's got on the table, his hand looking lonely all by itself, but shit, I'm not gonna do anything about it. "The compass, looking for direction, trying to find your way home," I say, nodding to myself. "Yeah, it fits."

Russia nods along, and he doesn't get angry or defensive like I would expect him to, the way I tend to psychoanalyze a stranger and verbalize my intuition to them can be quite rude and quite a jarring experience, but I didn't engage my brain-mouth filter in time, and there's nothing I can do to take back the words I've already said out loud.

"So will you come? Will you come with me on the weekend to Alex's?"

Right, we're talking about the weekend, where I get to meet his friends...right.

"Uh, well..." I hedge, thinking about being there with Russia, again like the pseudo-girlfriend, and not feeling horrible about it, wanting to spend more time with him.

I'm more than half-convinced that he's like a glacier, only showing the world ten percent of his hidden depths, but I'm hoping I'm not the *Titanic* about to get screwed over *hard*. "Uh. When is it?"

Maybe I can get out of this one...

Maybe I should get out of this one...

But honestly, what would it hurt showing up to a social gathering now that Elena is always hanging around with Beckett like she wants to? Katie's with Dean more often than not, and while she might be there, too, it'd be nice to get a change of scenery, a change of pace...

"Saturday at two. I can drive us there." Russia nods to me, a small smile playing along his lips, making my own lips twitch in a mirrored action until I tell them to *stop*.

I'm still not sure about this.

What do you want? Make up your mind already!

I want it all, is that too much to ask for!?

Don't answer that.

My eyebrows pole vault the length of my five-head. "Excuse me?" I lean closer to the table, even ducking down my head to check his injured foot underneath the table, as if making sure the injury still exists.

"You don't even know if you can walk without crutches, let alone move your ankle enough to drive. You sprained your right foot, and you probably should keep it elevated, but I don't know, I'm not a doctor." I raise my palms high, all *freeze*, and glance down at the breadbasket, knowing I *want* another one, but also knowing, on the other hand, that the bread's going to ruin my appetite for my gnocchi (I'm settling on gnocchi in a rose sauce).

"*I'll* drive."

"Yeah?" Russia's eyes light up, his smile as big as the moon, and it affects me, it does, crashing through me and making my heart flutter in my chest. "You'll come with me?"

God, he sounds *excited* to spend time with me.

It's very hard to keep reminding myself that Russia has given his heart to someone else.

Then that makes you the rebound, Soph.

I tilt my head at him. "That kind of reaction from you has me kinda worried, Russia." I turn towards the waiter, the kid asking us if we're ready to order. I order what I want, and Russia orders what he wants, along with an Orange Crush.

I hate how I find that adorable – someone looking so clean cut and has all those proper manners getting a super sugary fizzy drink.

He should be swinging back the most bitter coffee, darker than a black hole, but instead he's drinking what a little kid might, searching for the next sugar fix.

Hell, Russia looks one way but might be the complete opposite. Can he apply that logic to me, too?

He dresses well, he folds his napkin over four times to get a clean surface every single time he wipes his mouth. His manners are impeccable, the clothes he wears immaculate. But then he's ordered and Orange Crush, and he's got hidden tattoos – a literal compass, showing him the way to go.

I frown at him, trying to figure him out.

And my crush on him just seems to grow exponentially.

I'm so, so screwed.

· ♥ · ♥ · ♥ · ♥ · ♥ ·

"I'm just glad you'll be coming with me, that's all." And he does, look glad that is. "I'll text you my address right now. We have to be there by two, and he lives in Laval—"

"Laval?! *Laval?!*" I whine.

Russia nods in commiseration.

Even though we're going to be heading there on the weekend and the traffic going off island to Laval *should not* be as terrible as it is on weekdays, I still get flashback memories of waiting hours to get into the downtown core and going back to me childhood home back when I lived with my parents in the suburbs before they retired to Charlevoix.

It makes me nauseous, being in a car that long, but honestly it shouldn't be hours of traffic on the weekend. Hopefully.

I'm already nervous as is sitting next to Russia right now. What am I going to do when we're sitting in traffic together?

Passing out at the wheel is not an option.

"I know, I know. All of our friends got mad at him when he and his wife moved out there, but the houses were more affordable. Is that going to be a problem? Do you want to meet me there?"

I kinda love how conscientious he's being, how very aware he is that this might be an inconvenience for me. I don't live in the deep downtown core like Russia does, clearly only a few blocks away from the shop.

I frown at him, thinking. "It's my day off, actually. I can make it."

There's still a part of me that wants to ask what to wear, what I should look like, but I'm not doing that anymore, I'm not. This is what is, this is the Sophie you're gonna get forever and ever until the last tube of red lipstick is gone from this planet.

I'm done trying to change myself to fit someone else's expectations.

"Great. Awesome." The word sounds awkward in his accent, in his voice, like it doesn't come natural to him. His smile is doing something to my insides, and I don't know what to do about it.

Is this a date? Or are you being used to make him feel more comfortable and help him out since his foot is now messed up?

Time will tell, I guess.

Honestly, I don't think I can be left alone, not even for a second.

Russia makes me stupid, so *stupid*.

But what else is new?

·♥·♥·♥·♥·♥·

I spend too much of my time straddling the line between wanting to show off my tattoos at this get-together thing and wanting to hide them. I vacillate between wanting to make a good first impression, and then get mad at myself like what another person's opinion of me actually matters when it does *not*.

I remind myself that I'm doing this in some odd version of wanting to help Russia out, like it was somehow my fault that he was on his way to get tattooed by me when he messed up his foot, walked on it (like an idiot) to let me know what happened, and now he's got a bad sprain and is stuck with crutches.

I feel partially responsible when logically that doesn't make any kind of sense, but I've never been logical a day in my life, and I'm not going to start now.

I end up going with my *least* distressed black jeans, regular ankle socks (in bright red, because why not?), and a white long-sleeve shirt that covers up my sleeve tattoos, but still is kinda see-through so you can see the outline of them, too, through the thin material.

I've put my hair up, my undercut showing from the back of my head to just over the ridges of my ears, my twelve combined piercings in my ears visible, my jewelry matching across both ears, even though sometimes I like the asymmetric style, too. That's as much thought as I give to convention, to looking presentable.

Honestly, if Russia's friends are jerks, I'm bringing my car so I can basically take off whenever I need to and have Katie (whom I confirmed will be there earlier today, with Dean!) bring Russia back home.

I wince in the safety of my car as I watch Russia trying to navigate the icy sidewalk when I pull up in front of his building on Saturday at 1:25 p.m. sharp.

I'm caught in limbo of putting the car in park and rounding it to make sure that he doesn't fall again, messing up his ankle even more, and knowing that it might not be my place to do so. Honestly though, all my first assumptions about him have been wrong, and maybe he'd gladly accept the help, whether he has crutches or not.

I don't get to find out though, as Russia's able to get to my car, open the passenger door and slide inside in an inelegant sprawl that has the crutches pushing up against my roof and clacking together in a way that catches his fingers between them, making him swear in what I'm going to confidently say sounds like Russian.

I hiss in sympathy at the imagined pain already throbbing in my own fingers until he leans out and closes the passenger door, panting a little before he finally turns to me, his blue-blue eyes leaping with something that I could call excitement if push came to shove, and *I could* call it happiness at seeing *me* if you put a gun to my head and I admitted it before you pulled the trigger.

"Hi," he says, trying to get comfortable with the crutches out in front of him, maneuvering them around so they don't touch the gearshift, and putting on his seatbelt with a *click*, hands resting on his lap before moving to the heaters on the dash, practically shoving his fingers through the slats.

I frown. "Were you waiting outside long?"

Russia grins sheepishly but keeps his face turned resolutely forward, looking out the windshield while I turn off my hazard lights and look in my blind spot before starting to merge with traffic.

My GPS is keyed in with Alex's address and I let the posh voice direct me where to go, mispronouncing the names of the streets with a horrible English accent that makes me honk in laughter. Like, it pronounces the S in *Rene-Levesque*, which is hilarious.

"I overestimated how long it would take me to get downstairs. I apparently forgot there was an elevator in my building, and then I got hot standing inside with the heat blasting, so I came outside, deciding to wait, stuck in a vicious cycle of my own making."

I laugh, my feelings for him pressing up against my rib cage.

"How's the foot?" I ask, lowering the music. My Spotify playlist is not up for debate, and I'm not changing it if he doesn't like the Backstreet Boys—that's just his problem and no one else's.

"It's better, thanks. Thank you for picking me up. I appreciate it."

I nod, still looking straight ahead, noticing that this is the closest we've been outside of me doing work on him.

I don't even know why I'm impressed by his manners anymore. It's common decency, but really a hard juxtaposition of all the guys I've dated in the past.

"You look really great. I can't wait for them to meet you."

I balk at that, make some kind of noise that does not sound human at all. I cough, try to clear my throat of any more animal noises.

"Uh, can you grab my phone and search up some bakeries or something similar around here? I want to bring something for everyone," I say, keeping my eyes pinned straight ahead, fighting back a yawn because it's so warm and cozy in my car, and I'm starting to get just that much *a little too warm* in my winter coat.

I glance at myself in the rear-view mirror, my giant bug-glasses on that makes me feel a teeny, tiny bit like Audrey Hepburn and glamourous to a fault, my dark red lip looking vampy and sexy as hell, even though underneath the dark lenses my eyeshadow's neutral but still a little shimmery (because give me a shimmer or metallic eyeshadow or give me death!) paired with a winged eyeliner sharp enough to use as a weapon in a jiffy.

All in all, I'm real proud of my makeup and Russia hasn't even commented on it.

Well, we all know girls wear makeup for other girls.

Russia does as he's told, looking up the nearest bakery type place based on our location as I start driving in the general direction of the highway, following the instructions I'm being given over the speakers.

I park in one of the two parking spaces available right out front of the bakery, not even bothering to pay the meter since in this area you're allowed fifteen minutes before anything bad happens (like a ticket).

I glance at the storefront, the wood paneling snuggled up to the brick of the overall building, the way the glass at the very front looks like it would open up to a really beautiful *terrasse* come summertime (or really as soon as the weather allows for it).

I have to run around the car to steady Russia or else he would have planted his bad foot against the ground when he tries to get his balance, and he smiles at me warmly when I finally let him go.

"I swear, you're going to give me a hundred heart attacks today," I say. As if I wasn't already nervous enough as it is.

I'm meeting Russia's friends, and I *know* they're going to have questions about me, questions I'm not sure I'm ready to answer.

Why did Russia bring you here to this special moment?

I'm literally just his tattoo artist that has a giant crush on him. That's it.

We both walk inside (well, Russia uses his crutches) the little Greek bakery, Zachary, and we head to the glass counter, a girl looking about my age, no name badge in sight, standing behind the counter. She's got a smile on her face and a little bit of something that looks like chocolate frosting on her white apron and some on her cheek.

She catches Russia's eye, I can tell, and I tamp down on the would-be jealousy, knowing I'm reading too deeply into it, looking for something that isn't there, feeling something that shouldn't be there.

"Hello," he says, polite as ever and making me question my own manners, or lack of them.

Her eyes follow the length of him, down to the crutches, a bemused look on her face before she shakes herself out of it. Her eyes land on me, and she points to her eyes.

"Wow, your eyeshadow, it's amazing," she says, holding up her hand in an A-OK sign, grinning at me.

"Oh, thank you," I say, surprised, clutching onto my sunnies at the top of my head, all the better to see with once I'm inside. I tilt my head at her, getting a good vibe, knowing it might be a salesperson tactic, but honestly, I was going to buy from here *anyway* so there's no need for flattery. Although, it does feel nice for someone else to appreciate all my hard work since Russia clearly didn't.

I can feel him swing to look at me, nearly losing his balance on his crutches, the carpet underneath our boots sodden and a testament to how many customers this bakery gets—even if I've never heard of it before.

The girl behind the counter stuffs her hands in her apron pocket, and clips it onto her apron. She tisks to herself as she does this, her name displayed in English and in Greek (I think)—Chloe.

Even if this day's gonna suck, and Russia's friends won't like me and it's all a bust, and nothing will ever happen with him in the way I want it to happen, I know that Chloe's compliment is going to buoy me throughout the rest of the day, no matter how shit this whole meeting Russia's friends goes.

"What can I get you guys?" she asks, clapping her hands together, scratching at her cheek that has the chocolate frosting on it. "Oh, man, has that been there this whole time?" she asks, looking between the two of us, and Russia stays stoic, but I give her the benefit of the doubt.

I nod slowly.

"Well, I'm going to go over that for an entire year. So? What can I get you guys? Looking for cakes or a traditional pastry? Are you familiar with Greek pastries? Or is it for a wedding cake?" Chloe asks, shooting out the questions rapid fire.

I'm still trying to process about the whole 'wedding cake' deal, while Chloe wipes at her cheek, trying to distract us from the chocolate that's being removed from her skin.

I suddenly have the urge to want to be friends with her. I really, really do.

"Not...not a wedding cake," Russia sputters out, choking on air to the point where I have to clap on his back to help him breathe again. "No wedding cake."

Chloe looks like a deer caught in the middle of the highway, the headlights of impending doom coming too fast for any kind of escape plan to be made. "I'm sorry," she says. "I shouldn't have assumed..."

I shake my head at her, shooting her a reassuring smile. It *is* a bakery after all, and I'm sure they make delicious wedding cakes, and maybe one day, I *will* get married, but it might not be to Russia.

Hell, if we ever do, though, I'm coming right back here.

This place is good luck, I can already *feel it.*

"No, no, don't worry about it. We're just friends. I've never been here before, but we're going to a friend's house," I explain, wanting Chloe to get the full picture and the background story. I'm still absentmindedly rubbing at Russia's back and have to force myself to stop or *else.*

"Russia?" I ask, turning towards him. "What should we get? Do Alex and his wife like something in particular? I know Dean will eat anything, so I'm open to taking suggestions. What do you think?"

"Can I make a suggestion?" Chloe asks, bringing us over to the glass case where beautifully presented cakes and pastries are in the window, rounding the glass case to come stand beside Russia, pointing to different items.

I let Russia take the reins, not knowing one thing about Greek pastries although I will say unequivocally that *everything* looks delicious and like it's going to make me unbutton my jeans before the night's over from trying a bite from every single thing.

I buy a whole cake by myself, wanting it to come from me, and Russia decides to buy a pastry that I can't pronounce, along with a box of a dozen red velvet cupcakes that look too pretty with their fluffy cream cheese frosting; I probably won't want to eat it and risk ruining it.

But honestly, who am I kidding?

We thank Chloe once everything's been rung up, and I lunge to take one of their business cards off the counter, grinning at her when she sees me do it. I check their business hours and know that I'm going to be ordering from them for the shop more often than not, and that I'm going to have to hit the gym more if I'm going to be consuming these delicious-looking pastries on a weekly basis.

Honestly, though, life's too short. When in doubt, buy the eyeshadow palette and buy the delicious Greek pastries.

After securing our sweets in the back seat of my car, and watching Russia practically flip-flop into the passenger seat, letting out a sigh of exhaustion before wrangling his crutches inside next to him, I close the door for him, remaining totally unaffected when he gives me a grateful smile.

Yeah, right. Me? Unaffected when it comes to Russia? Yeah, no way.

I nearly get hit by some idiot on his bicycle in the *middle of winter*, yelling at *me* for having the audacity to round my car to get to the driver's side door where I'm parked. Some yelling and swearing ensues, and when I get back in the car to start my car, I'm already aggravated.

Lord help me if there's traffic on the way over to freaking Laval, I might just lose it.

"Are you all right?" Russia asks, and I just grunt an affirmative, turning my body to triple-check my blind spot for idiot Montrealers who think that taking their bicycles around the city is a good idea, acting like they own the freaking road.

I sigh, glancing in my rear-view mirror, then blind spot again before indicating and switching lanes, merging with traffic. I steer us towards the highway to eventually get onto the 15 N, headed towards Laval, the traffic a little slow and sluggish with a surprising number of cars on the road on this Saturday afternoon, but nothing to really complain about or lose my ever-loving shit over.

The drive over to Alex's home is pretty cool, and I don't feel like I'm going to die in an awkward silence—well at least not to the point that I'll fling myself out of my own moving car, but I'm still comfortable enough that I feel okay to drive, to have him so close and in my personal space.

There's light conversation as I drive us there, letting the voice living in my phone tell me where to go and when I need to change lanes and head towards which exit.

I'm too aware of Russia in my passenger seat, where he fidgets every once in a while, to get comfortable.

"You can lean the seat back, you know," I murmur to him, keeping my eyes on the road, my hands on the wheel.

"Uh, I'm fine. Don't worry about me."

"No, seriously, you'll mess up your ankle even worse. The seat's too close, just adjust it," I say, turning to look at him for a few split seconds.

"Sophie, I'm all right," he says, shaking his head. "I am. We'll be there soon anyway."

"I don't know why you're being stubborn," I grunt, hands tightening along the wheel as I drag my attention back to the road. I check my blind spot before indicating (like you're *supposed to do*), and switch lanes again the guy in front of me not driving fast enough for my liking.

"And you need to relax. I promise nothing is going to happen once we get there. I'm the asshole of the group, and if you and I get along, then you'll be just fine."

I snort, chance another glance at him, startled to find that he's being serious. "You're the asshole? Really?" I snort again, not believing a word he says. "I'm not sure I believe you."

Russia shrugs. "You met me at a time in my life where I'm looking for something else. I wasn't always this way. That's all I'm willing to say right now."

I clear my throat, cough out an invisible bug out of my throat. "Oh my God, you can't just end a conversation like *that*." I sigh. "Yup, fine, sure, no problem." I'm a bumbling idiot when it comes to this guy.

"Russia...I've got one more question until we get there, and I really want to hear your answer."

Russia fidgets one more time out of the corner of my eye. "I'm all ears."

How do I even begin?

"Why did you want me to come with you to Alex's place? Wouldn't another friend of yours offered to pick you up or something?" I ask, glancing over to him.

"Sophie, the road!" Russia yells, and I bring my attention back to the road, moving around the idiot who slammed the brakes in front of me, pulling my foot off the gas.

I continue down the highway, eyes pinned to the road ahead of me without saying anything else.

Russia keeps up the conversation on his end, probably noticing how my hands are practically fused to the steering wheel as we get closer and closer to our destination.

He talks about his hometown life back in Russia, how much he misses it. I let the words wash over me, my heart beating fast and hard in my chest.

I try to ignore the explosion of butterflies eating my insides, chewing on my stomach lining until I need to finally give myself a pep talk once I pull up the curb at our final destination.

I rush to get out of the car as Russia struggles on the other side, trying to wrangle his crutches and get them down on the ground to support his weight. I nearly slip on a patch of ice and want to yell at him while he maneuvers himself around to get at the desserts in the back seat.

"Are you serious right now?" I ask, waving my hand at his current predicament. "Just ask for help, would you? We can't afford to have that cake ruined, we just *can't*."

Russia's cheeks are flaming under the harsh afternoon light, the sun already starting to head towards the horizon even though it's definitely setting later and later these days, the countdown to ending daylight savings getting closer and closer.

"You already drove me here, and I'm used to doing everything by myself. Let me take the bag at least, I can do that. I'm not completely useless."

"Russia..." I start, then shake my head, hiking my purse higher up on my shoulder. I wonder if the dog treats I have yet to take out of my bag will become useful once we step inside the house, but that would be a thing I think Russia would have told me, so maybe not.

"Yeah, I guessed that already. Here, let me grab the bag. You all right there, or should I give you a piggyback ride like a pack mule?" I smile at him, but he just looks at me, not like he's willing to take the risk, or in disbelief that I could do it (I probably could under these conditions once I stretched out and limbered up and everything), but in a way that makes me hold my breath.

The snow swirls around us in a lazy breeze, being moved around under the harsh sunlight, like we're stuck in a snow globe together, picture perfect and ready for display.

Russia looks at me like he wants to say something, but I'm already turning away, my heart beating erratically.

I don't know what I would do if Russia's interested in me for real.
Good thing he isn't, huh?

I grab the bag and cake box from him when he doesn't actually move to give either of them to me, lock up my car, hike up my purse on my shoulder again and walk behind him as we head to the front door.

I follow him, step for step, like I'm going to catch him in case he falls on his ass, or try to hold him upright. As if that's possible with the way the bag is looped over my wrists, and my hands are occupied by a box of cake.

Fortunately, we make it up the driveway, the area having been heavily salted recently.

Alex's home looks cozy from the outside, and I'm hoping it's just the same on the inside. By the time we make it up the front stairs, Russia's panting, and I'm the one ringing the doorbell, giving him those few extra seconds to catch his breath while I shiver on the front porch, waiting to see how I'm going to be received.

I get a grateful smile in return while I try to school my face into being a bitch, but a *nice* bitch, pushing my sunnies up my nose to the top of my head, trying to ignore the fact that I'm going to be judged—it's going to be inevitable, I know, but still, it *sucks* being on the receiving end.

Alex is the one who opens the door. He's a familiar face, and he's wearing a welcoming smile that's big and wide. I blink at him, the smile a stark contrast to how I saw him the last time when I gave him the tattoo.

Alex's gaze moves over to me first, then to Russia and his crutches. He hastily waves us in, me going into the den of the beast first, only to be quickly followed by Russia and before I know it, I'm pulled into Alex's tight hug.

"Oh, okay, then," I laugh, arms pinned to my sides, still somehow keeping the cake box balanced in my left hand, not really sure how to proceed here.

I'm not in the habit of getting hugged by strangers upon entering their home, it only usually happens right *after* I tattoo them, and even then, some people aren't huggers.

Alex releases me just as quickly as he tugged me in for a tight hug, making me feel it along my ribcage, his hands going to my upper arms, smiling at me like he's won the lottery and I'm the idiot who gave him the winning ticket.

"I know it doesn't make a lot of sense, but I feel like your tattoo helped bring my son home. And I want to thank you for that."

I raise my eyebrows at him, shaking my head, not wanting that kind of power.

"I didn't do anything. I promise you I didn't do anything," I stammer, knowing that whatever little prayer, or whatever you want to call it, I said in my head while doing the tattoo isn't the reason that his son is home right now, but maybe it did help, in some small way. Maybe.

"Your little boy did it all on his own," I smile at Alex, who smiles back, bending his head down to look at our feet, like he can't bear to look at me as the emotion crashes over him.

I can't pretend to understand, but I let him use me as a pillar to hold him up until he feels strong enough to lift his head and look at the both of us.

"Shit," Russia says, and I turn to look at him once I'm fully released, still holding onto the desserts. He's catching his weight on the far wall, the crutches falling out of his grip to practically ricochet off the floor before falling at my feet like some kind of weird offering.

Alex lets go of me completely and stoops to grab them off the floor, and only then do I realize there's another person in the entranceway, a person I've never met before.

I place the cake box down by my feet (gently and carefully, I'm not a monster), and unzip my winter coat with my free hand, and swallow hard, knowing that something's going to change, something's going to *happen*.

"Hi," I say, introducing myself, hand out and ready for a handshake. "I'm Sophie."

The stranger smiles at me, and it's warm and genuine and immediately puts me at ease, as she moves towards me, a long-sleeved t-shirt with some kind of reference on it that goes right over my head.

She brings her hand up, her long brown hair hitting the middle of her waist, brown and wavy and pretty perfect and I bet she actually *did* wake up like that. Her makeup's understated, and her eyelashes are super long. standing this close to her I can totally tell they're not falsies, and I envy her.

I feel a swift and quick surge of it as her hand connects with mine.

"Hi," she says, grinning at me, looking at me like we're about to become best friends. "I'm Sera."

NINE

S hit, shit, shit!
   This is Sera? *She's Sera?*

What the hell?!

My hand goes limp like a dead fish in her grip, and I glance down in horror at our clasped hands, as if there's some other explanation why my grip has gone lax and all jellyfish-like. I clear my throat, cough into my free hand, trying to keep my smile in place, almost as if it's been screwed on, feeling my eyebrows pinching together.

What am I going to say?

Oh, so you're the one that Russia can't get over...

Yeah, I'm not gonna do that. *Definitely* not going to do that.

I'm so taken aback that I *almost* repeat my name again and then realize that we've been holding hands too long. Panicked, I drop my grip of her hand as if it's burning me, and she lets go of mine and the whole thing is awkward and weird, and my smile drops off my face as if I've taken a makeup wipe and swiped it right off.

"Here, let me take that from you," Sera says, leaning over to grab the bag of pastries and the cake box I've put on the floor to deal with my coat and boots, and of course I step into a wet spot and groan when the cold, icy water hits my toes.

If that isn't an omen, then I don't know what is.

"Oh, thanks," I mumble, surreptitiously trying to swipe my sock against a dry spot on the carpet, mashing my foot down so there's some kind of water absorption before I look over to Russia.

I notice that his own coat has been discarded, his boots are off, and his crutches are right up under his armpits. His gaze keeps swinging between the both of us with an unreadable expression.

"Hey, Russia," Sera says with that smile on her face, that perfect smile that makes you feel like you'll be friends forever. I watch as she walks over to him, arching up on her toes and kisses his cheeks, one on either side that makes that jealous monster inside of me snarl and growl and posture, but I know I'm not going to do anything about it.

There's nothing I can do to make him fall out of love with her and fall into love with me. That's not how feelings work. And honestly, I don't deserve to be a placeholder for the next best thing.

There's something magical, about the two of them together, though. Maybe it's the familiarity of knowing each other for a long time, but I think this is what a fairy tale looks like.

"I heard you took a tumble," Sera says, her laugh an undercurrent.

"Yeah," Russia replies gruffly, turning to look at me. "I wouldn't have made it to the clinic without Sophie, though."

Sera smiles even more brightly at the two of us.

She moves past me, tilting her head towards the house, as if she's the one living here when Alex is clearly an emotional mess, having disappeared with the desserts, and getting hollered at somewhere deep inside.

We follow Sera like puppies knowing we're going on an adventure, and I stay behind Russia until he stops moving forward and tells me to go on ahead of him, trailing behind the two of us with every sound of his crutches pushing into the flooring, two at a time in an odd gait.

My heart trips up in my chest as I keep my eyes pinned to Sera's back, a little surprised that I'm taller than her, like just by being herself she takes up more space than I do, and more of Russia's attention.

Jesus, I'm so not over Russia and my stupid crush on him... I'm being stupid, so stupid. How about we just try and enjoy ourselves, okay?

How about we just try and do that?

I release a pent-up breath, following Sera into the kitchen, being confronted with all of these people I don't know. I clench my hands into fists at my sides, as if that's somehow going to hide the tattoos I have on my hands and fingers. I'm introduced to everyone in the room with Alex doing the honors, having made me his pseudo-best friend as he comes to stand right beside me, pointing out people and naming names.

He introduces his wife, Theresa first, who's holding their son, a soft, serene smile on her lips even if her eyes are drooping with a bone-deep exhaustion, her body swaying from side to side as she tries to rock the baby to sleep.

It brings a lump to my throat, looking at the little potato of a baby, his tiny hands reaching up into his mother's hair, tugging sharply. Theresa just glances down at him with *so* much love that it makes my heart ache at the sight of it and reminds me just how much I miss my own parents, and that I'm going to have to make a trip to Charlevoix soon.

I'm then introduced to Josh, a stocky guy standing next to Elias, the two of them holding crystal glasses with something that could be whiskey, both of them nodding at me, looking me up and down like they're trying to figure me out.

All the while, Sera takes out the cakes and pastries from their previous homes and places them on the kitchen counter, exclaiming over some of them and putting them in the fridge for Theresa and Alex.

She finally turns towards me, walking around and behind me in a way that makes me shiver giving her my back (like, what, I'm going to get attacked?) to stand next to a guy. A very *hot* guy I have yet to be introduced to, who puts his arm over her shoulders and squeezes her close, smiling down at her in a way that *also* breaks my heart a little.

Oh, I was wrong. *These* two like they belong in a fairy tale, a portrait passed on for generations at a time.

Like, what do I have to do to get Russia to look at me like that? *What do I have to do?*

"This is my husband, Hunter," Sera says, and again, I hold my hand out for a shake, Hunter taking my hand firmly, but not like he's going to pulverize my grip anytime soon.

"And this..." Sera grunts as a kid who looks about nine years old careens into her by skating along the kitchen tile in his socks, yelping a little when Sera's elbow hits his head.

"Matty, why are you running around if you're not being chased?" she asks, looking down at him, putting both hands on his face, squishing his cheeks.

"Mom, come on, *come on*, I'm playing hide-and-seek with Uncle Dean's dogs! Pongo's going to find me, and I have to hide, okay?" Matty's turns around, looking over his shoulder for the pups and catches sight of me, his whole body stilling.

"You have drawings all over your body," he blurts, pointing out the ones on my hands, the outlines on my arms that you can see through my shirt.

"Wow, they look awesome. Hey, Mom, when can I get a tattoo?" Matty reaches back to tug at Sera's shirt, pulling down on the sleeve enough that it slips, and her hot pink bra strap is shown to the room at large.

"When you're eighteen, and not before then. And you have to prove to me that you're gonna like it forever and ever," she says, leaning down to kiss the top of his head, and Matty's not at the age yet where being shown affection by your parents isn't embarrassing or a fate worse than death.

It's adorable.

"Maybe we'll go together, huh?" She ruffles his hair, and I'm not sure who lets who go first, but it's a mutual decision before the kid slides over to the side and looks up at his dad.

"Hey, Dad, when can I get a tattoo?"

I'm looking at the back of Matty's head, and I can totally *tell* that the kid's got a shit-eating grin on his face.

"Get outta here, little man, or you're going to have to hide from me, soon," Hunter tickles his kid along the ribs, and the kid giggles, hunching over right away to get away from those hands.

"Go, play with the dogs. I'm sure they're smelling every inch of the place."

Matty waves goodbye to both of his parents, and Sera tugs on Hunter's sleeve, too. "When can I get a tattoo?" she asks, making him laugh by poking at his belly and ribs, and they're so cute I could cry.

It's only when I look around the room to find Russia, do I notice that he's resolutely looking away from the two of them, the sight of him making my heart practically shrivels up in my chest.

Unrequited love sucks, and it sucks *hard*.

I move towards Russia, reaching out to touch his forearm, to squeeze down on his skin. I sort of know how he feels. His blue eyes cut to me, and I hold my breath, waiting for him to say something, anything.

"Sophie, what did you want to ask me in the car?"

I bite my lip and shake my head. "Don't worry about it. I have my answer."

My name's being called, and I move over to see that Alex is showing off his tattoo to Josh and Elias, and they make the appropriate noises, but Alex is beaming like you've gone and put a glow worm up his ass. It's cute, and no one's been rude to me so far, and everything's going great.

"Can I do anything to help?" I ask Alex, looking over at him, leaving Russia to compose himself somewhere off and out of my peripheral vision. "I'm very happy that your son's home." I stifle the urge to hold my two thumbs up, like I would be trivializing the little guy's hardships and all that he's had to do to get home to his parents.

"Thank you," Alex says, head bowing down, glancing down at our toes. He sniffs hard, and my own eyes start to get wet, and when I look up, Theresa's moving towards him and hefting the baby up, hiking him up higher on her chest.

"Hold him," she says. "It'll make it feel more real that he's home, that he's with us."

"*S'agapo*," Alex says, the language unknown to me, but he leans close to his wife and kisses her softly on the lips, the cheek, and the forehead with such intimacy that I have to look away, like I'm seeing something that I really *shouldn't* be seeing, shouldn't be gawking at and longing for exactly the way I actually am.

"All right, all right. I need to sit down somewhere and tell the boy the ways of the world," Russia says, more boisterous now, putting on a façade that I can't hope to understand.

Don't I do the same thing, though? Get louder to drown out the silence?

Russia and I are more alike than I'd like to admit.

He comes closer to Alex, and the pair of them move off to the living room, just off the kitchen, settling down onto a couch.

Alex holds his son close to his chest, and they discuss "manly" type things, but I can tell from all the way over here that both of their eyes are shining with unshed tears.

I'm out of my element with all these strangers around me, and I really can't have Russia bailing on me, too.

"Yo, Sophie," Katie's voice calls out, coming out of an alcove somewhere with Dean in tow. "Ah, shit, sorry, the baby," she whispers, but baby doesn't say a peep, and when I glance over, Alex is holding him half-upright in his hands.

The baby boy's reaching for his beard, his hands slapping at his face, the exact moment in time that would make a fantastic tattoo, a memory that could be kept like this forever.

"Yo," I say, waving at Dean who's walking behind her, Pongo the Dalmatian, trotting behind his dad, eyes pinned up to Dean, tail wagging, nails not even rapping against the kitchen tile.

"Pongo!" Matty yells from somewhere in the house, voice distant enough that we all freeze and swing our gazes to the baby, but the kid's not scared. Pongo's ears go up, his head cocking from side to side, glancing between where Matty's voice came from and where Dean's standing next to him. Pongo plops his butt down, vibrating on the spot.

"Pongo, come and find me!"

"Okay, boy," Dean says, and Pongo's off at a trot, like he knows there's a tiny, defenseless human in the mix that isn't used to his presence yet, and Pongo disappears around a corner.

"Hey, Sophie," Dean says, running a hand across my undercut at the back of my head, the shaved parts over my ears, too.

"Sweet," he says, grinning at me, and really, is it really hard to believe that Dean Carter is one of my favorite people in the entire world? "Looking good, Sophie Kincaid," he says, tapping at my shoulders. "Shit, look at these pumpkins. Babe, why don't you have these pumpkins?" Dean laughs when Katie jabs him in the ribs with her elbow.

"I've got pumpkins elsewhere, and you've never complained about those," she says, the grin she gives him straddling the line of innocent to lascivious that has me looking away with a blush.

Only Katie, only Katie.

"No, but Sophie's looking like a tank."

"I know, right? I have to or my posture's going to be shit by the time I'm thirty-five," I say, flexing my arm a little for Dean, who fawns over my biceps because he's that kind of person, a golden retriever in human form.

"Hey, did she give you permission to touch her like that?" Russia says, teetering on his crutches he moved so fast into our conversational circle, making Dean turn to him and grab a hold of him before he succumbs to gravity. "Thanks, man."

Dean frowns at him, pointing a finger at Russia's nose. "Sophie and I are friends, man. Relax, relax. I'm sure all that stress is bad for your foot."

I shake my head. "Uh, I don't think it works that way, Dean."

"Sure it does," Dean says jovially, smacking Russia on the shoulder, upsetting his balance for a split second. "Look at him, all stressed and tensed up. Sophie's like my little sister, the one I never had, yeah?"

My cheeks burn at the implication of what Dean's saying, what he's *implying*.

"Uh, Dean, it's okay," I wave my hand at him, waving the whole situation off, like it's a bad stink I can dissipate even if I'm sure I've stepped in it now. "I'm just Russia's tattoo artist," I say, laughing it off, but it sounds hollow, even to me.

Katie's eyes narrow on me, crossing her arms over her chest, pulling all her *inner bitch* at her core, and turning her head to glare at Russia with all the force behind that stare.

"What? Why are you looking at me like that? What did I do?"

"Did you do what I told you to do? What we discussed the last time?" Katie asks, an edge of danger making my heart thrum in my chest, like a plucked guitar string, vibrating over and over.

"I've gotten around to it, yeah," Russia says, rubbing the back of his neck, keeping his stare pinned on Katie.

"Do you know what they're talking about?" Dean stage whispers, covering the side of his mouth with one hand, and all I can do is stifle a nervous giggle and shake my head from side to side, having *no idea* what's going on.

Matty's giggle pierces the room, and we all swing our heads back to the mouth of the hall, finding Pongo trotting beside the kid, practically skipping over to his parents, face red and eyes almost fever bright.

"Hey, Dad, I'm feeling kind of off. Can we check?" Matty asks, pressing his entire face into Hunter's stomach, Hunter's hand going to the back of his neck, his face in agony as he looks down at his little boy.

"Yeah, I'll get Sera's bag," Katie calls, heading towards the entrance, and Pongo sniffs at Matty's neck, sticking his nose into his throat, towards his mouth, tail not wagging anymore.

"Pongo, here," Dean orders, pointing down at his feet, and the Dalmatian looks between the two of them, his dad, and the kid he'd been playing with, until he finally relents.

Katie comes back with a purse that looks like a backpack, unzipping it already and holding a small pouch of sorts towards Sera.

"All right, kiddo, take a seat," Hunter says, carrying his boy to the kitchen stool. Matty nods slowly, seemingly out of it, like he's gotten into a bottle of beer and it's hitting his nine-year-old body *hard*. But that can't be what's happening, right? "Does it feel high or low?"

Matty shrugs, and Sera rips open the pouch, taking out a little machine, pressing it against the kid's upper arm, the buzz of the machine loud enough that I can hear it over here. She glances down at the machine, then starts pulling more things out of the pouch, making the kid bleed.

I'm about to say something, and I find myself moving a half-step forward, but someone's gently grabbing around my arm, jarring me out of the trance I've been in.

When I turn to look, it's Russia who's holding onto my upper arm and he just gives me a slight shake of his head, his blue eyes dark and sad.

"What's going on?" I whisper, my heart pounding hard against my ribs, worried, afraid because I don't understand what's going on.

"He's diabetic, Matty. Hunter, too."

"Oh," I say, not really understanding, not getting the full implications. I swing my gaze over to the trio of them, as Sera and Hunter's face, tight with worry now, glance down at the machine on the kitchen counter.

"Good news, buddy, you get to have some of that strawberry juice that Aunt Theresa likes so much," Sera says, glancing over at Theresa, getting a nod. Sera's clearly been here before, knowing her way around the kitchen, and sets out the glass for Matty and Hunter, the kitchen island separating them.

"Here you go, kiddo," Hunter says, holding the glass for him.

"Dad," Matty sighs, eyes fluttering like he's exhausted all of a sudden. "I can do it by myself. I'm not a little kid anymore."

"Yeah, well, you'll always be little to me," Hunter says, the forced inflection that *everything's okay* running hollow.

Matty sucks back the juice, drinking it down like it's water even though I'm sure it's terribly sweet. "Even when I'm bigger than you?" Matty asks, smiling at his dad.

"I'm gonna be bigger than Mom soon, too," he says, nodding to himself, then finishing up the glass completely, wiping his mouth with his sleeve, stopping himself after the fact to frown down at his shirt. "Aw, man."

"Clothes are meant to keep your body warm and not for cleaning yourself up. We have napkins for that, buddy," Hunter says, leaning down a little, bracing his weight against the kitchen island, keeping his eyes pinned to his son. "Let's just take a breather for a few minutes, all right?"

Matty nods, and Sera turns away, putting the jug of strawberry juice into the fridge, but even from this distance, even just looking at her profile, I can tell it breaks her heart, seeing them both like that.

And for some reason, I decide to play superhero.

"Hey, Matty," I say, coming closer to the kitchen island, hiking myself up on the stool, feet dangling when the kid looks over at me. Hunter's eyes sharp and predatory, like he's *allowing* me to come closer, and I nod to him, getting and receiving the unspoken message.

"Let me show you a couple of my favorite tattoos and how I got them. Would that be okay to tell you that story?"

Matty nods, swinging his stool towards me, and I roll up the sleeves of my shirt, the kid's face adorably surprised and shocked, pointing down at my skin, but not touching.

"This one," I say, pointing down to the hummingbird I have on my left forearm. The hummingbird isn't as bright as it was when I got it when I was nineteen and will need touching up before I hit my thirtieth birthday probably, but every single time I look at it, it makes me happy, and I think that's what tattoos should do—they should make you happy.

"The hummingbird is my favorite animal in the entire world. Did you know that they're the only birds that can fly backwards *and* upside down?"

Matty looks at me dubiously, his eyebrows pulled down in a questioning frown. He doesn't believe me.

"If I didn't see it, it didn't happen," he says, leaning his head against his hand, elbow to the kitchen island.

The answer is one I'd expect from a teenager, but I was like that at his age, too. I think Matty's an only child, just like me.

"Easy there, Matty, there's gotta be videos everywhere online. Have your parents show you sometime. Let's go to the next one," I say, pointing to the one on top of my left hand, a series of interlocking honeycomb structures, one of the strongest structures the natural planet has to offer.

And we go like that for the next ten minutes, me losing track of time, and when Sera and Hunter finally check Matty's blood using that little machine thing, nodding at him that he can go play but not to run around too much, I catch a glimpse of Russia looking at me, head cocked to the side.

Like he's trying to figure me out.

TEN

D inner goes by quickly, and I don't actually do anything absolutely hideous like drop my food in my lap, and I apparently get the seat of honor next to Matty. The kid's been asking me a ton of questions about my tattoos, harping on the fact that they hurt when you get them and then going around and asking everyone else if they have tattoos.

Hunter has some, Sera no, Katie not if you put a gun to her head, Dean yes, Alex yes, Theresa, no, and Josh and Elias just shake their heads, Elias admitting that he has a phobia of needles to the table at large.

Everyone's drinking beer or wine with dinner—lemon chicken and roasted potatoes, apparently Greek-style which I find out is *delicious* and I want to have this particular dish *always*.

I didn't know little kids would talk this much, but Matty sure does talk a lot, chatting with everyone in the room, and it just puts my sneaking suspicion that he's an only child further to the test, and makes me believe I'm right.

It's cute, though, and the way he talks to Russia and Dean, like he reveres them, right up there with his dad. He's a little cooler with Josh and Elias, so I guess he doesn't get to see them as much.

"How come you don't have long nails, like Aunt Katie?" Matty asks, glancing down at my hands currently over my belly, knowing I need to save room for dessert, trying to convince my body and my will that we're aligned in wanting to eat dessert when it shows up at the table.

"Huh? Oh, because I tattoo, and it's hard to tattoo with really long nails. They're pretty, though, huh?"

Matty's cheeks go red, and he nearly fumbles his glass of water, making a pained wheezing noise as he rights it, nearly sloshing it all over the place. He looks at me quickly to see if I've noticed, and I make sure to keep my gaze pinned to my empty plates, biting the meat of my inner cheeks so I don't do something stupid like laugh in the kid's face.

"So how's the tattoo going, Russia?" Hunter asks, rubbing a hand through Matty's hair, the length of his head, just a gentle pet that the kid loves and follows the pressure against his dad's hand.

Russia carefully wipes his face in that way he does, squaring up the linen, using one side to wipe, then folding it over before dabbing it delicately at his mouth, placing the dirty side up on the table, to be used again. "Ah, good?"

"Yeah, tell us, did he cry from the pain?" Josh asks, holding up his beer for me as if we're going to cheers but I don't have anything to cheers with, so I pretend I'm holding an invisible beer bottle, not wanting to leave him hanging.

"Uh, no. The upper back's painful. I know so."

"What? You have tattoos there, too?" Matty yells, and everyone shushes him, and he puts a finger over his lips, hiking his shoulders up to his ears, glancing left and right with his blue eyes—like his dad's—covering up his mouth with both hands.

Cute.

I glance up to look at Russia, sitting across from me, a smile on his face as he watches me and Matty interact, hands steepled in front of his mouth so I can't see the lower half his face, just have to infer by the rounding of his cheeks that he's smiling—or maybe it's a pained grimace, I just don't know.

"I've got tattoos pretty much everywhere, buddy," I say, nodding at him.

"How come so many? You have like hundreds!" he waves his arms around, nearly socking his dad in the mouth. "Oh, sorry, Dad, sorry. Hey, Mom, when I'm eighteen, which is *forever* from now, can I get a hundred tattoos, too?"

I keep my grin in place, not wanting to open up *that* can of worms.

"Hey, Sophie, please explain to my kid here how tattoos are done," Sera says, wrinkling her nose at Matty, whose neck nearly cracks when he turns his head to look back at me.

It's Russia who answers though, my mouth hanging open on a terrible would-be answer. "Sophie has to use needles to get the colors in your skin," he says, voice a little rough, a little thick.

"Aw, man. Needles? More needles? Ugh." Matty leans his head back, glaring at the ceiling like it's gone and betrayed him. "How can you like needles, Sophie?"

I shrug my shoulders, knowing I have to be careful here. I mean, the kid's not eighteen yet, and most shops won't let you get a tattoo without parental consent if you're under eighteen, so it's not like he's going to get tattooed tomorrow, but still, but *still*.

"I don't really like needles, I just like the tattoos I get from them." I wince, afraid he's going to ask another question, but his dad and I make eye contact, and I get a thumbs up from Sera, who's leaned over onto the table practically to see around her husband.

"Oh, okay."

I ignore the cold sweat forming along my spine, in between my boobs at the prospect of dodging a bullet with the kid.

"Hey, how do you know Uncle Tommy?" Matty taps his hand against my shoulder, his eyebrows pulled down in a frown, looking between me and Russia, swivelling his head, trying to work it out. "Are you his girlfriend?"

I choke on air, coughing into my hand.

Way to be called out by a kid!

"I'd like her to be," Russia says, making me hack into both hands, and Sera's shoving a glass of water towards me, rubbing a hand down my back, and how the hell is this happening? How? Why? Is he playing with me, too?

He's an asshole if he is; he really is.

"Here, I'll take her outside for some fresh air for a minute so we're not too loud for the baby," Sera says, somehow manhandling me until we're walking outside in our house slippers, me almost wheezing at the tickle in my throat, sucking back the fresh, cold air like I'm seconds away from drowning.

"Holy shit, *holy shit!*" I wheeze. "I know how to breathe like a normal human being, I swear." I'm embarrassed, and nervous, still trying to get air into my lungs.

Sera stands beside me, looking anxious. "Are you okay? Russia always tends to say what's on his mind, and it doesn't really matter what anyone else thinks."

"Yeah, I'll say. *Shit.* Why does he have to call me out like that?" I thump the area over my chest, trying to clear my airways even though I'm already breathing that much better, the cold starting to seep in my bones.

Sera tilts her head at me, arms crossed over her chest, huddled against the cold, and it's making me feel bad. "He's gotten better about it, about just saying whatever pops into his head, especially when it's going to get him punched." She grins, shivering a little.

I can feel my eyes going wide, bigger than basketballs as I bring up my finger to point at her, realization finally dawning.

"You? His crooked nose?" I point at my own nose, the bridge of it that certainly isn't crooked like Russia's.

Sera laughs, shrugging her shoulders. "He was an asshole to Hunter, and I punched him. Broke a knuckle, if I remember right." She makes a fist, and we both look down at it, like it's some sort of precious and powerful relic. "He likes you, you know. Couldn't keep his eyes off of you for as long as we've been here."

"Yeah?" I croak, hope leaping in my chest, trying to quash it down, trying not to really think about it, overanalyze and look at it from all angles.

"Yeah, of course. I honestly thought you guys were dating already, the way you're so comfortable around each other."

I can't believe she just comes out and *says* it like that.

"Oh, that's the whole tattoo thing. I've already seen him half-naked already, right? Plus, I touched him quite a bit to get the ink in his skin, so." I shrug, like it's supposed to explain everything. "There's that."

Sera shakes her head, frowning at me. "It's not just that, though. You were practically fangirling over him, or so Katie said. You live with Little Elena, right? I love that kid."

I bristle at the word kid. I can't be that much younger than her, but still, I also call whoever's at least a year younger than me a kid, so. "The traitor."

Sera brings her hand up, giving me a wave, hunching forward against the bite of the wind. My face is still on fire, and I'm trying to control my body temperature. "Hi, I'm Sera Delos, and I'm the original fangirl."

"Yeah, but have you ever fangirled over your client? Like, what is that? So unnecessary," I sigh, following Sera inside, but we stay in the entranceway, away from the conversation still happening in the dining room, a little alcove of privacy.

"I mean, I can't say that I have, but I knew my fair share of heartbreaks from loving fictional characters, and I think that's *worse*."

I laugh and it feels like we're connecting, like this could be the beginning of a friendship, maybe.

Just maybe.

"I...I'm kinda overwhelmed when it comes to him," I admit to myself, to her, because what better way to forge a friendship than telling Sera that I wanna bang her friend? Ha. "And even though he *says* now that he wants me to be his girlfriend, he never really asked me, never really said those words *to* me."

Sera sighs, exhausted. "That's Russia for you. Running ahead and expecting you to be right there next to him."

"I like him, I do, it's just, well, for the longest time I thought he wanted somebody else, and it keeps niggling in the back of my brain, you know? Like, is that a thing with him, am I just a placeholder? Did he choose me because I look so very different from the woman he's in love with?"

"Are you talking about me? It feels like you're talking about me," Sera says, not even beating around the bush.

I hunch my shoulders, the cold still clinging to my clothes. "I didn't think you'd know. Were you not supposed to know? I don't know what's going on."

"So let me give it to you straight, all right?" Sera nods to me, and I find myself nodding back. I just...trust her, for some odd reason.

"Russia...Russia's been my friend since before I started undergrad, like we were eighteen, nineteen, I think, when we first met. I've known him for a long, long time, yeah? Do you believe me when I say that?"

I nod, bobbing my head up and down. "Yeah, I do. I do."

"And I was an easy option for him, even if I didn't meet his standards at the time." Sera's looking at me like I should understand, but I don't.

"Standards?" I tilt my head. "I don't get it."

Sera licks her lips, nervous. "Russia used to be really into his image, how he would project himself to the world. It was very important to him then. And he's gotten better, he has; he's changed a lot over the past few years. But I'm not going to lie, he was an asshole, just like I'm a bitch if you get between me and my kid." Sera clenches her jaw, and she goes from friendly to *killer* in a second and it's giving me whiplash.

"Uh..."

"I'm telling you this because he's...softer with you. And the old Russia, he's had some misconceptions about looks and projecting an image, a façade to people. I think it's how he was raised.

"His parents are back in St. Petersburg now, have been for a while. And he's been watching all of us get married, have kids, and it's made him think about who he is, where he's going. He has been thinking about all of this for a while, I know he has. What I'm trying to say is that Russia doesn't love me, not really, because I would have been just an accessory to him, a 'girlfriend' he could show off but chose not to. He's grown up a lot. Hell, he's probably changed the most out of all of us."

I squint at her. "Have you seen the tattoo on his forearm?" I ask, slapping my own inner forearm, trying to jog her memory.

Sera shakes her head. "Outside of gatherings like this, I don't really see Russia. I have a nine-year-old, Sophie, and he takes up so much of my time, and then I have my husband, who looks like a grump but he's really a sweetheart. And then I have Katie, who I have to watch over more than all of them because Dean just finds it hilarious when she goes off." Sera sighs, a mom tired of her kid's antics for the millionth time, especially when that kid is a grown-ass adult.

"Come on, let's go inside before my nipples freeze off. Even standing near the door is too cold for me."

"Yeah, the barbells get really cold, and it feels like it takes me forever to get warm," I say, not thinking, freezing when I bump into her back, leaving the door wide open to the inner portion of the house.

"You've got...on your nipples? Oh, that's so cool. Shit, that's so cool."

I don't know what to do since she's still blocking the doorway and with another laugh she steps inside with me following at her heels.

"I mean, I could do it for you, if you wanted. The tattoo, too. Again, if you wanted."

"Don't tempt me," Sera says, leading us back to the kitchen and dining room area, rubbing her arms up and down.

"Don't tempt what?" Russia says, standing now with his crutches under his armpits, sagging his weight onto them so he's sort of hunched over, standing by the table, like he was coming to look for me. "Don't tempt you for what?"

"I'll kick your ass if you don't treat her right and punch your nose again," Sera says, pointing a finger at Russia, jabbing the air in front of his nose so he has to pull back in case she stabs him with her finger alone.

Damn it, I love Sera Delos. It's so hard to hate her.

She's given me a lot to think about, *a whole lot.*

I've gotta talk to Elena, I've gotta talk to Katie, and I *have to* talk to Russia.

He can't just lay down girlfriend bombs and expect me not to take cover.

But first, I have to *think.*

And then of course, there's dessert and I want to try everything.

"You told her about that? Come on, Sera, you were supposed to take it to the grave."

"Yeah, yeah. I've got the right to yell about my clout when it comes to that nose of yours. I'm going to shout it from the mountain if you're an asshole to her."

"I'm always an asshole," he says, and it sounds...sad.

"Hey," Sera says, her voice softening, and she looks like she wants to pull him into a hug, but stops herself, glancing over at me like I'm going to have a problem with it.

I mean, there *is* a squirmy feeling in my stomach, and I don't know what to do with it, or about it, but it doesn't get worse when Sera decides to forego touching him.

I honestly didn't think I was that person, but I like him, I like him *a lot*, and I know I'm screwed, screwed, screwed.

"That's not true. It's not, shut up and listen to me. Let's go back inside and eat some dessert, see how it ranks against my own *galaktobouriko*," Sera says, turning me to explain what the odd-sounding word is.

Turns out it sounds delicious, and Sera takes my hand, says something like '*Run!*' but I don't know why I have to run into the kitchen? Isn't that some kind of hazard with Matty running around and Pongo? Isn't that a bad idea?

She's a mom, for Christ's sake, what is she doing, adding to the anarchy!?

I glance back though, shooting Russia a smile over my shoulder, ignoring the way he smiles back at me and my dumb knees want to buckle at the sight of it.

But first, dessert.

Russia eventually heaves himself into the seat next to me, earning him a death glare from Matty across the table, the kid now sitting between Katie and Dean, but his nine-year-old anger is palpable enough that Russia promises to take him to a hockey game as recompense.

"Really? Just me and you? And Sophie?" he asks, but Hunter's swift to come to my rescue.

Matty has health issues, ones that need to be taken care of. He can't be away from his parents unless *someone knows* what they're doing and I'm sure I need some kind of training to understand what's going on with the little guy. The whole idea of being alone with him makes me nervous.

"Maybe your mom can bring you to my work one day? You can see me tattoo Russia over here," I say, and the kid beams at me, making me feel like the most powerful human being on the planet, his awe and happiness my power source.

Shit.

I love the kid, too. There's no doubt about it.

We eat dessert, and I'm able to hold the baby for a nanosecond (while seated because I don't tempt fate like that, no sir), nervous the whole while that the potato starts to squirm and squawk. Russia takes him from the pillow in my lap, expertly cradling him in his arms, clearly having done this before.

It's cute, and it shouldn't be cute, but it *is*.

I stop my brain in its tracks when it wants to take me down a memory lane that doesn't exist yet, one where Russia and I exist in a potential future together, where maybe one day I push out a little girl, or a little boy, and he holds them just like this, looking utterly in awe of the life he's holding. If I even want a kid, if I've changed my mind about that.

It ruins me when he starts speaking in Russian, calming and soothing words that I don't understand of course, but I like the *sound of them*, the cadence, the way he croons to the baby and the potato responds, squirming and reaching for Russia's beard, holding him close.

I glance away, giving myself a breather from the sweet scene, trying to relax myself and not jump to conclusions.

Russia and I say our goodbyes a couple of hours later, and I find myself liking everyone genuinely enough that I wouldn't mind coming back. I'm invited back to Alex and Theresa's house *any time, just let us know,* and Sera gives me a bear hug that I don't think I deserve and vows to call me at the shop for some questions she might have.

"What questions? What are you talking about?" Hunter asks, and Sera just grins at him.

Matty holds his arms out, too, wanting a hug, which I stoop down to give him.

"You come by the shop with your mom when you can. I'll show you what I can do."

Matty nods hard enough that I fear for his neck, but waves at me and Russia with both hands.

Russia and I both put our boots on, but none of those sounds are loud enough that you can't hear the *"are they gonna fall in love, Mom?"*

Shit.

We both sit in the car, waiting for it to completely warm up before I get us going, the silence almost unbearable as the windows start to fog.

I swallow my pride. "Russia, we need to talk."

ELEVEN

"All right. I'm listening," Russia says, turning towards me. What I was really hoping for was for him to take the conversational hot potato and hold onto it for a bit longer before throwing it back to me.

Fine, then, I've gotta be the one to take the reins.

I gulp, arrange my sunnies on the top of my head, flip the visor up because it's gone twilight-ish by now, and pull into the street, getting lost in the local traffic of Alex and Theresa's neighbourhood. I forgot to input the way home in my GPS so I can get out of here, trying to remember the way out.

"I want to talk about what you said," I say, glancing left and right, trying to find the street names and signs. "At dinner. Well, after dinner, after we all ate. At the table, to Matty." Jesus, could I have made that anymore awkward?

Russia snorts, rapping his fingers across the dashboard in a steady rhythm, not so much impatience but what feels more like a grounding technique.

It blows my mind since I think it's because *I* make *him* nervous? Is that right?

I get us onto the highway where my foot knows where to go, so I can sort of drive on autopilot following the signs to bring us back to the downtown core, glancing at him every so often.

"Silence is not an answer, Russia. Come on, just say what you want to say."

"I'm of a mind that you're driving right now, and I don't want to upset you."

"So you *were* talking the talk, just lying to the kid's face like that. All right, all right, I've clocked you," I say, switching on my indicator and changing lanes after checking my blind spots.

"No, that's not it. You just started choking and it's not like that did wonders to my ego."

My turn to snort. "Ego. Ha. Can't we just have a straight conversation?"

"Fine, I would very much like if you would consider being my girlfriend." Russia leans forward, turning his upper body towards me, giving me his full attention even if I can only glance at him in small slivers of time. I'm driving, after all.

Silence, the kind that makes me hunch over and ten and two my hands on the steering wheel, staring resolutely ahead.

"Uh..." I say intelligently. I don't know what I was thinking, like, I asked for an answer, but he just came out and said it, and we're sharing the same space and it's suddenly a lot, *too much* in such an enclosed space with the heat cranked up as high as it is.

"See? You still don't want to give me an answer."

He's right, *he's right*. "Didn't we skip the whole dating thing? Why?" I ask instead, blurting it out and *not* looking at him.

"Why what?"

"Why do you want to date me?"

Russia settles back into the passenger seat, heaving out a heavy breath that I'm not going to call a sigh, nope, not doing it. "Why wouldn't I want to date you?"

I huff now, worried. "Don't throw back a question with another question, what are you, thirteen? Matty's got better manners than you."

Russia snorts, laughing outright, trying to cover his smile with a fist, and I glance over, those butterflies mutating in my stomach into one giant wildebeest that keeps growing and growing until all I want to do is attack Russia with affection, and kiss that smile off his face.

Jesus Christ, really?

Really? This is happening?

"I feel like asking me to be your girlfriend and dating me are two different things?" I ask, turning to look at him, getting sucker-punched with his blue-blue stare that I have to look away and concentrate on the road or else I'm going to go up in flames.

"You've already seen me shirtless."

I honk out a snort. "Ha! I mean, true, true. We did go about it a little backwards, I guess."

Russia's smile is as big as a house when I catch myself looking at him, and he catches me looking at him. "Cute," he says, and my cheeks catch fire all over again.

If all of my blood could just *not* rush up to the surface of my face, that would be really, really great. *Really great.*

"Fine, whatever. It's all fine, totally fine." I white-knuckle the steering wheel, hunching closer to it like I want to become one with the car. Right now, that doesn't seem like a bad idea.

"Do you not want to date me?" It's only then that I hear the question *behind* the question—do you not want *me*?

And that isn't the case, not one bit. But I'm not Sera Delos, as awesome and amazing as she is, and I don't want to be anyone's replacement—I want to be their *first* choice, and I'm not entirely sure that's the case with Russia, even after my talk with Sera.

Hell, I wouldn't know what to do if I was someone's first choice. I'd probably run in the opposite direction as fast as I could.

We only know people so much, only know what *they* tell us, the rest is inference and some sort of perception and not all of us excel in those areas.

So, for now, I'm going to take it at face value but be careful and cautious.

"I didn't say that." I nod to myself, set on the course that I've put us both on, just like the same way I'm driving back to Russia's condo.

"Then what are you saying? Come on, Sophie, throw me a bone. A bone? Throw me a bone, right? Or am I having a stroke?" I glance over at him to see him frowning hard enough that his forehead's going to stay wrinkled that way.

"Throw me a bone, *throw me a bone*. No, that's right. It gets worse when I've been speaking with home all day. My parents called from Russia, and I find myself questioning every English word that comes out of my mouth."

"When did you and your family come to Canada?" I don't ask why they came to Montreal, that seems kinda rude to begin with. I stifle a yawn, just because I'm tuckered out from the day, a little heartbroken from seeing what poor little Matty has to deal with, and the conversation with Sera is still running around in my head, enough words in there that I can't seem to dodge them outright.

"I was twelve, almost thirteen when I got here, and my English was very poor. Don't even get me started on French," he says, waving his hand at an invisible foe, or like he's rubbing his hand across a whiteboard, erasing whatever's written there.

"Yeah? English is tough. I mean, I'm a native speaker, but it's tough. A lot of the rules don't make sense, and it doesn't help that like fourteen other languages make up a lot of the root words. What is that?"

"I know!" Russia slaps at his knee. "It's infuriating. And I still get my expressions mixed up sometimes or use the wrong adjective. Matty was talking to me about *My Little Pony* before, and I knew what a pony was, in my head, but what I said was 'micro horse' like an idiot. Made the kid laugh, though, so there's that."

I stifle a laugh, too, just because it's funny, not because I'm laughing at him. "I'd like to learn Russian, hell, I'd like to learn any language. I was able to take Spanish in high school for four years, but you know, if you don't practice it, you lose it. I'd like to learn more languages, though, seems like you could make a lot more friends that way."

"Is that what you're missing—friends?"

I nod slowly. "It's harder to make friends when you're older, no? Elena and I talk about it all the time."

Conversation goes back and forth like that until I'm finally pulling up to his condo building, sitting in front, double-parked with my hazard lights on, locking up my car after helping Russia out of the passenger side, walking him up the few stairs it takes to get to the entrance of his building.

We're both inside the inner doors to the building, but Russia hasn't used his fob to enter the lobby yet, and we just end up looking at each other, like we've exhausted all the topics of conversation in the car, or now that we're out in the air, conversation is just that much harder in such an open space.

There are other people coming into the building, boisterous and loud, and Russia hangs onto his crutches, staring down at me like I'm the question to his answer.

"What?" I ask, tilting my head at him, scratching at my cheek. "What is it?"

"I want to see you again," he says, followed by, "Can I see you again? Tomorrow night? I can make us dinner."

"Here?" I point down to the ground at my feet, like Russia's going to conjure up a kitchen and start cooking right here and now. Obviously not. "I mean, at your place? Uh, well," I rake my brain for details about tomorrow's shift, and honestly I should be done around seven-ish, right around supper time. I could, I could definitely make it tomorrow.

The question is, *should* I?

Why not, though, why not?

I'm tired of wanting and waiting when I can have him right now, even if I get heartbroken, even if this ends up going nowhere. I've been whining about having something special, but I don't think I'm going to get special unless I *try* for it first.

Isn't it worth it to take the chance?

I don't look like I'm a scaredy cat, I know. The tattoos and the predilection for that kind of transient pain in inking my skin or piercing parts of my body for shits and giggles takes a certain kind of bravery to embrace the pain for fleeting moments and then get on with life.

But this?

Heartbreak, too, is transient, it doesn't last forever, it's not never-ending.

So why am I hesitating? "Depends on what you're cooking," I say, choosing my words carefully. If he knows how far gone I am for him, that's it, that's the end of the road, I'm sure of it.

Russia frowns, thinking about it. "Steak and potatoes?" he suggests. "I make really good gravy for the steak."

I grin. "I bet Dean taught you how, and that's not a thing you actually know."

Russia smiles at me, the smile turning into a grin—game, set, match. "I don't know, I guess you'll have to find out."

Yup, he has me there. "I guess I will. You have my number. Let me know what to bring."

Russia shakes his head. "Just yourself. That's all I need.'

And *damn it*, do I blush hard enough to become a beacon from outer space.

I cough into my hand, clearing my throat, and do an about-face and turn away, waving my hand in the air, awkwardly waving goodbye to him from this angle. I call out another *bye* and head outside, get inside my car and start the drive home, knowing I've got some company.

Elena greets me at the door, Beckett standing on our couch, jumping up and down like a little kid (even though it makes more sense that adults would do it all the time since no one can tell them not to—kind of like getting to eat cake for breakfast), punching the air in front of him, watching the hockey game currently on screen.

He bellows once and then falls back and flops onto the couch, impersonating a dead fish, before kicking at the air and snarling.

"Told you!" Elena yells, moving over to him and running her hand on his belly and tickling him, which honestly, *is* adorable, but I also don't want to choke on all the noxious affection and *love* permeating the room.

Maybe it'll be different once I fall in love, once and for all, finally. I don't know.

I'm not really holding my breath.

Their affection with each other is gross in the way that eating too much cake is gross—it's awesome in small doses, but then you get kinda queasy when it gets too much, drowning under all that sugar.

And boy, do they have *sugar*.

But I love that for my best friend in the entire universe, I really, really do.

"Hey, Beckett," I say to the living room, the two of them turning into snuggle-bunnies on the couch, and I hope nothing starts to come off that *shouldn't* be coming off.

I glance back at the back of the couch, Beckett's mitt rising up in a wave and then flopping back down with a *smack,* and it doesn't take all of my brain power to figure out what just happened.

I won't get sexiled—Elena's still shy about that even though I told her I have the world's best noise-cancelling headphones (not the best *best,* but pretty close) and won't hear a thing, but it's a no-go most of the time, and Beckett's always patient with her, always, always, and I just really love them together.

But right now, I need my best friend, I need to talk to her, to unload, and Beckett's in the way.

I sigh, heading to the fridge for the case of sparkling water we keep in there, all bubbly and delicious, and wish fleetingly yet again that I'd stolen one piece of that dessert *gala*-something for lunch tomorrow at the shop. That would've been great.

I plop my bottle down on the counter, looking out over the island and into the living room, at the TV where the game keeps playing, and the two of them are ensconced in a world of their own making, and I don't want to disturb that. Elena *deserves* that time alone with Beckett, and my whining isn't going to necessarily put her in the lovey-dovey mood with her boyfriend.

Except Elena springs up from the couch like an Italian version of a lemur—or is it a meerkat—those critters that just lift their heads and look around in the Serengeti, I think, blinking at me as if I've gone and called her name.

"What's up?" she asks, sitting upright, then swinging her leg over Beckett to come over the back of the couch, sit on the edge and look at me, legs swinging.

"Did you have a good time? Cousin Katie's still there, I think. *She* had a lot to say."

Good thing I wasn't drinking any sparkling water, or I would have drowned for *sure*. "She did not. Don't make shit up right now. I've had a rough day."

Elena shakes her head, a knowing smile on her face, like she knows *everything*. "That's not what Katie told me," she sing-songs, kicking her feet in time with each syllable. She glances back over her shoulder, the period counting down, the last minute of play for the Habs against the Bruins, and I know not to talk when the last minute of play is on.

Hopefully there won't be any whistles blowing, therefore stopping the play and making sixty seconds feel like *forever*.

I clear my throat, watching the TV but not *seeing* anything, running through the day in my head, and the final blow when Russia asked me over tomorrow.

God, he's asked me over to his place tomorrow and I'm going to go crazy starting from now.

What do I wear, what do I dress like, since I'll be going right over after work? Heh, I won't even have to move my car. I'll keep it parked behind the building in the lot and just walk the six blocks to his building.

Yeah, *yeah*.

I come back to the here and now with Elena waving her hand in front of my face. "You okay?"

I nod slowly, still not sure myself. There's a lot going on in my head, in my heart, and I need to figure it all out sooner or later.

"Let me say good night to Beckett, and I'll come meet you in your room, okay?"

"I don't want to ruin your night."

"You're not ruining anything, you never ruin anything. Sisters before misters," she sings, like that guy in that movie. She flicks me in the forehead, and I nearly bop her one until she prances away, and I leave them to their kissy goodbyes, wishing I could do the same with a certain someone, too.

I run through my routine and remove the day from my body – makeup, leave my hair loose and run a brush through it, and change out of my clothes. I'm rubbing at my aching scalp when I hear the door close, the lock twist and the security chain slide home. Seconds later, Elena's knocking on my bedroom door (like she's always ever done), and flopping down on my bed, face first, kicking her legs up and down in utter joy.

It's a good look, even if I can't see her face.

"What happened?" I find myself asking, lying down next to her, belly down, up on my elbows and feeling that twinge in my back even if I'm too lazy to do my stretching exercises right now.

"Beckett. He's just so...*so*...ugh. I love him a lot. I hope I continue to love him a lot." Elena nods, brow furrowing a little as she thinks about it.

"Of course you will. Obviously."

Elena sits up on her butt, and I roll over onto my back, making a Sophie bed angel, swiping my duvet with arms and legs, my left wing getting ruined by Elena sitting cross-legged next to me.

"So? How did it go?" Elena asks, smacking down on my hand until I stop moving. "I was just teasing before, you know? I know you always make a good impression, even if some dicks have bad first ones of you."

I shake my head. "It's not that, not that at all. Everyone was really nice to me, sweet even. I got to hold a baby. I broke out into a cold sweat and I was sitting down, but I did it. He's so tiny, Elena. A potato that makes noises and cries and has the longest eyelashes I've ever seen."

Elena nods, keeps nodding when I glance over at her.

"Tell me what really happened."

She knows how to cut through the bullshit, my best friend, even if she can't see it for herself sometimes.

"Well, I met Sera."

Elena claps a hand to her mouth. "*Shiiiiit.*"

TWELVE

"Yeah," I huff, plopping my arms and legs back down on the bed. "*eah.*"

"I mean, she's really an amazing person, and Matty and Hunter, too, but I haven't talked to him so much so I feel like I can't really give an opinion on the guy, you know?" Elena pats my arm in what I think she means to be consoling, but it just isn't, it *isn't.*

"How the hell am I supposed to compete with her, huh? How the hell am I going to manage that?" I grunt, squeezing my eyes shut tight.

"Well, just like you've told me a hundred times before," Elena says, exaggerating, we both know it, "we don't compete with other women. We just don't do it. Sera is amazing, yeah, she's a great mom, and friend, and Katie loves her to death, hell, everyone loves her to death."

"Not a lot of people love me," I say, squeezing my eyes shut even tighter, watching the kaleidoscope of colors burst behind my closed eyelids, sniffing hard through my nose, taking the option to not cry, thanks, but we'll see what we're gonna get.

"You know that doesn't matter, you know that. We don't compare ourselves to other people, and what we can do for other people. Well, what we can do for other people *only.* You don't exist to accommodate other people, you don't exist solely to be there for other people, Sophie."

I grunt, blinking my eyes open until my eyes get adjusted to seeing again in the brightness of my bedroom. "Remind me to put some money in the pot for your therapist. She always knows what to say, *always.*" I punch the air in front of me, shaking the bed.

"I'll tell her, don't you worry. But come on, you're so awesome and amazing, and so cool, gah, can you even imagine Russia not liking you, wanting to be with you? You, Sophie? Really?"

"I don't know, I don't know. Like, he says stuff, but my brain's always thinking about Sera, even if we talked while I was having my near death experience. I don't know, the way he keeps looking at her, though. He has to still be in love with her, right?" Elena sighs, thwacking me with a pillow.

"Hey, I didn't ask to get beat! What are you doing?!" I fight back, sitting upright, and grabbing the pillow away from her.

"What? Did you hear something different?"

"I want you to stop doubting yourself, stop comparing yourself to Sera. Sera's married, she's *married*. She's not the kind of person to steal someone away."

"It doesn't matter if she steals him away if he's already given a part of himself to her. That's the point!" I wiggle in the bed like a little kid having a tantrum. Yeah, I've got doubts bigger than the rings of Saturn, but Elena's not letting me mope.

"Hey, stop that. You're being dumb. Why would he ask you to be his girlfriend if it was actually like that?"

I turn to frown at her. "Who told you that? Katie? I'll kill her," I snarl, lifting up a fist and vowing vengeance, then letting my arm flop back down 'cause I don't have the energy.

I've never been this cut up over a guy in what feels like forever, and granted, I haven't precisely been in this kind of situation before. I'm getting blindsided by my own stupid feelings.

I don't know what made me look at him and go, *yup, he's the one I'm gonna like now until forevermore*, but here I am, upset about it. "And he said that he wants me to be his girlfriend in front of the whole table, too. You think he was doing it in front of Sera to show he's moving on or something?"

I get flicked in the forehead for my trouble, and I clamp a hand over the wound, like Elena's gone and rattled my brain *hard*.

"You're being stupid," Elena repeats, back to the first-grade taunts. I mean, they work just as effectively, so it makes a lot of sense.

"I know I'm being stupid. You're supposed to be my friend and *tell* me I'm *not* being stupid! That's your job!"

Elena shakes her head, aims up another flick until I grab both of her hands and she finally relents. "My job is to tell you the truth, and I'm doing it. What a load of shit! Look, I don't know the guy that well, I'll admit it. But you talked to Sera, right?"

Of course she knows about that. Katie knows everything, and now Elena knows everything.

I nod miserably. "Yeah, I did. She basically just told me the same thing you did, but I'm paraphrasing it really heavily, and that's the gist of it. She doesn't believe that Russia ever loved her, that she was just convenient for him to latch his feelings onto, and like, yeah, I get that, I do. It's easier to do that than take a chance on someone new, someone who could really hurt you than the person you've always got hanging around."

"But what?" Elena asks, fingers still ready for a forehead flick.

"I didn't say anything," I sigh, folding my hands over my stomach, wriggling my toes, staring up at the ceiling, waiting for the answers to appear up there, give me some guidance, like that compass I inked on Russia's skin.

Tell me where to go, what to do, but the *vegvisir* doesn't work like that apparently.

"Yeah, but you're thinking it, I can tell."

I huff out a laugh, but it sounds exhausted, even to me. "I don't want to be anyone's replacement. I don't deserve that."

"No. No, you don't."

"But I also don't know what I don't know," I say carefully, the weakest part of me wanting to have dinner at Russia's place tomorrow evening. What if he's the special I've been waiting for?

"True," she says, and I want to smack her for agreeing, for *not* being the voice of reason. "So what are you going to do now?"

"I think I'm going to go over for dinner tomorrow, see what Russia has to offer."

"Is that a sex joke? Did you just make a sex joke?"

I groan. "No, I didn't. Relax, relax. I'm just gonna go have dinner and *see*, and then I think I'll know."

"Know what?"

"If he's worth my time. If there's a veritable shrine to Sera Delos in his condo, then I'll have my answer."

"I don't think it works like that, but you do what you have to do, yeah?"

I nod. "Yeah. *Yeah*," I stress the word, trying to convince everybody in the room that I have my shit together.

Spoiler alert: no one has their shit together, no one, at least not a hundred percent of the time. It's called being a human being, a stressed-out meat ball carrying around a brain that likes to malfunction more often than not.

·♥·♥·♥·♥·♥·

I tried—and failed—to *not* think about dinner with Russia the entire time I was working. There were brief moments of respite, sure, working on tattoos, losing myself in my work, times when I was drawing out ideas and sketches for *new* tattoos, too.

But in the lulls between, cleaning down my station and my workspace, I would let my mind drift as the work got repetitive, my hands moving on autopilot over the flow of shading, my brain flitted over to what it would be like, having dinner with a man I find attractive, a man who finds *me* attractive, and leaving all the baggage out of it.

I'm no one's placeholder, but I still have to see, I have to *know*, need to hear it from Russia, and no one else.

With a final check of my reflection in the women's bathroom at the shop, and one final adjustment to my hair so it falls long and wavy down to my ribs, pulling it back over one ear to show the already-fast-growing undercut (or it just feels that way whenever I freshen it up), and a touch up of my lipstick, I leave the shop after winter-proofing myself, pulling on the giant hood of my coat over my head to not get any hat hair for the six block walk over to Russia's place.

The days are getting longer now, the sun dipping down just past a quarter to six in the evening and you can already start to smell the wet spring just lurking around the corner, waiting for the dying winter winds (and wet snow) to cease and desist.

It's pretty dark by the time I make it to Russia's at five past seven. I get buzzed up after finding him on the panel, and taking the elevator up to the eleventh floor, doing a shoddy two-step all the while, like I've got to go pee or something, which I don't.

I knock on his entrance door to his unit (number 1111) and nearly take a step back when he opens the door looking harried, his blue eyes too big for his face, his eyebrows lifting up towards the ceiling and his face screwed up in worry, a deprecating laugh falling off his lips.

It's the smell, though, the *stench* of burned meat that makes me take a step back.

Russia ushers me in with a sheepish smile, his head bowed low as if I'm some kind of queen passing by one of her knights and he doesn't get the chance to look at me.

It's *loud* in Russia's home, the hood over the stove on an all-time high, and the patio door's been opened to let the cool night air in along with some snow swirlies that I swear weren't there by the time I made it inside the building.

It stinks in here like charred meat, and Russia's hopping on one foot trying to bag the ruined food and toss it outright, glancing at me when he's done, hands on his hips.

"So, I screwed up," he admits, blinking at me, shoulders hunching in like he thinks I'm going to verbally whip him for messing up dinner. Yeah, right.

"Okay," I say, nodding, unzipping my coat, knowing that the wonderful perfume is going to permeate into my clothing sooner rather than later, but it doesn't really matter. There's laundry detergent for a reason.

"That's okay," I reassure when Russia looks completely forlorn over the idea of ruining dinner.

"I just really wanted to make you supper, and I screwed it up." He looks so adorably crestfallen that it makes my heart twist.

Now is not the time to be freaking out over how cute we find him, right?

"It's fine. Really, really fine."

"But you're starving. I know you don't eat regularly," he says, referencing all the times he's caught me eating meager snacks when he's come in for a session, and I know I have complained more than once about how hungry I get.

"And I was going to have everything ready, and I know how to cook, I just...wasn't paying attention and I lost track of time."

I shrug, not trying to make him feel worse. I *am* hungry, sure, but it's not like I can't stave it off until we order something delicious, and it takes its time getting here.

"We can order something. There's this thing...on our phones?" I lift up my phone and point to it, as if I'm trying to teach a late Boomer how to use the internet.

He smiles at me, shaking his head. "Yeah, yeah. We all know home-cooked meals are better."

I shrug again. "You want a pizza, or were you stuck on steak and roasted potatoes?" I ask, pulling up my favorite food-ordering app.

"Hey, no, no, no. Let me," he says, and when I look up from the tantalizing menu options displayed on my phone, Russia's frantically patting at his jeans: front pockets, ass pockets, then glancing around like a puppy confronted with too many toys and is having a vicious bout of executive dysfunction before Russia hops over to the dining room table and snatches his phone up.

"Do you want pizza or something else?"

We settle on an all-dressed pizza with green olives on top, a topping he never considered before and which I assure him that he'll never eat pizza the same way again.

"It'll ruin you for all other pizzas," I say, taking a seat at the dining room table, letting Russia pour me a glass of white wine. I don't know much about wine, and if he's trying to impress me with the bottle, it's a lost cause. I ignore the hot prickle in my chest, wondering if Sera would know, if she would appreciate it.

Russia smiles at me though, his eyes soft and warm, and I feel myself unhunching, unfurling, like a flower searching out the sun.

"This was not how I envisioned the night going," he says on a half-sigh, grabbing his own glass and pouring himself some wine. "I had it all planned out."

I flush under his gaze, twisting the stem of the wine glass between my fingers. "Yeah? Bet you were going to be a real Romeo, too."

Russia shakes his head. "Well, for one, I wasn't going to ruin dinner. I was late coming back from that bakery we went to yesterday—"

"Zachary," I supply, remembering our server, Chloe, and the awestruck look she gave him, which I mean, she's allowed to do, of course.

Stop going green with envy. He's not completely yours yet...or is he?

Russia nods. "Yeah, and I had a hell of a time finding parking, and then trying to get my crutches under control. The shop owner, well, Chloe's the granddaughter of the shop owner I learned, the woman we met yesterday." He points her out in the air, like she's right here with us, trying to jog my memory.

"And she even helped bring out the dessert I got from the shop, because I couldn't carry it safely to the car. We should keep going there, everything I've tried so far is amazing." He nods at me, like he didn't just lay down his cards where there is a future that I'm a part of.

Huh.

Huh.

I clear my throat, rapping my knuckles against the table in a one-two rhythm that lets everyone in the room know that I am definitely *not* calm, cool and collected.

"If it's anything like that dessert we had yesterday I'm going to be the size of the moon before the end of the year."

Russia shrugs. "Sounds like it'll be worth it."

"So I want to ask you something," I say, not having planned any of this, but we're not eating, and we're not watching TV, and we're definitely not kissing so now is as good a time as any.

Russia nods. "All right. I just got incredibly nervous," he says, giving me a shaky grin, laying his hands flat out on the table, like I might just start hooking him up to a polygraph of all things.

I bite at my lip, watching his eyes catch the movement, making my belly swoop and tumble and do some impressive acrobatics.

"Is this our first date?" I ask, wanting to be sure, circling around the central issue. I'm not going to flat out *ask* if he's still in love with Sera, not yet. I can still walk away at any given moment. I can make a run for it, move cities, fly to the moon, the usual.

"Yes."

I nod, slapping my hand against the table. "Good."

"Good?" Russia tilts his head, bringing a hand up to cradle his head, looking at me like I'm the most important person in the room.

Huh. *Huh*.

Well, this is no good for my heart, all of this attention from him. Definitely not good at all.

I nod again, surer of myself this time.

"Why are you looking at me like that?" I ask, my voice dipping down into a whisper. I'm usually loud, but here and now, facing Russia, I'm careful and quiet.

"Like what?" he asks, just as carefully.

I swallow hard, glancing away from those blue-blue eyes. I clear my throat, rearrange myself on the seat. Anything to distract myself from the fact that Russia's looking at *me* like I'm the special one.

"Was yesterday a pre-date?" I force myself to ask instead. I force myself to lift my head, to be *brave* in a way I've never had to be before and look at him. I take one last fleeting glance at our hands on the surface of the table – mine tattooed, and Russia's looking clean and pure.

I think about how Sera looks nothing at all like me.

I think about it all.

I watch as Russia mulls this over, then finally nods. "Yes, it was. It's important to me that you like my friends. They make up a big part of my life."

I nod along. "Yeah, it totally sucks if you guys can't hang out together without there being this massive friction between personalities. No one's saying you have to pledge allegiance to them and promise to save them during a...zombie apocalypse, or hell, the end of the world as we know it, but you also kind of have to not be that person who drinks the only water available if they're on fire."

Russia blinks at me then bursts out into laughter. It's a good laugh too, enough to make me grin back at him.

I made him grin, not Sera, *me!*

Notice how you're the only one bringing up Sera here?

"Yeah, that's true. So, tell me, what was your favorite thing that you did today?" I frown at him, not understanding the question. He flushes and stammers. "I just want to hear about your day, how it was."

Russia waits for me, looking genuinely excited about hearing all about it.

My heart trembles in my chest, and I can feel myself slipping from like into something a whole lot like love. Oh, I'm not there yet, but I can see myself getting there, day by day by day.

"Oh, well, uh, I finished up a really beautiful tattoo today. I had a client who had a...I'm bad with the medical terms, but this young kid, a freshly minted eighteen-year-old, had to have a portion of his thigh excised—cancer. And he's been through like a million medical procedures, and he had the world's dreamiest smile," I say, placing my head on my hand, anchoring my elbow to the table, still fiddling with my wine glass, not daring to take more than a few sips.

"And he came in with his parents, and they all talked about what tattoo he was gonna get."

"What was it?" Russia asks, voice whisper-soft, sitting there, riveted to my story.

I pull in one last deep breath, ignoring the heat in my chest, the way my heart beats faster.

"We decided on a mechano-cyborg type of artwork, and I was really nervous, since it's not my forte. And with scar tissue, it's tricky, not to mention every single person is different. The shop has had clients with no scarring at all come back when their bodies started to reject the ink, it's just...a person-to-person thing.

"But this kid, Liam, he was so good throughout all of the sessions, and his parents were always with him, which I found to be incredibly sweet—just there to support him, his dad holding his hand when the kid had to practically pulverize it for the pain."

"Your job...it can be quite emotionally taxing."

I like that Russia realizes that, that he's starting to understand. Not a lot of people really do, or at least, that's been my experience.

"Of course it can. I mean, with Alex, I felt so weird and awful doing that tattoo, like I was tempting fate by stamping the potato's feet into his skin."

"Potato?"

I wave a finger at him, nearly knocking the glass over. "All babies are potatoes until they start sprouting hair. It's just the way it is."

"What if they come out with hair?"

I blink at him, rearing back in horror. "They can do that? That's so freaky," I shiver. "I've never seen one with a full head of hair. Like tiny wisps, yeah, but not like mine." I place my hands around my head pointing to the volume of the waves.

Conversation goes even easier after that, me showing off a lot of my artwork on my work-related Instagram account, Russia asking me a ton of questions about shading and colors, and just seeming as interested as can be about my work, about what I can do.

It's nice, really nice.

He ends up loving the pizza with green olives (because he's not a monster), and as the night winds down and we end up watching *Rocky IV* of all things, Russia judging Dolph Lundgren's accent (the guy's Swedish after all), I end up learning some Russian words, too.

"*Dobriy vyecher*," I fumble with the syllables, trying to move my tongue around them.

"Good," he says, and I sit up straighter at the praise.

"Any more I should know?" I ask, turned toward him, the knee I've hiked up onto the cushion pressing into his thigh, his arms sprawled along the back of the couch, his bad foot spread out in front of him.

Russia grins, and my belly swoops at the sight of it.

"I don't know, I'm blanking. What do you want to know?" He tilts his head to the side, playful, flirtatious, and honestly, this might be one of the best first dates I've ever had.

I ignore the flush in my cheeks, *ignore it*. "What would you call me in Russian, when you want to be sweet to me?" My heart gives a painful squeeze in my chest, but I still want to *know*, whatever he says.

Russia glances at me, his blue-blue eyes darkening, something flickering behind them. He licks at his lips, and I follow the movement with my eyes, entranced. He hums while he's thinking and I just sit there, heart beating too hard, too fast, waiting, waiting, *waiting*.

I hold my breath.

"I used to like *zvezda moya* a lot, but I don't think you're my star. Stars are so very far away, and I would like to keep you close, if that's what you want, too."

I smile at him, trying to make a joke out of it. I'm so bad at this whole thing. I have to make a joke out of it or I'm going to *expire*.

"If you're asking me if I'm a cuddler and would win gold at the Cuddling World Championships for Canada, then *yes* is the answer." I notch my chin high, waiting for him to digest that information.

I've noticed that most of the guys I've dated aren't against cuddling, they're against *asking* for it, of *needing* it when really, it's kinda the best thing in the world.

Russia grins at me again, holding out a hand for me. I place my tattooed hand in his, watching the way he holds onto me like I'm precious.

His blue eyes bore into mine. "I could call you *zolotse moya*, which could mean something like my gold, or golden one." He lifts his other hand slowly, running it along my golden hair.

"I like that one," I confess on a whisper, leaning in closer to him, trying to catch what he says next. "Any others?"

He purses his lips, turning away to look at the screen while I study his profile instead, and damn, it's a *nice* profile. "*Krasavitsa* for beautiful, but that's overused in my opinion. Then there's *meelaya* for darling."

"I want *that* one, the one you just said." I shiver, and I'm sure he can feel it. "I've never been anyone's darling before."

"You don't want to hear any more?" he asks, turning towards me now, his face even closer than it was before, and I can't seem to catch my breath.

His eyes are a pure blue, no flecks of gold or green in them, just a pure blue that entrances me as much as it terrifies me.

I let out a slow breath and move closer to him.

I want this, I want this so bad. Why can't I let myself have it?

"*Oomnitsa* would suit you well, too, my clever one." Russia's eyes flutter when I move even closer. I lean close to press a kiss to his cheek, and I move my hand to his other cheek as if for balance, but I really just wanted to feel his beard.

So yeah, that term of endearment works on me, too.

"Anything else?" I ask, pulling away, waiting for Russia to focus on me, and *only* me.

I hold my breath, waiting.

Waiting.

THIRTEEN

M y heart kicks hard against my rib cage, a violently fluttering bird that has nowhere to go, nowhere to escape to.

Russia looks at me, his eyes a darker blue hue, and we're so close, we're practically sharing the same air.

It feels inevitable, too, that we've both come to this very moment, like we were always meant to be here together even if I have doubts, even if I'm not sure about him a hundred percent.

But God, I want, and I want, and I *want*, and I'm tired of playing it safe.

Life *is* pain, in one way or another, you just have to learn to live with it, and I'd like to think I'm better at it than most.

"Would you let me call you *meelaya*, Sophie?" Russia moves even closer, close enough that when I lick my lips, I end up licking his lips, too. Russia groans deep in his chest, the sound chasing a wildfire across my skin.

"As long as you're not calling me a bitch," I whisper, my eyes trained on the spreading smile across his mouth, transfixed.

"No, no, never that, Sophie." His eyes flicker up to mine, but he still looks to be waiting when I close that scant distance between our mouths and kiss him, nothing but touching our lips together in the briefest kiss before Russia wakes up and starts kissing me *back*.

I lose my breath, the pressure of his mouth against mine, a stark reminder of how very much I've missed being kissed, missed being this close where my body heat feels like it could melt all the remaining snow on the entire island of Montreal.

We kiss, giving each other tentative ones, still learning what it's like to be this close to one another, and when I swipe my tongue along his bottom lip, Russia freezes for a split second where I think I did something wrong.

I feel the shudder underneath the hand I have on his other cheek, and when I start to pull back to ask if this is still okay, Russia surges closer, wrapping an arm around my upper back, pulling me closer until we're a tangle of limbs and he's falling backwards. My belly swoops in the same way it feels like doing a roller-coaster drop with my eyes closed, in the front cart.

"Okay?" he asks, pulling back for a second before I'm nodding quickly, wanting more of his taste, especially when his mouth opens under mine, sending the right kind of fireworks all over my skin, heat pooling in my lower belly.

I don't even know how long the kissing goes on for, the kisses to his mouth blurring with the kisses to his cheeks, the bridge of his nose, moving up to kiss the crinkles at the sides of his eyes that I find so incredibly endearing and up to each fluttering eyelid, up to the middle of his forehead where he's been holding a lot of stress lately.

"Sophie," he murmurs my name against my lips, even as I'm sprawled on top of him, my body electrified for something more, more, *more*.

"Yeah?" I force myself to pull back, to check in with him, and end up sitting up, straddling his hips, hands on his chest, looking down at him. "What's up?"

Russia blinks up at me, a flush along his cheekbones, mouth parted so he can catch his breath.

I grin down at him, my hands splayed out across his chest, wanting more kisses, a thousand more kisses, a *million* more kisses.

"I don't want you to think that I invited you over so I could sleep with you."

I snort. "Please, Russia, if you were gonna do that, all I gotta do is hurt your other foot and then I'll be running away and you for *sure* would never catch me." I pat his chest in a *good boy* pat. "I don't feel that way, like I'm being pressured. But I also want more kisses, so are you buying or selling?"

His eyes flutter closed, and he pulls in a deep breath through his nose, my entire body practically rolling with the movement. Russia's hands go to my hips, not bruising or anything like that, but just gently holding me in place, like he doesn't want me to get away, but loose enough that I can make a run for it if I need to.

Not that I want to, I'm exactly where I want to be.

"*Meelaya* means my darling. Would that be okay with you, to call you that?" he asks, and my throat tightens up at the pet name.

It's old school, for sure, but baby or babe was never really *my* preference, and I love *love* that he asks me for permission to use that particular term of endearment with me, *for me*.

I nod, feeling his heart race underneath the palm of my hand, like he's just as enthralled by me as I am by him.

"More kisses now?" I ask, my watch lighting up as I twist my wrist to move over his chest properly, not feeling bad about copping a feel, moving slowly, though, and gently so I don't freak him out.

Russia's blue-blue eyes stare up at me, his dark-as-soot eyelashes framing them, making me feel like I'm looking into the blue sea, clear enough to lose my balance, to forget where I'm standing, where I am, *who* I am.

"You want to be my girlfriend?" he asks finally, and I nod at him again, then verbalize it.

"Yes. I expect those Greek pastries we had today every time you come and see me, or we see each other. Can you do that?"

Russia smiles, a flash of his white teeth, his hands tightening just a fraction on my hips. "Yeah, I can do that, *meelaya*."

Ah, I didn't know I would like the sound of that so *so* much. He's gone and taken all the power back, and I'm going to be the weak subservient one, all by the sound of the Russian term of affection that has me wanting to melt in a Sophie-sized puddle of goo.

"What do you want to be called? What should I do for you?"

Russia closes his eyes, trying to hide the brief look of surprise I caught on his face. But I caught it all the same and saw it for what it was.

"Has no past girlfriend of yours ever asked you that before?"

Russia shakes his head, his eyes still closed, and one of his hands moves up to my upper back, applying some pressure and *oh*—he wants a hug.

I don't quite stifle the laugh until I'm flopped on top of him, and then we're both laughing, Russia's arms like steel bands around my back and waist, squeezing me close.

"Is this what you wanted? All you have to do is ask, you know. I *love* giving hugs, as long as you want them."

"You could not be in the mood one day," he muses.

"Russia, that doesn't mean that I'm *never* gonna hug you again, or that same day. Maybe I need to recharge my 'hug' batteries and I'll get back to you with a rain check or something. Were you not hugged as a child?" I ask, trying to make a joke out of it, but I feel him tense up underneath me.

"Well, I'll hug the crap out of you every day if you want. I'm sure Josh and Elias and Alex wouldn't say no, either."

"It's different with them," he says, and I just nod, rubbing my cheek against his shirt. I really could fall asleep like this, and it'll be the best kind of nap, the one where you feel energized rather than the kind where you wake up feeling worse than when you went to sleep in the first place.

"It doesn't have to be. You know Dean will hug you hard enough until you actually fart."

Russia laughs underneath me, and I lift my head to look down at his face, eyes roving over his features, memorizing the way his face looks when he's laughing, when he's happy—all because he's with me.

Fireworks burst in my chest, and the world seems a little brighter in the face of all the stuff that's going on in the world because I happen to be here, snuggled up against him, watching him laugh.

"Why are you laughing? He's super strong! Montreal's very own Thor, if you hear Katie talk about him." Russia leans up to press a kiss to my mouth, dropping his head after kissing me three more times in a row, like it's all for good luck, and a girl can find herself wanting good luck kisses *all the time*.

"Yeah, Dean would hug me if I asked." Russia goes quiet, rubbing my back up and down, and we're quiet for a time, still getting used to being this close with one another.

I like him just as much in the quiet moments as I do in the moments when we're talking, when I'm tattooing him, when I'm meeting his friends.

It's where you find the measure of a person, when they're quiet, I think, reading their features like you would pages in a book, reading between the lines at what's implied but not seen explicitly.

"Sophie?" he calls, and I rouse myself enough to lift my head to look at him, and at this angle, we're still super close, close enough to purse my lips in a silent demand for a kiss.

He smiles and obliges me, before wriggling underneath me to plant his elbows into the couch, leaning back on them, and by default making me sit up properly or else my spine's going to bend in a way it's definitely not supposed to.

"Yeah? Ah, what time is it? You've got work early tomorrow, huh?"

I don't know how Russia does it, working in an office for a dumb number of hours a day, working hard *and* long hours, but at least the commute isn't shit, which matters *so* much during the winter.

"Yeah, I'm sorry."

"Why are you apologizing? I didn't mean for the time to get away from me like that. I gotta go get my car."

"Wait, you left it at the shop?"

I nod. "I'm not going to drive six blocks and try to find parking around your building when I had a guaranteed spot. Like I would willingly shoot my stress levels through the roof. No thanks."

"All right, let's go."

"Wait, what are you doing? You plan on hobbling over to my car?"

Russia nods, pushing me a little until I flop back on the couch, discarded as he gets himself upright and hops towards the kitchen, leaning against the wall to put on his boots. "Yeah, you can drive me back, so I don't slip and kill myself."

"Hey, that's not funny. I could save you all this trouble by going by myself, you know that, right?"

"And you know that I care about you enough not to let you walk alone at this time of night. Just let me walk you. I'll have my crutches as weapons."

I shake my head at him, knowing he's being dumb, but still it settles my heart rate enough at the prospect of the both of us walking together to my car. Montreal's a city with crime like anywhere else, and there's nothing that anyone can do about it.

So I'm grateful for the walk to my car, but it takes three to four minutes for Russia to get into my car and for it to warm up completely, sitting in idle while I crank up the heat and beg my car to hurry up to get all of the engines fired up and the heating system to be working like, *right now*.

"How's your foot? We nearly went down like the *Titanic* right before we got to the shop."

Russia snorts a laugh and turns to look at me. "Are you all right? I didn't hurt you?"

"Yup, I just got thwacked by your crutches and I have to say, they're not really that much of a weapon with how light they are."

"Jesus, Sophie, I'm not going to hurt anyone," he says, and I take it to mean *hurt* in all ways—physically, mentally, emotionally, spiritually.

Don't hurt me, Russia. Don't hurt me, please.

Please?

"I'm sorry I hit you though, while I almost lost my balance."

"That's okay," I say, throat a little tight now as I glance down at my wheel, having forgotten my gloves in the shop, and refusing to touch the icy steering wheel right away before the heat starts kicking in. I want to feel like I'm living inside of a volcano before I even think about driving Russia back to his place.

He yawns, covering it with both hands, and it's what decides me to get him home earlier. I don't have to be at the shop until 11:30 tomorrow, and I'm an early riser anyway, and I'll head to the gym after Elena leaves for the day, getting my morning errands out of the way before heading into the shop to do my work.

Russia's gotta be in the office early-early and I want him to get as much sleep as possible.

I drive us back to his building, taking a whole lot longer than expected when I hit a red light that takes a whole entire *two years* to turn green, and only then am I able to pull up in front of his building, turn on my hazards, and move to open my door to help him out.

"No, no, it's fine, it's fine. You don't need to take care of me so much."

"And if I want to?" I hit back, leaning close and looking down at his mouth for a second too long.

"Then I'm going to have to do something drastic," he says, eyes pinned to my mouth.

I lean in close and press a gentle kiss to his mouth, my bones nearly melting at the sound and feel of his sigh against my lips.

"Please be careful driving home," he says, pressing one last kiss to my mouth, then two to my cheek, always in threes, which a girl can come to *expect* after having it done a few times, you know?

"I will, I will. Now go inside before you freeze your ass off. I'll talk to you soon."

"Count on it, Sophie. Good night, *meelaya*," he says, making me flush red hot.

I nod, trying to stifle the gurgle that wants to come out of me, somewhere between a half-coo and an aborted giggle that'll sound worse than it is, but Russia just laughs, kissing my cheek one last time before opening the passenger door, the light in the car nearly blinding me with its brightness.

I wait until he has his crutches pinned underneath either arm, closing the door behind him, locking them up, and he waves at me one last time from the lobby when he notices that I'm still waiting by the curb.

The drive home is done on automatic, my brain knowing which direction to go in, the trek the same one I do five times in a given week, and I can let myself *think* about what happened tonight, after freaking out all day, I'm definitely wrung out, a rag left out to dry, limp and wrinkled.

I had a good time, and I feel hopeful about Russia and me.

When I get into the apartment, Elena's yawning at the TV, sitting in the middle of the couch, phone pressed to her ear. She waves at me when I come in, and I wave back, like we're little kids again, unable to use our words to say hello. I toss my keys in the catch-all bowl we have that's full of change, and a thimble of all things, a few hundred or so safety pins because you never know when you're going to need one.

I hang up my coat, toe off my boots and pad into the living room, plopping on the couch and allowing myself to sag sideways, leaning on Elena, my head pressed close to the phone by her ear, too. I can hear Beckett clear as day.

"So I'll see you when I get back in town, three days from now."

"Yeah, of course. We have Zoe's birthday to go to, and I need you to help me pick out a present. Well, 'help me confirm my present choice' is a better phrase for it."

"As long as it's not Habs-themed then she'll love anything you give her, baby," Beckett yawns on the line. "All right, I'm calling it a night. Sweet dreams, sweetheart. Love you."

"Love you, too. Safe travels and don't do anything stupid. Be safe."

"Always. Good night."

"Good night." Elena pulls her phone away from her ear, starts rolling her shoulder backwards and forwards so it's no longer a comfortable perch to rest my weary head on, the jerk.

"You guys are so stinking cute, my teeth are hurting. *My teeth*, Elena. Shit."

Elena shrugs her shoulders again, and I have to forget about leaving my head on her shoulder for a second longer; I don't need my brains scrambled, thanks.

"So...how did it go?" she asks, the question loaded.

"Let me rest here and I'll tell you all about it," I say, not wanting to move right now, not wanting to do much of anything.

We both stare at the TV, some kind of show that has monsters and shit and a jump-scare that makes my entire body jolt into a standing position and has me halfway into my bedroom, Elena closing the TV behind me, running into my bedroom with me.

I tell her the story in fits and starts while running through my night routine: skin care after removing my makeup, pulling on my pajamas with the polar bears on them, reading socks pulled all the way up to the knee even if I don't plan on doing any reading whatsoever.

"So it's all good, right? You had a good time? He was sweet?" Elena nods, because that's exactly what I've been talking about all this time.

I nod slowly, carefully, crossing my fingers while I get into bed, and Elena moves to the doorway, closing it behind her after wishing me a good night.

I don't know why I stare at the ceiling, blinking at the shape-shifting shadows playing across it, a sliver of waning moonlight dancing across the surface.

I just don't know why.

FOURTEEN

"Hello?" I groan into the phone, having overslept on this beautiful, extremely sunny Monday morning. I blink at the harsh sunlight, phone pressed to my ear, trying not to doze off since apparently there's another person on the line.

"Hello?" I try again, clearing my throat, my morning voice sounding like a life-long smoker when I've never touched the things.

"Sophie?"

I hum. "Yeah, hi, Russia. Morning." I keep my eyes closed, shivering underneath my blankets in a way that has nothing to do with the cold.

"Did I call too early?"

"I'm surprised you called at all. Phone calls are weird, don't you think?"

"As opposed to talking in person?" he asks, sounding more confused than I am this fine morning.

I nod to myself, humming into the phone again, blinking slowly so I don't get blinded by the harsh sunlight streaming through my half-opened curtains.

"Yeah...you know. When I talk to you, I want to see your face. It's a nice face," I say, still half-asleep, slowly waking up to the dawning horror that I'm actually saying *exactly* what I'm saying. Who am I, really? And what am I doing this early in the morning, flirting like this?

"Well, I'm glad you like my face."

"I don't *just* like your face, though. You know that, right?"

"I know you're an artist and can appreciate symmetry, I get that. Except for the bump in my nose."

I snort. "Yeah, yeah, I know all about that bump and how you got it," I laugh, trying to picture Sera taking a swing at her friend for saying something rude. "Sera told me it was because you were a dick. Were you a dick?" I ask, to confirm his side of the story.

Russia grunts on the other end of the connection, almost like he's been hit with something. "I was extremely rude, and I deserved it."

I'm quiet for a second—not a lot of people would admit that outright, like maybe never. Especially to someone they're starting to date, someone they want to make the best first impression for—where we end up projecting the shiniest version of ourselves, hiding all the muck and dirt.

"Yeah?" My voice comes out on a whisper.

"I did deserve it and I'm reminded of the fact every single time I look in the mirror. I was insensitive and basically an asshole, and I paid for it."

"Did Sera cause any lasting damage?" I ask, probing for the answer I want.

"No, I can breathe just fine. I just look a little different is all."

"I can't imagine you without it, actually. I don't think you would be half as interesting without it. Like me without some of my hand tattoos."

"Or the ones along your collarbone," he adds, sighing into the phone. "I wish I didn't have to work," he says, and I ask him all the pertinent questions about his job (finance—kill me now), and I nod along in my bed, closing my eyes and just basking in the gloriousness of his voice and the way it sounds pressed so closely to my ear.

"Did you fall asleep on me?" he asks, his voice warm, and I can *so* tell that he's smiling right now, his voice changing with it, like I've gone and made him happy.

Shit, I hope so. *I hope so.*

"Nope. Not at all. Not me. Just listening to your voice."

"Yeah, *meelaya?* I like listening to you talk, too."

I laugh, snorting a little, and scissor my legs under my blankets because it's getting hot in here, but I'm too lazy to actually kick off the blankets. "Well, thanks. Nobody's really told me that before."

"I also really like how you don't care what I think."

I freeze a little, because boy, do I have him fooled.

Which is good, I guess, or else he would have too much power over me and that would just suck since he'd have all the cards and I'd end up with *nothing.*

"In general, I do care what people think," I say, trying to keep my statement as general as possible, throwing him in there along with the rest of the people on the planet.

"But not when it comes to me...generally."

Russia's laugh is low and delicious and who knew I could fall head over heels with a laugh? Who knew?

"I like how caring you are," he says, sighing into the phone, an unfortunate sound coming through the mic of his phone, halting all talking. "That was my chair, more precisely me moving on the chair and I didn't fart in the middle of a serious conversation."

I get startled into laughing and laughing, so hard and loudly that Elena throws something against the wall we share, and I have to stuff my face into my pillow to keep from getting even *louder*.

"Ouch, ouch, my abs, my *abs*. Why?" I laugh, sniffing now, just picturing Russia on his super-expensive office chair (because that's just the vibe I get, that he believes he deserves nice things and that includes office furniture), letting one rip. I giggle like a little kid, losing it all over again, Russia joining in on the fun.

"At least I got to hear you laugh," he says, making me sniff hard and hide my face in my pillow again, denying the existence of the blush. If I don't acknowledge it and pretend it's all from the heat of my pillow and nothing else.

"Yeah," I say, sobering just a little, sniffing and wiping at my wet eyes. "What are you doing now?"

And it goes like that, the both of us losing time talking to each other, debating over which *John Wick* movie is best, and since I haven't seen the other two (and confess my fear of watching the other two to him), we make plans to watch them together the following evening with me being invited for an actual homecooked meal that he promises me will be good.

We had to reschedule our *John Wick* night for another three weeks later.

I ended up pulling the late shifts, and Russia has a normal morning-hour type job, and we couldn't make our schedules match up

He surprised me, though, with phone calls every single day, with conversations about growing up as an immigrant, conversations about high school, and all the high points of his life.

We talk about everything that makes up a person.

Russia asked me my favorite artist, and I couldn't give him just the one.

We talked about my tattoos, and all the other ideas that he has for ones he wants. We talk about books and movies, and how Russia doesn't have a sticky memory for details.

We talk about his friends; and I've already gathered that he's one of the more serious ones in the group, but I'm not that close yet with Elias and Josh, so I can't make a call one way or the other.

"I had a bad day at work today," Russia admits, his voice heavy with every single weighted word.

"Do you want to talk about it?" I ask, lying down in bed, my phone pressed to the half of my face, my eyes closed. I don't want to fall asleep on him, but I just might.

"I don't know. Would you listen to me?"

"Of course I would. Tell me what happened."

"I...I made a mistake. A big mistake. It cost the company fifty thousand dollars."

I keep my silence, trying to equate the fact that someone's yearly salary was lost in a single day. "Okay."

"Okay?"

I hum. "You feel pretty awful about it, huh?"

"That's one way of putting it. I...I felt like a failure today."

"So, maybe this will make you feel better, maybe it won't, but I'm going to try anyway. When I do tattoos, even after doing them for long enough now, I *still* get pretty nervous."

I can hear Russia smiling on the other end of the conversation. "Yeah? You didn't look nervous to me when you did mine."

"Oh, I'm good at hiding *all* of my feelings, but that's another story," I mumble, pulling the covers up and underneath my chin. "And I'm making art, right? And it can look different from the original idea in mind, right? I always feel like throwing up a little after the big reveal, hoping the client loves it." I hum to myself. "And I've made mistakes before, and someone had to fix my mistakes probably with a cover-up tattoo, but the point is, it'll be fixed."

"Are you trying to tell me everything's going to be okay?"

I squeeze my eyes shut. "I'm doing a bad job of it, huh?"

Russia laughs, and it's so lovely that I hear myself sigh into the phone. *Yup, I've got it bad.*

"No, no, this helped. I wish I could see you, though. Ask for a hug."

"Should I deploy Dean for emergency hug services?"

Russia laughs again, a happy chuckle. I hear rustling over the phone, and I can picture him in his own bed. "No, I'm not that hard up. I can't wait to see you tomorrow."

I groan. "Stop being sweet to me."

"Why? Do you not like it?"

"Nah, I like it a lot. It's going to be a problem."

Russia laughs again, and I'm happy that I could make his day just a little bit better.

"It'll make me want to be sweet to you all of the time."

I squirm in my bed, not allowing my brain to wonder if he's ever said that to Sera. "Prove it," I say, and Russia laughs again. It sounds a whole lot like a promise.

I dress more casually since it's basically going to be a movie night, with nothing but BB cream on my face that just covers up my dark under-eye circles that are genetic and I can't really do anything about them.

On the one hand, I don't want to look like a walking corpse, and I don't usually leave the house without a winged eyeliner (and depending on my mood, the sizing of it is different, too), but I'm wearing joggers and a giant color-block hoodie that's warm and cozy, and I braved nothing but a puffer vest and nearly froze my nipples off in the drive over to his place.

"Hey," he says, leaning in to kiss me on the cheek when I cross the threshold into his home, the smell of his laundry detergent invading my nose, and then the *delicious smell* of the food he's making for us making my mouth water.

"Oh my God, *what is that?*" I ask, looking around the kitchen to the immaculate counter tops, not even a dish in the sink or a stray glass of water that has been used throughout the day, greasy from fingertips or lip gloss (well, at least in my particular situation) hanging around either.

"What's that smell? I'm dying."

"I hope you're hungry." He grins, winding an arm around my waist and tugging me into the kitchen, opening the oven up for me so I can see the homemade pizza (with green olives!), and some chicken wings on the top rack, all of the smells coming together—nirvana for my nose.

"Is it ready?" I ask, and Russia leans down, pressing a laugh and a kiss to my cheek, lingering there for a second so that his beard starts to itch just a little against my skin.

"You hungry, *meelaya?* Food'll be ready soon, I promise. What can I get you to drink? Sparkling water?"

"Ah, so you've found out my deepest, darkest secret—my addiction to sparkling water. Yes, please, and thank you!" I sing-song, grinning at him when he fishes out a Perrier from the fridge, handing me one of those mini-bottles that you get in cases instead of the big-ass bottles. "Did you get this just for me?"

Russia shrugs, and I'm taking that as a *yes.*

Huh.

The oven timer beeps, and Russia dons his bright red oven gloves (cute!) and takes out the food that I immediately start salivating over, waiting for him to plate it. We bring it over to his couch, where he's set up everything so I don't accidentally go slopping food all over myself or his furniture.

He cues up *John Wick 2* for us, and I'm already asking questions—didn't they call John Wick 3, John Wick: Chapter 3 Parabellum? Why not just call *it* Chapter 2? Don't people know that continuity matters?!

To which I get laughed at and then told to be quiet, which you know, I *do* have a bad habit of talking during movies, and it drives Elena insane. Looks like I'm in the wrong, *this time.*

"It's called *Chapter 2,* anyway," Russia says, after looking it up on his phone, turning the screen towards me so I can check for myself.

I grunt an affirmative sound and shut myself up by eating more pizza, my eyes pinned to the movie, watching for a whole twenty minutes straight before Russia laughs at something said on screen that doesn't make a whole lot of sense given the subtitles.

"I'm guessing they didn't translate that well, huh?" I whisper, not looking away from the screen, torn between watching Keanu Reeves kick ass and watching Russia's face, which is *just* as interesting.

"Okay, okay, the movie was good, but it wasn't *as* good as the first one. You know I'm right," I say, blowing Russia a kiss as he walks back into his kitchen, disposing of our plates after we nearly had a battle to the death over who's going to do the clean-up, which I lost valiantly but got a lot of kisses instead.

"So does that mean that you don't want to watch the third one?"

I gasp. "I said *no* such thing. Unless you have work to do? What time is it anyway? I don't know, how are you feeling? You have to be in the office earlier than I have to head to work tomorrow, so you let me know how you feel."

Russia's blue-blue eyes almost glow even from this distance (between his kitchen and his living room), like he doesn't really believe what I just said.

"What? What is it?" I ask, heart beating a little faster now from my worry. Did I say something wrong?

Did I?

Russia shakes his head, heading over to his fridge and pulling out a baking sheet and popping it in the oven. "Any allergies I should know about?" he asks, looking over his shoulder at me, freezing in the act of putting the sheet in the oven.

"Mango," I say, shrugging when his eyebrows hike up his forehead. "I know, I know, it's weird, but as long as I don't eat it directly, I feel good. No itchy tongue, here."

"Okay, but nuts are okay?"

I nod. "You? Are you allergic to anything that I should be worried about?" Russia shakes his head and pops the stuff in the oven, setting the timer before coming to sit next me only after grabbing me another bottle of sparkling water.

See? He's being sweet, and I'm having a hard time.

Wow.

"Thank you," I murmur twisting the cap with that satisfying hiss of expelled air, drinking it down even though it bites at my mouth and throat, making my nose itch, because Russia's being sweet to me and it's making me *thirsty* for more things other than water.

Shit.

"So? Do you want to watch the third movie with me?"

Hell, I'll do anything with you.

I clench my jaw to keep *that* particular answer to myself, and to myself *only*, pulling in a deep breath through my nose and letting it sink in that we're having a movie night and it's fun and casual, and I've been kissed a few times, and I don't feel like I'm going to throw up from being nervous.

Win-win-*win*.

"Yeah, if that's okay."

Russia nods. "The cookies should be ready in fifteen minutes," he says, stammering a little when I gasp so loud I end up choking on nothing but air.

"You made *cookies*? Are you kidding me right now? Did Elena or Katie give you a handbook on how to keep me happy? Honestly..."

Russia grins, and I don't even control myself anymore before I'm putting my palms on either side of his face, his beard soft and a little prickly at the same time, pulling him in for a kiss, sighing against his mouth like I've missed him when I only saw him the other day.

Maybe that's what love is, huh? Missing someone all of the time?

Maybe, maybe, maybe.

We kiss until the kitchen timer beeps, and we only stop because I don't want to eat charred cookies after he's painstakingly made them for us. That's really the only reason why I let him go. I ignore the way my body's flushed and warm, my cheeks holding enough heat to power an entire city bigger than Montreal.

We watch the third movie cuddling until I realize that Russia's a pretty good cuddler, always checking to make sure I'm comfortable that I basically just nod and let myself go boneless on top of him, only asking him maybe once or twice if his arm's going numb.

We don't move for the entirety of the movie, me being audible with my reactions, which makes him laugh so I milk that for all it's worth, wanting to get that kind of reaction out of him until he's murmuring to me in his mother tongue more often than not.

They *sound* like sweet words, terms of endearment, softly spoken and whispered, and I wish I was sneaky enough to pull out my phone from the pocket of my joggers and pull up any old translating app to figure out what the hell he's saying using the audio feature.

But I'm not that sneaky, and I'm also sleepy on top of him, all snuggled and warm that I'm pretty sure I doze off for only five minutes before Russia's gently shaking me, rubbing his hands up and down my back in an even more soothing gesture, so I'm *definitely* not getting up anytime soon.

"*Meelaya,*" he says, voice deep and crooning in my ear, making me sigh out loud, which somehow makes him laugh. "You should get up now," he says, but he's the one who holds me tighter to his chest, like he's the one that doesn't want to let go.

He starts talking in Russian, while I rub my face into his T-shirt like some kind of kitten searching out all of the tactile affection if he's going to give it to me without me having to ask. "I wish you could stay, but we both know you need to get home. I'll give you some cookies for the drive home?"

Well, that makes me lift my head and blink at him. "Cookies? For me?"

Russia smiles, his eyes practically twinkling with it. "Anything for you."

"But you made them," I say around a yawn, covering my mouth up quick and slowly rolling myself up into a seated position, not liking this new turn of events one bit. "I don't want to take away all of your hard work," I say around *another* yawn.

"What's the point of working hard if you can't take care of the ones you want to take care of, hmmm?"

I blink at him, knowing that what he said is important, helping me understand the way he ticks, but my brain's not fully online yet, and I'm still warm and sleepy and I wish we could go back to kissing for hours and hours and forget about all of our responsibilities and obligations.

I blink at him slowly, watching his face, just as he watches mine. "You want to take care of me, Russia?"

Russia nods. "If that's what you want as well, then yes. I would love to take care of you, however, whatever, that looks like."

I cover my mouth, thinking, then drop my hands back down into my lap.

"I'm a lot to take care of," I admit, knowing myself, knowing what I want and need on a daily basis. "It's going to take more than just pizza and cookies."

Russia nods again, slowly, mulling it all over while I think my heart's going to beat its way *right out of* my chest. I hold my breath, waiting for his answer, waiting for him to tell me I'm wrong, or right, just to tell me *what* he's thinking.

"What else?" he asks, leaning in closer and pressing a kiss to my cheek. "What else do you need?" He presses a kiss to my forehead, then moves to give me a kiss on my neglected cheek, and I'm holding my breath for so long that I get a little dizzy.

I exhale on a woosh, blinking at him, wanting this, wanting *him*, in a way I've never really wanted anyone before.

"I need kisses and hugs, especially when I'm upset. I need you to understand that I'll spend hours of my days off sketching and working on new techniques, hanging out with Elena and Katie because I love my friends and I love hanging out with them."

Russia nods, prompting me to continue.

I gulp but ultimately decide to just go for it. Maybe he's the guy I've always though he's going to be—maybe he's that special someone it feels like I've been waiting around for, why it never really seemed to work out with anyone else.

"I need you to want me for me, for Sophie."

Russia nods again, reaching for my hand. "Who else would I want, *meelaya*?" He tilts his head at me, clearly confused, but I don't say what

I'm thinking, nope, I just keep it locked in my chest, not allowing it to be uttered into existence.

I think it, though, all through getting a plastic container with almost *all* of the cookies because Russia is seriously a prince among men, and then a really *great* kiss goodnight. I think about it all the way down to the visitors' parking and inside my car, starting it up without waiting for it to heat all the way through, shivering all the way home.

I think about it a lot.

A lot.

FIFTEEN

Monday mornings don't really suck for me, but today's the day from hell.

I woke up late...and rushed to work without putting on lipstick. Bekah noticed and stopped mid-sip in her Tim Hortons coffee, pointing at her mouth, then back at me.

"Yeah, yeah. It's one of those days," I say, feeling *naked* without lipstick or gloss, not even a tinted lip balm, not *anything*.

I had rushed through my morning workout, over-exhausting my legs and abs, and I know I'm going to feel it every single time I get on and off my rolling stool while working, hell even when going to the *bathroom*.

It's unfortunately going to be one of those days where squatting is going to kill me, I just know it.

I rush to get ready for my next client, running behind on sanitizing my station, wanting it to be freshly done by me, just in case someone used my bench when they needed to. The open space is usually assigned by artists in the shop at the time, but it's not like we sign our names to it, making sure we stay there forever.

I do my first tattoo of the day, a pretty watercolor ballerina on the upper back of a girl about my age, and she took the pain like a champ, her boyfriend holding her hand the whole time, talking to her, making her laugh as often as he could, just trying to distract her from the sting.

When I'm done, I get pulled into a hard hug, the kind of squeeze that hurts my lungs, but I suck up all the good energy while I can, waving goodbye to her, wanting to grab a snack, turning towards the back room when I hear my name.

"Sophie, Sophie!"

I know that voice, I *know* that voice.

I turn, and yup, there he is, Matty with Sera following after him, hiking her purse up on her shoulder, a bucket of coffee in one hand, and both she and the kid are holding paper bags. Sera's got hers balanced on top of a box of a dozen donuts, the smell of glazed sugar and fried dough wafting into the shop, and since we're all just a bunch of animals, we all start circling closer, like hyenas eyeing a gazelle—or whatever hyenas eat.

Aren't hyenas scavengers? I don't know.

"Oh my God, what are you two doing here?" I ask, glancing down at the box of donuts I've been handed. Bekah and even Jake come out of the breakroom, and Remy is in the back with a client yelling at me to save him some.

There's a ruckus of noise and audible sniffs as I open the box, seeing the dozen donuts, making my mouth water.

"Hey, hey, it's mine, *mine*," I snap, closing up the box and taking a step back, putting me next to Sera and Matty coming up on my other side, like we're going to get into a fight over it.

Which I'm not above doing. They're *donuts* and I haven't had a donut in a thousand years and now I have *twelve* of them.

Is this what true power is?

I don't have another client for a couple of hours, and I know Remy's finishing up his appointment, so there's an artist on backup if I decide to mosey on down to the back room and take some time to myself earlier on in the day rather than not. I offer Jake a donut, a toll for the ferryman, or the boss-man, who lets me go on break early, and then hand one to Bekah, making sure she has some, too.

Jake's thanking Sera for the coffee and the eats, and Sera's talking to him, pointing out one of his tattoos, an obscure reference to a show or movie I never really understood and always forgot to look up.

"Oh, wow," Sera keeps saying, looking like she wants to touch, but her hands are still full until Jake sees the vat of coffee she brought over and takes the stack of paper cups and covers, putting them on the reception desk.

"That's like a reference within a reference," Sera says, pointing down at Jake's forearm, and Jake's got on the kind of grin that would incinerate the panties off any woman, even married ones, probably especially *married* ones.

"How did you even do that? You got Gallifreyan somehow into the shape of the Sonic Screwdriver even though it's a circular language. Wow, that's amazing, truly."

Jake looks half in love with her already, and I wonder if that's her charm, the kind of true power that she has, bringing people closer to her, not to manipulate or use, but just by being warm, so incredibly warm that you can't help but like her, learn to *love* her, almost straight away.

I don't have that superpower. I don't, I don't.

"Hey there, little man," Jake says, waving down at Matty, not going for a handshake like some guys might. What does a nine-year-old know about handshakes, seriously.

It doesn't get past me that Jake's golden skin flushes underneath Sera's stare, the way he sort of unconsciously starts turning his left arm so Sera can see without *really seeing* the other nerdy tattoos he has there.

Sneaky, but not so sneaky.

"Sera, let's go in the back. Come on, Matty," I say, stopping for a second to hand the kid a giant binder that might be half his body weight, but he assures me that he can carry it. "Follow me."

We head down the stairs at the back of the shop, towards the back room where we seat ourselves at the only table where most of us eat lunch, shoot the shit, nap on the table, whatever. It's empty now, and I place everything down. Sera puts the bags down, too, only to reveal muffins in each of them.

"Sorry to barge in like this. Katie gave me your address, and it's a Ped. Day for Matty, so it seemed like a good idea to pass by. You're not incredibly busy are you? I could totally just drop all of these off and meet you some other time," Sera says, waving at everything she brough.

I shake my head. I'm not busy for donuts, no way.

"It's like you want us to pledge our souls," I blurt, glancing up at her to make sure she knows that I'm joking. Honestly, though, there's not much we won't do for some sweet food. None of us here at The Red Seal really eat regularly (re: optimally) when we're working.

"I'm buying if you're offering," she says, making me laugh.

Matty sits down next to me, and it makes feel me incredible for no real reason at all.

"How are you guys doing? God, thank you for all the treats, it was so unexpected. Wow, so much food."

"Mom always does that," Matty says, nodding at me like he's telling me a world-renowned fact of life. "She always brings too much of any food, especially dessert, and it makes everybody happy. She says it's important to try to make other people happy with little things like that."

"I'm happy, super happy that I have donuts *and* muffins. I haven't eaten much today, do you mind?" I ask, flipping the box open and grabbing a donut that's vanilla frosted with all the sprinkles on top, because I am a child at heart, and sprinkles really *do* make me happy, along with glittery eyeshadow and long-lasting lipstick.

"Mom, can I have one?"

Sera freezes for a second, then glances down, her cheeks blooming under a harsh blush that has nothing to do with makeup, but more like shame or embarrassment. She breathes hard for a second, then glances up, smile in place, pinned there, like one of my drawings on a peg board.

"How about we share, like your doctor suggested, hmmm? We haven't even had lunch yet."

"Ugh, *finee*," the kid says. "I get to pick though."

Sera shoots him a glance and the kid's shoulders hike up to his ears.

"Can I please pick which one?" Matty asks, leaning close to the table now, glancing down at the nine leftover donuts, making his analysis, his very own pros and cons list.

"Better. Yeah, go ahead and choose for us." Sera looks into her purse again, pulling out that pouch thing I saw last Saturday—was it only Saturday and not a whole year and a half ago? —putting it down on the table. "Let's just check your sugar first, here."

"Mom—" Matty turns his head to me, nervous now, when I've already seen this. Maybe the kid forgot that I was there the last time, too.

"Oh, do you want some privacy?" I ask, already done with half the donut, grabbing a paper napkin to deal with my sticky fingers. "I'll just go and wash my hands."

Sera looks at me, the smile in her eyes and just a little bit across her mouth.

I head to the bathroom, forcing myself to do my business, then wash my hands thoroughly, hoping to have given them enough time. When I step back out, Matty's almost in tears and I somehow feel like it's my fault.

"I'm not saying no forever, Matty, you know how this works. You can't have the half-donut right now. Let's just wait until your sugar comes down a little. Is your pump at the end of its batteries?" she asks him, and Matty checks something at his waist. He shakes his head.

"But I *do* want it now. It's going to suck later."

Sera looks at him, blinks. "Kid, when has a donut ever sucked *later* in the history of the universe? When has that happened, huh? Tell me. I'd love to know."

"Mom—" he huffs, putting his head in his hands, like the world's crashing down around him and he's making the smallest target possible in hopes of not getting hit. We all know it doesn't work that way, it just doesn't.

"I hate being a diabetic. I wish I wasn't." It hurts to hear him say those words, to hold his head in his hands like he's not sure he can hold himself up without the support of his hands.

Sera shakes her head, smiling sadly at him, where he can't see her. "But you are, Matty *mou*, and I love you with all my heart. Your dad loves you with all his heart, too. Come on, have some water. Didn't you want to look at the binder of artwork anyway?"

"Well, Dad's bigger so he's gotta love me more." Matty lifts his head and *grins,* and the world seems all the better for it, lighter, *happier.*

Sera gasps, affronted, and I know the danger's passed us by now, the tightening in my throat is going to ease at any given second, just to let me breathe a little. "Excuse you, your dad doesn't love you more. I would win that contest. If there were Olympics in loving Matty MacLaine, I would win gold, and your dad would win silver."

"But he's bigger than you," Matty keeps insisting, smile bigger than the room, but I watch him close the donut box, moving himself away from temptation.

I don't know a lot about diabetes, but I know you have to watch your portion control and keep limiting how many carbohydrates you eat, adjust insulin levels after every single meal, which also depends on the amount of activity you did for the day, how much emotional energy you expend at any given moment.

And needles.

So many needles, punctures to fingers even though there's sensors now, like little plastic caps embedded into your skin for you to scan your blood glucose levels. Punctures in the lower belly, upper arms, thighs.

Punctures every single day, *multiple* times a day if you don't have a pump because those can be pricey.

While I couldn't sleep last night, I learned a little bit about diabetes, specifically *juvenile* diabetes. I had to stop reading at a certain point, angry and sad until all the emotion was too much, and I ended up conking out more exhausted than ever.

"That doesn't mean anything," Sera says, adamant, waving away the fact that her husband is, in fact, physically larger than her. But based on presence alone? Sera's got him beat, for sure. A hundred percent.

"Mom—oh, hi, Sophie!" Matty waves and there goes my heart, tumbling into love with the kid, wanting to protect him at all costs, fight against anyone or anything that'll make him sad.

"Do you mind if I take the donuts upstairs? They're going rabid up there," I say, winking at Sera, hoping she understands what I'm trying to do.

"Rabbit? Are they turning into rabbits?" Matty asks, glancing between the two of us, head swivelling from side to side at a speed that's bound to hurt. "No way that's happening."

I snicker, because yeah, English is weird. "I'll be right back," I say, nabbing the closed box and bags of muffins and bringing them back to the reception desk in front, leaving them with Bekah where everyone can see them, sniffing around like dogs that have caught the right kind of scent.

Jake comes out of his office on a mid-jog, and I grin at him, jabbing the air with my pointer finger. "She's married, man. Lay off."

"Happily?" he asks, tilting his head, his face a big, fat mood.

"Yeah. That's her kid. Don't be an ass."

Jake nods. "Right. All the great ones have been snatched up, I swear to Christ." Jake sighs, shutting himself in his office, almost kicking the door shut when it sticks, needing privacy to mope.

When I head back. Sera is sitting back in her seat and Matty's walking around the room, fascinated by the drawings pinned there, some handwritten letters that we've accumulated over the years—ten times more personal than emails, even though getting any kind of thank you after the initial reveal is *something awesome.*

"Mom, I want this one. Oh, yeah, and this one, too! Shit."

"*Matty,*" Sera groans, looking up at the ceiling, but she's grinning just like I am.

I don't know why it's so funny when little kids swear. It's like they don't know what's coming for them the rest of their lies (re: adulthood) and swearing from now just makes it that much funnier, I guess.

Whatever it is, Matty comes traipsing back to the table where both his mom and I are sitting now, and he fishes into his jeans pocket, pulls out a quarter and hands it over to Sera.

"Bad word," he mutters to himself. "They're all so *fraking* cool, though. I'm gonna get a hundred when I turn eighteen, just watch!" He glances down at his arms, covered by his long-sleeved shirt, but still probably envisioning what all that ink will look like about nine years from now.

"Technically, *frak* is also a bad word, but I'll let it slide for now," Sera says, crossing her arms over her chest, letting Matty explore the room (which is not that big, granted). "Sorry to bother you, but is there anywhere I can refill my water bottle?"

I hold my hand out for the water bottle, and she hands it over. I come back two seconds later, and then Sera's calling to Matty to drink some more water, and the kid grudgingly obliges, even over protests that *he's going to have to pee in three fraking minutes*, which earns him another loss of another quarter.

I don't know what game they're playing, but I want *in*.

Matty's looking over the binder now with everyone's artwork in there, his eyes as big as pizzas, his fingers tracing along some of the outlines, asking questions about colors and shading while Sera and I talk small talk, the *worst* kind of talk, until it starts to get interesting.

"So I was wondering if I can book an appointment with you to get my nipples done," she says out of the crook of her mouth, Matty absorbed by whatever's in the binder, a whole table and a half away.

I nearly choke on the very air I'm breathing. "Uh, what?"

"Is it weird for you? I don't want it to be weird for you. I'll book something with anyone you recommend."

I think about Jake piercing Sera's nipples and want to *die*.

"I mean, it's weird now because I know you. Does that make sense?" I shrug, not wanting it to be awkward between us; I like her too much.

Sera nods, pushing her hair off her face, tucking it behind her ears. "Maybe I should start smaller. Maybe I should do my helix first, or conch." She points the areas out, pinching the areas between her fingers as if testing out her pain tolerance. "I heard nipple piercings can take up to a year to heal. Does that sound about right?"

"Yeah, and you'll never be more aware of your boobs ever since they sprouted. Mine took a year, but I also like, banged into them all the time. I can't even tell you how many times I've hit them with dumbbells doing upright rows." I demonstrate the movement, holding pretend dumbbells in both hands, palms facing my body, knuckles out, and pulling them up towards my neck.

"Oh, shit, that must have *killed*," she says, sliding back that quarter that was on the table back towards Matty, who fist pumps in the air, trotting over from where he'd been standing to grab it with a *"score!"*

"Yeah, and your husband can't touch them for that long, too."

Sera sighs, like that would be *bad*. I mean, fair. "I really wanted them, too. Yeah, maybe we could try piercing my ears. I really like what you've done, but I'll look up some ideas and what I think will suit me."

I nod. "I can do your ears no problem. We've got some really pretty jewelry back in the shop, if you want to take a look, and lots of different budget options."

Sera snorts. "Does Russia know? About...?"

Oh, *oh*. "Nope. It's literally for me to know and him to find out."

Sera laughs, a peal of laughter that invites me to join in, and Matty comes rushing over, demanding to know what happened.

How to explain nipple piercings to a kid who gets quarters when bad words are said?

I'm not gonna do it, definitely not gonna do it.

"I've gotta say that's not the only reason I came by. Matty had a ped day, and it was nice going around town with him, getting groceries and stuff, and we decided to pass by, just to say hi. I know we've taken up a lot of your time, but I'm hoping the donuts and the muffins made up for it."

"No, I'm so happy you guys showed up. I'm going to be living off those donuts and muffins for a thousand years. Like, my boss will give me a raise for having a friend like you bring me treats, you really have no idea." I halt after letting my mouth run off, after saying *friend* after I've met her like only twice.

We should be rivals; she has a piece of Russia that I don't think I will ever get—but how can I hate her? *Why* would I hate her?

That's not right.

"Good, I'm glad. I'll call the shop and make an appointment so you can fit it around your tattoos, okay?"

I nod dumbly as she stands up, ushering Matty over to her, the kid closing the binder carefully as if there's something precious inside and hefting it to bring it over to me.

"Let's go, kiddo. We're headed home," Sera says, ruffling the kid's hair, which he painstakingly puts back in place, and I've got half a mind that the kid is half in love with *me*, tattoos and piercings and *all*, even without my favorite lipstick.

Looks like we've got a contender.

"Thanks for having us, and enjoy the treats," Sera says again, letting Matty lead the way back up the stairs and into the shop where all the magic really happens.

"Yeah, enjoy them, Sophie," Matty says, bringing my attention back down to him. Holy shit, he's cute. "And tell Uncle Russia that we say hi, too!" Matty waves, his entire arm moving along with his entire body, and that's super cute too.

How can I compete with Sera Delos? How?

And honestly, why would I want to?

SIXTEEN

R ussia's back on his two feet (mostly) by the end of the following
week, when he comes into the shop for his next session.

We're starting on the shading today and we'll see how much I can get
done before the session needs to be over. It's different now, that we've
shared kisses, that he's made his "intentions" clear, for lack of a better word.

Like I'm in some sort of Regency novel and he's the rakish duke that
wants me only for my virginity.

Sorry, pal, you're a little late to that game, yeah.

I let myself bask in the happiness at seeing him again, even though we've
talked to each other every single day—sometimes not for long (I can barely
hold phone call conversations to save my life, always multi-tasking and
talking out loud is the thing that goes first), other times long text messages
on a giant thread that begins with half-formed thoughts and ends going on
tangents.

It's nice, super nice.

After I finish up, Russia waits around for my shift to finish, and I end
up introducing him to Jake, my boss, as my boyfriend, and Jake gives me
the most monumental shit-eating grin that I want to die on the spot, dig a
hole into the ground and live there forever and ever.

I can't do that, obviously, so I stand there and take it, pointing at Jake
viciously once Russia's already out the door on the official first day of Easter
break (my ass it's the first day of the long weekend when it's still ten below
and I swear I saw a few snowflakes driving into work this morning) and

mouth the word "*Sera*," and Jake snaps his mouth closed and disappears from my line of sight.

I wave bye to Bekah, pull on my coat and step outside into the fading sunlight—which feels glorious, *glorious*—now that daylight savings time is over, even if it sucks losing an hour of sleep.

Russia holds out his hand for me, letting me make the decision, and after glancing around to make sure no one's watching how I'm going to transform into a puddle at his mere touch, I grab onto his hand, his grip firm against mine, and I don't actually combust, which is great, but *also* I'm holding Russia's *hand*. We walk carefully since Russia's gait isn't at a hundred percent yet and make our way to that restaurant we went to the first time we ate together, the one after I brought him to the clinic.

I order pasta—because when am I not ordering pasta? —and Russia orders us a bottle of wine, white, like he's noticed I prefer even though I'm pretty sure he likes red more.

Still, it's a nice gesture and there's already heat blooming in my cheeks, my body practically hunching in on itself, suddenly shy. It doesn't make a lot of sense, either.

I was the epitome of a total professional touching him and tattooing him, even if I'm looking at him in a different light now, studying the contours of his body not in the way a graffiti artist would look at a particular section of wall or building and see the end result.

Instead I find myself looking at him now like I'm going to be getting opportunities to touch those areas because he's going to *let* me touch those areas, and because I want to, want to find out where he's most ticklish (even though I think along his ribs is a good bet).

Everything's different, but still kinda the same.

"Sera came by the other day," I say, not really understanding why I'm bringing it up since it's none of his business who shows up, but I know on some level that I'm testing him, testing his reaction, heart beating *hard* in my chest, my breath rattling in my throat.

And I keep doing it, keep vomiting up the words.

"She was really sweet, actually, bringing everyone donuts and muffins."

Russia raises a single eyebrow in a silent question as his mouth tightens, his jaw clenches, the hands holding onto his napkin-wrapped cutlery flashing white.

I've gone and touched a nerve.

I know I have.

So what do I do?

I keep pressing the stupid thing, making sure the pain makes him lose his mind.

"Yeah, and Matty came, too. He wanted to see some of my artwork, and I'm pretty sure my boss, Jake," I say, unnecessarily since Russia *just* met the guy, "fell in love with her at first sight."

"She's married," is all Russia says, the words heavy and loaded, and I feel my spine straighten, my body lengthening, like a pufferfish that makes itself look bigger in the face of an enemy.

Russia's not my enemy, though. He's not.

Why are you doing this, Soph? Why?

Because I have to know for sure, once and for all.

I don't ever want to be second best, that's just not fair, and not what I want to sign up for.

Nope, not me.

Maybe that's just an excuse for not wanting to be someone's first, though, Soph, because that's some scary shit, isn't it?

I nod, glancing down at my nails like I'm the supervillain with all the time in the world, the hero captured and under my control while I lay out my evil plans for him to understand what he's going to be missing out on.

I lick at my lips, take a sip of my wine, the coolness soothing the raging fire inside of me, the drumbeat of blood pounding along in my head, at my ears, the base of my throat.

"I know that, and Jake knows that," I say, watching him get flustered, his body rigid, sitting all the way across from me. It's not the right kind of answer to give, the implications clear—that Jake *knows* that, but he's still willing to take a shot, regardless if she's married or not.

And maybe there's an implication there, that Russia should take his shot before Jake takes his...if he wants to jump on that particular opportunity.

I hold my breath, watching and waiting for his answer.

"Sera wouldn't do that, she wouldn't do that to Hunter," he says, shaking his head like a wet dog trying to dispel himself from all the evil moisture. I don't know who he's trying to convince—himself or me.

She wouldn't do that to me... The words are left unspoken, but that doesn't mean I don't hear them, loud and clear.

My heart trips up, slip-sliding in my chest like it's been dislodged, like it's taken one too many hits in my twenty-six years of life, and now I'm staring at Russia, a man it would be so easy to love, who clearly loves another.

There's no other reason why he'd be so invested in her, in her reaction to another man wanting her in the way that Jake clearly does.

Russia...Russia hasn't gotten over her, he just hasn't...he's in love with another woman, and it just had to be Sera freaking Delos, who's done nothing to return his affections.

What am I supposed to do now? What the hell am I supposed to do now?

What am I going to do—hate Sera for having a place in his heart, when I've met her and know exactly what she's like?

How can I possibly hate her when she's done nothing wrong, done absolutely *nothing* wrong?

It's like hating the sun for rising every day or hating the rain that makes all the trees grow.

You *can* hate the sun and the trees, the rainfall, the oceans and seas, but you'd be dumb to try and stop them, to try and stop others from loving them in your stead.

So it comes to this.

Our menus lie discarded on the table, neither of us paying attention to them, and when our waiter approaches out of the corner of my eye, I just give him a subtle shake of my head, and the kid gets the message: *stay the fuck away, we're not ready yet.*

"I don't know, Jake's a good-looking guy," I find myself saying, advocating for cheating and I'm starting to hate myself for it, but I can't take it back now, I can't *unsay* it.

It's like I'm watching myself from the outside-in, watching myself screw this up for me, self-sabotage at its finest.

I'd have to be stupid not to see that Sera's so clearly happy with Hunter and Jake can suck it and wait for his own dream woman to come along, one who likes his tattoos just as much as Sera appeared to. It can't be that hard, surely.

"Sera would never fall for somebody like that," Russia continues, his words almost guttural now, pulled deep from his chest like they have to be pried out of him.

"Somebody like *that*," I repeat slowly, leaning back in the booth, my back pressed tightly to the back of it, creating as much space between us as I possibly can.

My heartbeat's erratic now, and my palms are getting slick with the nervous kind of sweat that makes me feel out of control. "What do you mean? *Somebody like that?*"

Russia shakes his head, doing his own version of creating space between us, pushing against the edge of the table as if he can pin me with it even if the thing's anchored to the ground, my foot right next to the table leg.

"Somebody like that, somebody who would try to lure her away from her husband." He sounds...disgusted, and there's something moving behind his blue eyes that I don't really have a name for.

"I thought you said she couldn't be lured," I snap back, watching his neck tighten as his head snaps up, like I've called him to attention, or there's an invisible thread linking him to me and I can control his movements—the puppet meets the puppet-master.

But that's not the case at all.

My face feels wooden and not my own, my features at rest like I'm about to go to sleep, even while I push and prod and hope for more of a reaction from him, digging down deep for the truth of the matter.

Who is he going to choose? Sera or me? *Sera...or me?*

"No, you mean somebody who *looks* like that—tattoos and piercings, looking like they've gone through life *living* it, loving it, not following the rules," I supply, Russia looking at me as if I'm the stranger, like he doesn't know me at all.

My brain brings the images of us kissing last week forward, a memory to reminisce and cry over because I know what I have to do.

I know, but it's just going to hurt like a bitch.

"Someone like that, Russia?" I prompt, ice crowding in around my heart, making it hard to breathe. "Someone who looks like me?"

It hurts, God, it hurts, knowing that he *thinks* that, but doesn't actually say it, his silence another kind of slap I wasn't prepared for.

If I were ever to meet his parents, would he want me to cover up completely, cover me from throat down to my toes, hiding everything that makes me...me? Would he be so ashamed to be seen with me like that?

What about his friends? Do they think that, too? Was it all just a farce?

Russia shakes his head, his eyes pinning me back against the booth and it feels like I can't move unless he releases me from his stare. His voice is steady and even when he speaks. "Sera's the most loyal person I know. I don't care about this Jake guy, even if he is your boss."

Ah, so he's going to play *that* card. "Sera's the most loyal person you know?" I add the emphasis where it's needed, watching his face start to change from complacent, bemused to angry now as I attack one of his friends, attack the woman who has his heart, who doesn't believe that he loves her as much as he is able.

How did I get involved in this soap opera—how did this happen to me?

"Yes. She is. The kindest, sweetest person I know." His blue eyes blaze with the hottest kind of fire, the hottest part of the flame is always the blue part, and he burns me right through.

"Why are you talking about her this way? I thought you liked her, and I thought she liked you." He says the last part like he doubts it, and I get it, since I'm the one asking questions, pushing for answers that I want to hear.

"Loyal enough to never want anybody else?" I ask, hating the insinuation—I don't know what she goes through every single day, taking care of her son, watching him and his blood sugars, being there, a pillar for him to lean on when he's exhausted and tired of living in that way, only nine years old and sick of his life as a diabetic. I don't know *that* story.

Wouldn't it be easier, though, for her to have fallen in love with someone like her friend, Russia? The one who seems to know her best?

"Sera doesn't make assumptions on character based on looks alone, she cares about how you *act*, what you *do*, and sometimes what you *say*," Russia stresses on a labored breath.

The silence stretches and I wonder if he's going to do it now—if he's going to bring into question everything I've already been thinking about, about the two of us, about the lingering feelings he has for her, clear as day underneath the high-noon sun.

So I do it for us both instead when he takes too long, once and for all.

"I think I'm going to refer you to another colleague of mine, Remy, to finish up your tattoo. There's only the finishing touches left anyway and then you'll be good to go." The words tumble out of me before I can fully process them, but I'm not taking back anything I just said.

It's for the best, it's the for the best *for me*.

"Why? Why are you doing this?" Russia asks, and I sit there, my spine unbending, hard enough to snap. "Why are we talking about Sera like this? Why does it even matter?"

I close my eyes, her name ricocheting in my head like a litany, a prayer, a curse.

I want to shout in his face, to yell at him—doesn't he know, didn't he think I would find out, that I wouldn't know how much he cares for her?

Every question I'm asking about Sera is really about *him*, about what he'll do when he gets tired of me, when I don't meet his expectations of being the perfect girl of his dreams—Sera Delos.

I have too many tattoos, have piercings in private places, I don't wear my hair in a boring haircut even if Sera's hair looks glorious. I wear colorful makeup and I have an eyeshadow palette addiction (I have to collect all the shades with every kind of undertone—cool, neutral and warm), and so many lipsticks that I've lost count.

I don't look a thing like her, I'm not strong like her, taking care of her kid in a way that's gentle and friendly and looks to be like she deserves the mother of the year award ten times over.

Me?

I can't compete with that, can't *compare* to that. *And I shouldn't have to.*

"Russia," I say on a sigh that burns my throat, that knots me up, and makes tears burn in my eyes, sting my nose. "I think you should figure out what you want, *who* you want."

"Why? What? Sophie, I don't know what's happening here, but I promise we can go and talk somewhere private to discuss it."

"Well, I don't want to discuss it, and I don't want to eat with you anymore. Please, just make a decision and tell me what you decide. I don't want to compete for your love, that's not fair to me, and it's not fair to you. Okay?"

Russia shakes his head, looking lost. "I don't even know what you're talking about, we were going to have supper and then we started talking about *Sera*—"

Her name's like an invisible knife lodging in my ribs—between the fourth and fifth to be exact as watching *Game of Thrones* has come to teach me.

"I want you to figure out what you want," I say again, getting to my feet, holding up a hand to stop him from moving. "I'm going home, I need some time away from you." Could I have phrased that better? Sure. But it's the truth, no matter how much I pretty it up.

"Sophie..."

I shake my head, ignore the pleading tone in his voice that turns my legs to lead, that makes my knees want to buckle to sit back down at the booth again, to pretend the conversation didn't happen, that he didn't rise up to defend her like *he's* the one who had something to lose.

"Sophie, please. Let me just order us food to go and we can talk about it. Did Sera do something to upset you the other day? Is that it? Do you want me to talk to her?"

I clench my jaw tight, tight, tight, grab my coat and pull it on. "I need to go home now, Russia. Get home safe, yeah?" I say, zipping up my coat and leaving the restaurant behind, that look on his face branded into my memory, even as everything inside me starts to *hurt*, the kind of hurt you feel when you look down at the open wound, seeing once and for all the piece of yourself that you've lost.

I end up running to the shop, grabbing my shit in a whirlwind of activity, holding it in, *holding it in*, keeping myself contained.

If I can just get home, if I can just *see* Elena, she'll help me figure out what I need to do to drown this pain away, to forget about Russia and his tattoos and his terms of endearments that I've learned to say by myself, in near perfect pronunciation I've practiced them so, so much over the last week.

I just need to get home.

.♥ . ♥ . ♥ . ♥ . ♥.

The apartment's empty when I trudge inside, Elena clearly not anywhere in here, clearly with her Beckett. And I can't help but be jealous right at this very moment, that he's taken my friend away from me when I *need* her here.

I keep making these sounds in my throat, whimpers like Pongo would make for a treat, but I'm alone here, and I head into the shower where I can't distinguish the tears on my face from the water running down in a stream over my head and body.

I replay the whole conversation again with Russia, the way I was *instigating* all of it, stepping my foot in it while I waited for Russia to show me the truth, not asking it from him, but taking what I wanted and only what I wanted to see, to hear.

I feel a little sick, stomach flip-flopping, even as hunger claws at my stomach lining.

It's not until I drag myself into bed, freshly washed skin and hair, running through the motions of skin care and hair care, that I glance down at my phone, find Elena's text message: *Staying over at Beckett's. Don't wait up! Wish me luck!!!*

I can't bring her back here, *make* her come back here when I made this mess, when I demanded to know the truth.

Russia—Tommy—has *never* said my name in the exact same way he's said Sera's, like it's a gift in his mouth, a precious gem that shouldn't be swallowed, but admired.

So there's my answer.

It's the one I wanted, yeah.

I shuffle under my sheets and covers, the bed unmade because the bed's *always* unmade, burrowing underneath all the layers and layers, my fuzzy reading socks on, my phone on *do not disturb*, and my laptop sitting next to me, taking up the space there instead of someone I love, sleeping in the same bed next to me.

I pull up *John Wick* again, watching it for the millionth time, and when *that* scene shows up, I let myself cry again, great, racking sobs as the grief tears through me.

There's something incredibly cathartic about watching John Wick bring the pain (and so much murder) and revenge to those who had wronged him.

It helps me sleep, even if the lines in Russian stir something inside me I didn't really acknowledge was in there: that I've gone and fallen in love with Tommy Ivanov—and he doesn't love me back.

SEVENTEEN

I t feels a lot like I screwed up the next morning, as the sun's too bright, the day already half-gone and having gotten away from me as I struggle to make sense of the time, and my place in it.

Right, so Elena never came home, and I'm alone in the apartment and I can't get her to make me something delicious for breakfast.

I'll be alone forever if I keep this up...

I sigh loud and long since no one can hear me, spreading my arms and legs out in my bed, taking up as much space as possible, nearly throwing my laptop off the mattress, and hence my precious John Wick.

I'm able to keep it from falling completely onto the floor and I'm taking that as a good omen that everything will be all right, that everything's going to be *fine*.

Russia just needs to make up his mind.

Who does he want—me or the perfect Sera Delos?

Who's he gonna choose, once and for all?

It's not my problem if he wants to pine after a married woman, one he insists will never let him see the light of day (and she said just as much, too), but it is kinda sad, and I'm mad as hell that it's *making* me sad.

Hearts are stupid things—they should just keep on keeping on, doing the whole shuttling the blood to the rest of our bodies, not getting involved with other human beings, being weak and fragile and *in love*.

It doesn't make a lot of sense, no, least of all to me, but here I am, in my bed, pining for a man who has to come to the decision if he wants me or the perfect Sera who will never look at him because she's *happily married*.

Why am I letting this happen? Why am I letting him make the decision?

Am I going to go crawling back when he says he chooses me? Will I ever trust his word?

What the hell, Sophie, what did you do? What did you do?!

I hear the door unlock, Elena calling out a hello into the apartment, padding over after some time to knock on my bedroom door. I grunt an affirmative sound, doing it a second time until she comes inside my bedroom, looking at me as if I'm roadkill and she's pitying my lost life at the hands of a set of wheels.

Nice.

I flap a hand at her, and Elena comes closer to my bed, to the burrito I've rolled myself in the constricting kind of comfort that might make me panic in a couple of seconds, fighting to get loose. But right now I'm swaddled like the baby I'm acting like and wishing things were simpler, back to that time *before* I met Russia, before I tattooed him, before I lost my ever-loving mind.

And my heart.

Can't forget about my stupid, *stupid* heart.

"Hey, you're off today?" Elena asks, and I nod at her, making another groaning sound. "I'm gonna make French toast, you want some?"

As if I'm going to say no to French toast when I'm feeling lower than low. *Yeah, right.*

"I'm not going to make you some if you don't talk to me, though. What's wrong?" she asks, heading out into the kitchen, knowing that the mere *mention* of French toast will lure me out of my room like brains lure zombies out in the middle of the apocalypse.

I groan even more loudly, just to be making a sound than anything else, head to my bathroom to wash off the night sweats, wash my face, brush my teeth, making myself feel human despite the gaping hole in my chest, despite my heart hurting.

Isn't it better though, if you never see him again?

Why play second fiddle? Why?

"How was last night?" I ask, watching Elena's pale face get taken over by an epic blush, one that crawls down her throat and chest through the V-neck she's wearing.

"Huh. That good, yeah? Cheers to Beckett," I say, lifting my mug of coffee that has been set in front of me like you'd throw a steak at an enraged guard dog, hoping he takes the bait. I do take the bait, take a big slurp, scald my mouth, and my chin starts to wobble at the pain, the pain all over my body, and I duck my head, put my coffee down so I don't drop it on myself, and wipe at my tired, gritty, swollen eyeballs.

Didn't I cry all my tears last night? Didn't I do this already?

"Hey, hey, what's wrong, what happened? Did I ruin the coffee for you? What, what?" Elena asks, coming around the island to stand in front of my stool, her hands coming down to my shoulders. It's enough prompting to claw my arms around her and squeeze her tight, my tears soaking into the shoulder of her shirt.

"I'm sad," I say between tears, heaving in breaths, my mind stuck on the moment where Russia kept saying my name yesterday, kept *saying* it in that way of his, so very different from Sera's. "My heart, it *hurts*."

Elena's arms come around me, too, and she ends up rocking us from side to side, and I wonder if this is how she hugs her students when they're having a hard time, if they seek that kind of comfort from her.

I hope they all know that they're lucky little shits to be getting an Elena-hug, one where you feel every cell in your body coalesce and be *present* in the moment, and despite the pain, her hug's an anchor to the present moment, reminding me that I'm still here, despite whatever it is I'm feeling.

"Tell me what's wrong, won't you? I swear, I leave you alone for one night and everything goes to shit."

I wheeze out a half-laugh. "No, I can be left to my own devices," I say, pulling my head back, and Elena leans over to grab the roll of paper towel, ripping off a couple for me to mop up my face and blow my nose.

"Clearly not. Look at you, you're a mess." She says it with an affection that's deep as the Marianas Trench. "Come on, French toast will help a little, and you can tell me about it."

I help make the mix for our breakfast, Elena keeping the conversation light, being as she's private about what happened with her and Beckett last night, and that's fine, as long as she's happy.

And she is, I can tell, the way she keeps humming under her breath, a dreamy smile on her face as she goes about frying the bread in a buttered pan, the smell driving me crazy, the vanilla extract and cinnamon we put inside the egg mixture making the ultimate difference—my idea, naturally.

There's a choice of powdered sugar or maple syrup—or *both*—and since all I want to do is get high on the sugar and head back to bed. I'm glad that it's my day off and that it coincided so nicely with my heartbreak. It means I don't have to put up a front in front of anyone at work, so it's fine to get my sugar high.

"So…" Elena prompts, and I slurp down some more coffee, delaying the inevitable.

"Yeah, Russia and I aren't a thing anymore, even before we got really started," I blurt in one rushed breath, getting it out as fast as possible, like ripping off a bandage.

Elena ducks her head down, rubbing at the middle of her forehead, like she's rubbing away a sharp pain. She lifts her head and squints at me, all Italian-Canadian attitude that has bloomed day by day since she got away from her family (*the idiots*). "So I really *can't* leave you alone by yourself for one night."

"Hey!" I jab my fork in the air, which she only squints at, daring me to do more. I gulp down my delicious French toast, ignoring the way I can't seem to really taste-*taste* it, but my brain's filling in the gaps in sensation. "It's not my fault."

"Yeah, but I know you, you're the one that did the talking and the convincing that you shouldn't be together, right?"

I narrow my eyes at her, thinking back to a time where I pulled the same card. Am I a serial breaker-upper? Is that me? I shake my head.

"Yeah, well, this time, I've got a proper excuse, yeah? Russia, he's in love with someone else. You know it, I know it, *all* of Montreal knows it, too. Okay? *Okay?!* And I'm better than that, chasing after a guy who *can't* love me back because there's nothing left to give."

Elena sighs, pushing her plate away and I know she means business. Nothing can turn off a DiNovro off food unless it's real serious business.

"Explain it to me again, using words this time."

"Don't talk to me like I'm stupid."

Elena's dark eyes flash, getting bigger in her face, handed down by generations and generations of Italian grandmothers that wielded all the power in their respective houses.

"I'm not talking to you like you're stupid, but I'm not understanding. So help me understand by explaining it to me."

I drop my fork on my plate with a clatter, startling at the sound.

"Look, Russia loves Sera. The great Sera Delos who's actually a really amazing person that I wish I could be friends with. Like, she brought fucking muffins and donuts *just because* the other day at the shop and wanted to book a piercing appointment with me. Which I'm going to have to cancel because I can never look her in the face again after dumping Russia—for good reason, though, don't get me wrong."

"Who told you that Russia's in love with Sera?"

I blink at her, like I'm four chapters deep into a book and she's still asking me about the opening paragraph of the story. "Huh? Katie, Sera, hell, Russia says her name like it's a prayer."

Elena keeps blinking at me, rubbing a hand over her mouth, slow enough that I can see a smile creeping over her lips.

"Why are you smiling, why the *hell* are you smiling? You're supposed to be sympathetic with me right now. I want chocolate chip cookies. I *demand* chocolate chip cookies. Please? Pretty please with a cherry on top?"

"You're kidding me, right? You're kidding me right now," she deadpans.

I shake my head at her, my belly swooping at her words. "Huh?" I say eloquently.

"You're basing this off the way he says her *name?* What the hell, you think you're Shakespeare or something? Sophie, oh my god, *oh my god*."

"What? What is it?" I can feel my stomach starting to sink down to my toes, my whole body slumping with the weight of it, with the knowledge of it. I chose this, nobody else, I made the decision for him. I chose me over wanting to be with him, I did this, *me*.

"Russia's had girlfriends in the past, yes. I only know this because Katie has been trying to get the guys girlfriends since forever so they can stop ragging on her about when she and Dean are gonna get married—you know how she is—and Russia hasn't been with anyone in the past two years. I don't know about casual shit, and I don't need to know, and frankly, I don't think you absolutely need to know either, other than the both of you being careful, obviously."

"Jesus, Elena, you're not my doctor."

"Excuse me for caring about you and that includes your lady parts."

I snort, the aching in my chest subsiding a little, the undertow of it not quite so harsh, and I can catch my breath. "Lady parts. Ha." I sigh, looking down at the single piece of French toast left over. I want to eat it, but I can't. "I think I ate too much."

"Sugar coma?"

I nod again. "Sugar coma. Leave everything, I'll wash up later. I'm gonna go to bed and mope about my life decisions, question my existence just to add to the pile of shit I'm *already* going to be thinking about."

"Sounds like fun," Elena says, grabbing up our plates and placing them in the sink, eating the last piece of French toast so it won't go to waste. "Mind if I join?"

"I don't know," I say, squinting at her when she turns to look at me, her gaze assessing. "Are you going to convince me to get back together with Russia, a man in love with another woman?"

Elena shakes her head and rolls her eyes. Rolls her eyes—at me!

"No, I'm going to talk some sense into you and then you're going to make the decision on what you're gonna do."

I flap my arms up and down, like a Sophie-bird. "I've already made a decision! It's been done, DiNovro! We've been had!"

Elena glances at me, walking towards me and pointing the way to *my* bedroom, as if I don't know where it is, as if I don't own half of this apartment. Rude, rude, rude.

I flop onto my bed like a petulant child, swiping my loose hair from my face so I can actually see her, lying down right next to me, jostling me over so that we can both have room on my double bed.

My laptop gets sacrificed to the floor (gently, gently) and we both are on our backs, staring up at the ceiling, like we could be the only two people in the world, looking up at a starless sky, looking at all of that inky black and wondering where we're headed.

Where are we headed? Where am I headed when all of this just sort of sucks so much right now?

Did I make a mistake? Did I?

"You're one of the coolest people I know," Elena starts on a long-drawn breath, and I look over at her.

"That's a given. I mean, *look* at me."

"I said one of, *one of*, Jesus. Sera's another."

"Oh," I say, as if that's bad. I like Sera, I do. It's nobody's fault that Russia's heart is a jerk that's latched onto her. It's fine. *Fine.*

"And I know you took one look at Russia and lost your shit."

"No shit was actually lost, for the record," I say and get thwacked in the arm for my shitty (ha!) humor. I blink up at the ceiling, letting the silence stretch, waiting for the inevitable snap.

"And most of the time, you're pretty invincible, until you met him. You felt like the world was swaying, that you couldn't get your bearings. It feels a lot like that, falling in love with another person, like you're not so sure of what's up or down or left or right until you look at them and realize—*oh, I'm supposed to be here, and they're supposed to be next to me. That's how it is now.* It can be how it is, that way you can move through life together side by side. Doesn't that sound wonderful?"

I nod slowly because it does. I just don't know what it has to do with me—with me and Russia.

"Russia doesn't love Sera, I know this for sure, because he doesn't look at her the same way he looks at you, like you're the magnet in his compass, like he'll always come back to you."

"Oh, shut up, none of that makes any sense," I say with a wobbly voice.

It's the most romantic thing I've ever heard, but I'm not going to tell her that. She'll have one on me for the rest of my life if I do. I'm going to have to name my first born after her, if I even decide to have kids in some sort of future.

Elena leans up, putting her head in her hand so she can look down at me. I flex my double chin at her and she smiles, but it's quick and gone in a flash, wanting me to be serious for once.

"He doesn't love Sera, you're just using that as an excuse to stay away from him. You know it, I know it, pretty sure Russia knows it, too."

"He does not know it because *I* didn't even know it."

"Really? You're gonna play that card with me now? Really, really?"

"*Really, really,*" I snark right back. "Fine, I pushed him, I pushed him to talk about her, and he did, and I know he loves her, Elena, I just do, I can't explain it, don't ask me to."

"You know you can love someone without being *in love* with them, right? Like I love you, like you love me."

I blink at her, flopping over onto my side so I'm facing her properly, thinking about it all, pulling the trigger on admitting it all.

"I'm scared." I squeeze my eyes shut, those same words that Elena uttered all those weeks and weeks ago coming out of my mouth. "It hurts this much now, what's it going to be like when it's over?"

"What's the point of starting any tattoo then, if it isn't going to come out *exactly* how you envisioned it? Come on, you know better than that, you *do*. Russia loves you, is *in love* with you."

"How are you so sure, huh? When did you become the resident expert on relationships?"

Elena shrugs, bashful now. "I don't know. I'm not, not really. But with Beckett, it's easy—not hard at all. I feel safe when I'm with him, and he's so gentle and careful with me, being exactly what I need when I tell him I need it. I don't know, I just...I want to see you happy, and I think being with Russia will make you even happier. Maybe...maybe you're the one that decided for him, though, the one that made sure he chose Sera instead of you, and you made it clear that you're not willing to take his heart when he has the memory of her in it."

"What the fuck? What the fuck, when did you get so deep?"

Elena snorts, flopping onto her back. "I'm not sure, it just makes sense. You told him to make the decision, but you decided for him. You made him choose by *not* letting him pick you. You didn't even give him a chance."

"Because he was going to pick Sera."

"No, he wasn't. He loves you, you stupid idiot. He loves *you*. You, you, you!" Elena jabs her finger into my shoulder with every syllable, and I'm pretty sure it's going to bruise.

"Ah, quit attacking me, I get it, I get it."

"No, no, you don't. Katie told me that she and Dean had to go and pick him up from a bar last night—he nearly got thrown out or something—and he whined about you the whole time. Whined. The whole time. *All of the time.*"

I turn onto my back, wiggling my toes, staring up at the ceiling.

"I don't know what to do."

Elena sighs. "Nope, not yet, you don't. But you will. You will."

"Scarily ominous."

"Didn't mean it to be. You're his first choice, Sophie, you just have to choose if you want him to be yours. Like, is Russia your first choice, too?"

Shit.

Shit, shit, *shit*.

EIGHTEEN

- -

I 'm surprised the next day at work when Jackie, the kid with the new chest tattoo, comes to see me. The healing on her chest looks spot on, nothing concerning or anything like that, and she timidly asks me to do a hand tattoo for her—a geometric heart on her left hand—"*so I can remember that it's still there, even when I'm hurting, it's still intact, you know?*"

I had to go and close myself off in the ladies' room for a good cry, my eyeliner shot to shit, but I totally forgot about bringing my touch-up foundation to conceal the redness in my cheeks and nose like I didn't just have a breakdown because I'm *still* out of sorts on Sunday morning.

It's fine. *I'm fine.*

"Shit, this one hurts so much more," Jackie says through clenched teeth, and I glance up at her, checking in to make sure she can handle it. The geometric design means I have to spend more time on it, and if the kid needs a break, she needs a break.

I can always go grab a bite to eat at any of the restaurants down or up the street—staying as far away as I can from *that one.*

There's a Lebanese place two doors down, and I could scoff down my body weight in garlic potatoes inundated with garlic sauce, stink enough that I'd kill forty vampires on the spot. I'm thinking about it as I do the outline to her tattoo, as I start (lightly) shading in the different facets of the heart, turning it into an impenetrable jewel instead of the fragile muscle it really is.

It takes me a couple of hours, and when I'm done, all I can do is smile down at her left hand, hold onto it, give it a squeeze, smile ever wider when she squeezes back.

"Thank you, it's beautiful. I can't stop looking at it," Jackie says, hopping down from the bench as I wipe it down, sanitize it, wrap it up for her, go over care instructions one more time, as if she's forgotten how.

Jackie pays for the tattoo, and I sigh, clean up my station, get rid of what needs to be gotten rid of, and slump in my stool, swinging from side to side absentmindedly until Remy yells at me to stop the cacophony of squeaking.

Too bad.

I breeze through the shop and head outside, the day actually nine degrees above zero and it's starting to *feel* like spring, enough so that I can make the walk to the Lebanese place without my coat on, basking in the warmth after the long slog of harsh winter we've barely left behind.

I order my food, finding myself spacing out more than once when asked about my order, and end up walking back in a little bit of a daze. When I get there Katie DiNovro is standing in the middle of the shop, arguing with Dean.

Well, shit.

I wasn't expecting this.

"I'm getting the tattoo," Dean says, his face scrunched up adorably, and I don't know why Katie even pretends that she's not affected, the *whole shop* is affected.

"Okay, fine. But I'm not helping you moisturize it," Katie says viciously, crossing her arms over her chest. "And if you have another allergic reaction, I'm going to kick your ass," she says, voice laced with an anger that hides a well of worry.

"She loves me, I swear she does," Dean says to me as I walk closer to them, shivering a little from the temperature change. Bekah's got thyroid issues and the kid's always freezing, so the heat's always a little high, even though she's got her space heater turned on underneath the desk.

"Of course I do," Katie says, leaning in close to press a red-lipstick kiss on his cheek. Dean clutches at his cheek like he's never going to wash it again, which is the gross kind of cute, but still cute.

And still practically light-years away from me getting for my very own version of it with a person who's name rhymes with *fuchsia*.

"You want another tattoo?" I ask Dean. "You should've told me. I would have waited to go and buy some lunch." I hold up my paper bags by way of explanation.

"How about you take your proper hour off owed to you, and we can go eat in Dean's car, or outside on the bench over there. It's beautiful today," Katie says, pinning her stare on Jake's closed office door.

"Yeah, okay, I can do that. It's less depressing than eating alone in the back room with nothing but my phone for company."

"'Atta girl," Dean says, lugging his hulking arm around my shoulders and steering me towards the door. I get a nod from Bekah, who's overheard everything—Dean's not the quietest of human beings, and he went and fell in love with an Italian who doesn't really understand the meaning of an indoor voice, or better yet, understand the need for it, but flouts the rules anyway.

We head outside, round the building to the back lot, my coat on but unzipped, the two of them wearing lighter coats for the warmer weather while I'm still sporting the hulking mass of a winter coat now that defends my fragile body against temperatures of thirty below zero. I'm gonna start sweating soon, but that's fine.

It's nice to have company, and it's a nice break to the day.

"Here, have some potatoes," I say, opening the steaming bag and putting the container down between Katie and I. Dean presses up against her back to look down at the offerings of food, grumbling about some sort of spice that I don't hear or understand. "Aren't you guys going to eat?"

"No, I'm just going to watch you eat," Dean says, blinking at me owlishly.

I grin at him. "Weirdo."

"The best weirdo you know," he snaps back, then leans away from Katie and presses up against her back, the added weight of him against her making her lean forward.

"So why are you guys really here? Like, I get why Dean wants more tattoos, but I also know you don't just randomly show up. I know your schedule's even more hectic than mine, so."

Katie shrugs, the blue-red lipstick she's wearing reminding me that I need to buy that particular shade, too.

"We took a chance, figured it was close to lunch time, and Elena let me know that you had the earlier shift today, so yeah, we figured you'd get some free time for yourself. How's your day been so far?"

It's not like she doesn't care, but we both know why she's here, we both know it's because of me and Russia, well *not* me and Russia, as it were.

"Good. I did a sweet geometric piece on a repeat client."

Katie makes a noncommittal sound, swiping up a potato with her fingers and eating it. I have a feeling Dean doesn't mind garlic breath, not when it comes to her.

I gulp down the tightness in my throat and eat my pita sandwich with the deliciously seasoned chicken. The turnips make everything that much better, along with the extra container of pepperoncini unearthed from the bag when Katie snoops around.

"Are we going to let her eat first, or do you wanna do this right away?" Dean asks, turning and leaning forward, his elbows planted on his monster thighs, glancing over at Katie and me.

I gulp down more food. "I don't know, am I going to throw up my lunch because of what you guys wanna talk about or nah?"

Dean points a finger at me, then boops his nose for some odd reason. I don't get it, but it doesn't mean I can't *appreciate* it. He fights with the parts of his hair that come loose from the tail at the top of his head, pushing them back over his ears, but they don't stay where they're supposed to, and he keeps grumbling to himself about *bad haircuts ruining everything*.

"Well, surprise, surprise, I came to see how you're doing, how you've been."

"Elena," I say as way of explanation.

Of course Elena would talk to Katie about it, maybe not divulge my deepest darkest secrets, but yeah, it could have come up in casual conversation, sure.

"No, Russia. When he was whining about you at the bar the night before. I've never seen him that drunk. Russia's *never been that* drunk, okay? He was the mother hen most of the time if we went drinking together, never let himself get that loose or that out of control, all right? I've never seen him like that, and I've known him for a long time, like, almost half of my life at this point. He's never been like that, not ever."

I blink at her, mouth gone numb, losing all the ability to taste my delicious food. "Never say never."

"Shut up and listen," Katie snaps at me.

"What she means to say is that she values your friendship a whole lot and would like for you to get your head out of your ass and figure out what it is that *you* want," Dean supplies, nodding his head, still hunched over at the waist, elbows planted on his knees.

"Thank you, baby," Katie says, turning to give him an award-winning smile.

"No problem. S'what I'm here for."

I roll my eyes. "It's rude being that lovey-dovey in front of the broken-hearted," I say, flapping my hand at both of them, delving down into the bag for the napkins, swiping delicately at my face because lipstick and I forgot to pack this particular shade (seriously, it's called *dragon blood*) in my purse this morning.

Katie's eyes go sharp and deadly. "And whose fault is that?"

"I already had this talk with Elena yesterday, okay? She tried to convince me that he doesn't love Sera anymore, I get it."

"What?" Dean squawks, sitting upright fast, hands on his knees. "Katie, what the fuck? When did that happen?"

Katie looks back at him and twists her body so she's facing the front instead of me alone.

"Are you serious? When we met, he thought he was in love with her, wanted to do something about it when she and Hunter got together, like an ass." Katie's face pinches closed, like she got seared by a bad memory.

"What? How did I not know this?" Dean asks, rearing back, blinking in horror like he *just* realized Santa Claus isn't a real thing and is reeling with the betrayal at being *lied to* all this time.

"It's fine, don't worry about it." Katie pats his hand placatingly, but Dean makes a grab for it, threading their fingers together. "You..." Katie turns to me, eyes narrowing in that DiNovro stare that I've come to learn well. "Explain yourself."

I already half-know that I made a mistake, that I ruined this for myself, that I was using Sera as an excuse to push him away.

But I only half-know it, the other side of me is still steeped in fear, still marred by past experiences where I didn't fit the part to be someone else's girlfriend. Seriously, though, opposites attract, but birds of a feather flock together—maybe we're just too different.

You know that's not true. He gets your jokes; you guys are more similar than the way you look.

I'm not the wild child that everyone paints me to be—that's old-fashioned, thinking in that way.

"I don't know, I just, I got scared, and he always talks so highly of her, and it's my own damn fault, because she's so lovely and I always just thought that I could never compare, never measure up."

Katie sighs, long and exasperated, weary. "What am I going to do with you. What am I going to do with *the both* of you?"

"I vote to send them to a deserted island, and the bonds they form trying to survive together will get them to where they need to be in the end. Mainly in love and happy, and they can watch really awesome sunsets together, too. Bonus." Dean gives himself a high-five and I kind of want to hug him really, really hard.

Katie's lips twitch at the corners, but she doesn't deign to reply—it'll probably only encourage him.

"That's a lot of out-of-pocket expense," I say, eating some more, the misery in my belly making me full before *I* want to be full. This emotional crap is no joke. "Who's fronting the cash to get us there?"

"Don't look at me. I just cook for a living," Dean says, hands up in a *freeze* motion, still holding onto his girlfriend's hand.

Katie shakes her head, looking like she wants to wring both of our necks. "Okay, listen up. Tell me, are you all right?"

"I'm sad, sure, but I'll get over it." I shrug, because I will get over it, and Russia will be another regret like some of those *unfortunate* tattoos I got when I was eighteen.

Katie nods, bites at her crimson-stained lip. "That's not what I'm asking, not at all. I'm asking if you can live with your decision, that it's not going to be a regret you'll have later on."

"I mean, I regret some of my tattoos, but I still keep them on my skin. I might regret it later, but maybe it's better this way, you know?"

Katie's brow furrows, and she shoots me a death glare. "It's not better this way, you know it's not better this way. Dean knows it's not better this way. Come on. Own up to it, own up to being scared. Own up to letting it rule your head."

My eyes start to well up and Dean looks about ready to panic.

"Quick!" he says, pointing at my face as my chin starts to wobble. "No, no, kitten, you have to fix this, we have to fix this. I don't want Sophie to be sad, what the hell?"

Dean stands up as the tears fall down my face, and my food tastes awful (through no fault of the restaurant. It's just everything's numbed today and that includes my sense of smell, my taste buds, my will to eat my entire body weight in food.

Dean comes to my side of the bench, plopping down, a giant at my back, sheltering me from the oncoming storm.

Why is he being so nice to me? Why couldn't he be Russia?

Why did I do that to Russia, test him in that way that was completely unfair?

Why did I let that insidious voice in my head get in the way?

"You could never see him again," Katie says, as if she knows something I don't, but maybe I'm reading too much into it, like I always seem to do. "You live in the same city, but you could never pass him by in the street ever again, never see his face, never hear him call your name."

It hurts, it *hurts*, to think like that, to feel it in my chest, sharp as any needle I use on a daily basis.

"You've fallen in love," Katie says, just a statement of fact.

"Like an idiot," I say, wiping at my cheeks with my hands, and Dean pets my head, like I'm one of his dogs he's trying to soothe, which still feels nice, even if I am a human. "I think he's great. I really, really do."

Katie nods, inviting me to continue.

"He's a baby when it comes to pain—I've seen eighteen-year-olds handle it better than he does, but he lets me carry on, like he's trying to impress me by suppressing it. Idiot, he's such an idiot. He loves his friends, anyone can see that, the way you've become his family. He loves Matty, too, even though I haven't heard him talk about kids, not even once, when we hang out. And..." I sigh, wiping at my cheeks roughly enough to hurt my face.

"And he calls me 'darling,' and it's all I want, to be treated that way, not like I'm the one who's fickle just because of the way I look. I know, I know, I've been projecting, but what can I do now? What can I do?" I sniff hard, using napkins to mop up my face, blow my nose. "Is my mascara all over my face?"

Katie shakes her head, reaching forward to squeeze along my forearm in reassurance.

"Then why don't you tell him all that?"

I shrug, like it's answer enough.

I've been scared to, been scared of being rejected. I haven't liked someone in so long, haven't been in love like this before, and it's so new and raw that I don't even know what to do with it, how to press it down, to fit the confines of my heart when it feels so big, so unmanageable, like whatever's pumping in my chest doesn't belong to me, and only to me, anymore.

But I guess that's the point, isn't it?

That's the point.

"No one says you need all the answers right now—you don't. You need one answer, to only one question," Katie says, her dark eyes piercing me through, reading all of my contents, like being analyzed underneath a microscope. I don't like the feeling at all.

"Yeah?" I croak, sniffing hard enough to keep the snot from dripping out. Ugh, I'm a mess, a *mess*. All I want to do is go home and crawl underneath my bed covers and sleep the sleep of the dead.

"Do you want to be with him?" Katie shakes her head when I open my mouth to talk. "I'm not asking if you think he's in love with someone else, which I know Sera talked to you about, but you don't want to listen, so we're glossing over that," she says, waving my fears off.

"I'm not asking if it won't work out, or you don't think you look a certain way, or whatever. I'm asking one simple question: do you want to be with the man you love?"

I hesitate, I do.

I allow myself that one moment to reflect, to contemplate what it would be like—my life without Russia.

I could fall in love one day with another faceless man, but it won't be Russia, it won't be him. I won't look into his blue-blue eyes and see love and affection there, he won't burn any more steak dinners, and he won't call me *meelaya* anymore.

I nod slowly, feeling like my heart could burst, pressing against my rib cage, too big for my chest, for my body.

"I need to talk to him," I say, matter-of-factly. I nod to myself, decided now. I glance at Katie, as if seeing her for the first time. "I need to talk to him and let him know everything that I'm feeling, like an adult. Shit."

Katie laughs, the sound loud and boisterous, and Dean joins in and gets up from his seat behind me to lean down and kiss that laughing mouth, the both of them a picture-perfect couple that would look *beautiful* as a tattoo. Maybe I should talk about the potential for that to Dean.

Maybe.

Shit, I want *that*, I want that so freaking bad.

I just need to talk to Russia first, just need to lay it *all out* there.

No big deal.

Shit.

NINETEEN

I make us reservations at *that* restaurant, the one where I started all this shit, and leave him a text message, even leaving a *voice mail* on his phone that I will be there, at the booth we were in last time (if I can beg and plead my way to it and make it seem like it's life or death), and now I have nothing else to do but wait and *think*.

I've taken care with my makeup, trying to mask the redness under my nose, the redness in my cheeks from swiping all the time to take care of the onslaught of tears. My hair's straightened, silky-straight down my back, hiding the undercut from view, my hair parted right down the middle so you don't even see my ear piercings.

My hands are adorned with rings—gold and silver—bringing even more attention to the tattoos on my fingers and hands, the comforting weight of the jewelry giving me something to twist and turn as I wait for Russia to show up, watching my phone and the time he has left to show up.

I'm dressed comfortably, my hoop earrings big enough for a car to drive through them, my makeup leaning towards the neutral side, foregoing the eyelashes today. My lips are in a pale pink color, not my usual red or wacky colors that I like to use to complement my smoky eye looks.

I wore my black Doc Martens, just needing that extra bit of comfort, that style that I needed to make me feel better about myself, like I'm ready to take down an army, all by my lonesome.

I'm sitting at the booth now, leaned all the way back against the cushion, wishing I'd chosen the other side of the booth to get a look at the door, keeping my eye trained on it, to make sure that I can see him walking towards me, but it's too late for that now, too late to switch seats as it's already five minutes out from the time I told him to meet me.

I know he read my text message, I saw the notification, but whether he shows up or not is another question entirely, and then I'll really have my answer, once and for all.

I link my hands together, and stare at the opposite side of the booth, the empty space, where I hope Russia will be sitting across from me a lot sooner rather than later.

My stomach lining has been sacrificed to the vampire butterflies in my belly, and the heat along my neck and back from my hair is starting to make me sweat, making me want to put my hair up in a top knot and fuck this façade, fuck this effort.

I keep my hands linked together so they don't shake, my phone beside me, screen black, glancing down and tapping the screen every few seconds or so hoping I'm going to see a notification there—a message from Russia telling me that he's on his way.

The screen stays black, though, no matter how long I stare at it, wishing it'd light up with *something*. I even become too afraid to touch my phone, to wake it up from its sleep state so I can see the empty screen, no notifications, all the while marking down the time until eight o'clock sharp.

It doesn't help matters that I'm practically the only one in the restaurant on a Tuesday night, even though it's supper time—the weather's so nice, a lot of people are choosing to grab something quick and eat outside in makeshift picnics on benches, in cars with the windows rolled down.

The city comes alive in the spring as soon as the weather turns, and sooner rather than later, *terrasse* season's going to be upon us, where pedestrians like me are going to have to share the sidewalks with encroaching tables from all the restaurants taking up space, everyone eating outside, enjoying the beautiful weather before winter comes around again to bite us in the ass.

I hold my breath, trying to decide if I should check my phone, glancing outside to see if he's coming from a long way off, so I can *prepare* myself.

I do it fast, a lightning strike of movement that has me clocking the time against the screen of my phone—another five minutes (or so) before Russia's supposed to meet me here, and we can talk, and I can grovel and apologize, and we can air all this out, and I can tell him that I love him, and everything will work out.

A measly three hundred seconds to go while I wait here, holding my breath, struggling to breathe.

This *might* have been a bad idea, just giving him orders like that, instead of requesting him to meet me somewhere, like a normal person, but it doesn't matter now, when all I have to do is wait, my waning patience getting crushed underneath my heavy heart.

It doesn't help either that I have an eager beaver of a young kid for a waiter—fresh into university if I'm gauging it right, probably just finishing up his first year at McGill or Concordia, or maybe one of the French universities like UQAM, or UdeM, even though we're not really in that part of town.

"Can I get you anything to start, or are you still waiting on someone?" The kid asks in French, the word *someone* being emphasized, and I swing my glare over to him, even though none of this is his fault—it's my fault, *I* screwed up, *I* was scared.

"Still waiting," I croak, cough, and clear my throat. "Can I get a glass of water, though?"

The kid nods, his head jerking up and down. "I'll bring a couple of waters, no problem. I'll be right back." He smiles, practically prancing away to his workstation and pouring the glasses of water from an icy pitcher of water.

I turn back to look at the opposite seat, still empty.

I touch my phone again, watching the minutes pass me by now, nothing but three minutes left, my heart starting to squeeze down now, making it hard to breathe, hard to be here by myself, staring at the space opposite me.

I won't die if Russia never shows up, I won't. That's not how life works.

But I'll find myself wondering in the quiet moments between work and family and friends, in between *living* as much as I can. I'll remember tonight and wonder what would have happened between us if I hadn't chase him off, if there could have been a future for us, a future where we could have been happy together, for as long as we wanted.

I know the time's running out, the sand running through my fingers, the hourglass losing time, slipping away and away, ready to start over.

I click on my phone again, checking the time.

One minute, nothing but sixty measly seconds until he's supposed to show up.

I sit up straighter, taller, thanking the kid who brings over the glasses of water, while I keep staring intently at the other side of the booth, like I'm thinking about a game of pin-the-tail-on-the-donkey.

I'm alone now, waiting for Russia to show up, to suddenly *appear* there, to materialize in front of me, and I want to reach out, to hold onto his hand and make sure that this is real, that he is real.

But the booth remains empty as I glance down at my phone, the clock ticking over onto a new hour.

I slump, the muscles in my body curling in on themselves, making myself a smaller target. I stare down uncomprehendingly at the menu beneath my hands, wondering how I'm going to sit here and pretend like I can eat something when it feels like I won't ever find joy in food ever again.

That's transient, I know, that feeling won't last forever.

But I loved and I lost, and I'm certainly not the first person to have gone through this, certainly won't be the last.

But no matter which way you cut it, it sucks, and it sucks *hard*.

I sniffle, grabbing the napkin blindly, rattling my cutlery, to bring it up to the corners of my eyes, still worried about my makeup, my understated look that made me look the part for him, toned myself down because I couldn't come up with anything spectacular, wasn't inspired when I looked down at my eyeshadow palettes to come up with something that was totally *me*.

I made this understated version of myself, not to fit in—no, not really, but to show myself that I could, if I wanted. I don't have to be so loud all of the time, I don't have to shine the brightest in a given room, as long as Russia looks at me like I *already do*.

My knee gets bumped underneath the table and I freeze, holding my breath, keeping my head down, caught between wanting to know and *not wanting* to know, afraid to get the confirmation that this might be some cruel joke.

Maybe it *isn't* Russia, maybe it isn't him at all, just some rando guy trying to pick me up like has been known to happen, and really, I'm not in the mood to chase this stranger off acting like he's some kind of shark in the water, scenting the blood of a weakened fish.

I grit my teeth, clench my jaw, try to stifle the sniffle, but you can't really hide that when you're afraid snot's going to ruin your face, so I sniff hard once, then lift my head.

Oh.

Oh.

"*Meelaya*, why are you crying?" Russia asks, his coat still on, his cheeks and the tip of his nose pink, his breath coming out in pants. "I got here as fast as I could."

My lower lip starts to wobble, and I duck my head fast, pressing my napkin to my face, sniffing hard to get the tears as far away from my tears ducts as possible, pulling in a deep, deep breath.

I glance up again, just to confirm, *confirm*, that it's Russia sitting across from me.

"You're here," I say, my voice breaking at the tail end.

Russia just smiles, reaching out a hand, and I'm half-afraid to break the illusion, to figure out that this is all some kind of fever dream, that I've conjured him up in my head and I'm still in the throes of my nap, stuck in my bed after work, contemplating what to wear, how to present myself for tonight's apology.

"Yeah, I'm here."

I tentatively reach out, making a noise in the back of my throat when I finally touch his skin, then place my palm against his own, watching his fingers wrap around my hand not in a bruising grip, just a reminder that he's here, that I'm here, that we're both here *together*.

"I'm sorry," I groan, looking up at him. Is it possible that he got even more handsome in our time apart?

Was it really only two days ago where I screwed up so badly and accused him of loving someone else when he hasn't *shown* me otherwise?

"I'm sorry I accused you of not wanting to be with me when you've told me, when you've *shown* me that it's just not the case. I'm sorry I was worried, that's on me," I say, squeezing his hand a little tighter now, wanting to make sure he stays put. "I'm sorry that I couldn't tell you how I felt, before. I'm sorry about that."

Russia holds onto my hand now with both of his, cradling mine between the two of his, like he doesn't want to let me go either.

"Can I talk now?"

I nod quickly, throat tight while I keep sniffling.

"I didn't expect you to reach out actually, and I thought you were done with me," he huffs out on a laugh, but we both can hear that it's at his own expense.

"I just...I've been called a lot of things in my life, have been loud when I wanted the attention whether it was good or bad." He points to the crooked edge to his nose. "I got this because I was mouthing off, being obnoxious, being an asshole."

"I know," I say, nodding. The sound of her name from his lips doesn't hurt as much anymore. "I know that."

"Did she tell you that I thought I was in love with her?"

I nod again, more slowly now, carefully.

"I thought I was, because we were friends, and it's easy I think, sometimes, to fall into love when a friendship is already there."

"It can be easier, sure," I say. "You're comfortable with the person, up to a certain point, and they know some of your faults, what you let them see."

"Sera and I were never really that close, though. We would hang out, sure, but I never really got the chance to know her, to *see* her. Not like I see you, not like I want to know everything about you. Half the time she was making references, and I couldn't figure them out. I got annoyed with them, but she made me feel special. And I selfishly thought that it was only me that she could make feel that way, when that wasn't the case."

I shake my head, finally, *finally* getting it. "She does that to everyone."

"Yeah, she does, and when I realized that, belatedly, when she got engaged to Hunter, that she had found the man who makes *her* feel special, I just... How could I step in front of that, keep her from that, when she wouldn't feel the same way with me, couldn't? She loves Hunter, and Matty, and they love her back just as much, more even, because she deserves that."

I nod again, my throat so tight, the pain so acute that I can't bring myself to speak, to say anything of value right now, just sitting here, stewing in my emotions.

"And I love you, Sophie Kincaid."

My stupid chin wobbles again and he makes a cooing-like noise at me, reaching over to capture a couple of tears that have escaped, thumbing them away from my face. "Yeah?"

"Yeah, Sophie, I do. Do you think you could love me back?"

I nod quickly, clutching onto his hand. "Yeah, yeah, *yeah*."

Russia smiles, getting even more handsome, more beautiful with it. "I don't want you to ever think that there's someone else in my heart, *meelaya*," he says, and my throat bobs, and it's hard to keep the sniffles contained.

Jesus, someone's going to think something bad's happening over here when it's something *good*, so, *so good*.

"Does that mean I can finish up your tattoo for you?"

"Yeah, you can. I'd be honored if you would finish it for me."

I nod, glancing down at our clasped hands, holding him just that little bit more tightly.

"Okay, *okay*."

Russia brings our hands up, pressing a kiss to the back of my hand, and I let myself sag against the table, tired and excited, elated and nervous about our next step, what that's going to look like—but it doesn't even matter, doesn't matter *what* it looks like, as long as it feels good for the both of us, as long as we *take* the next step, *together*.

"Never thought I would be here," Russia says, and I frown.

"Here? What do you mean? At the restaurant, or with me?" I'm still feeling raw, still jumping to conclusions, my grip spasming around his hand, tightening.

"I don't know if you've noticed, but I'm not the most out-there kind of person. I had virgin skin before you inked me. Got tattoos, even if it was a dare, to get you to notice me."

I snort, watery and tired sounding.

"That sounds like some sort of kink that I'll have to research later," I say, grinning at him, my heart eighteen times too big for my chest, for my body, for this *restaurant*. "Of course I noticed you, of course I did. Don't you remember how dumb I acted?"

Russia shakes his head, a soft smile along his mouth that I'm going to be kissing later. "You don't remember how dumb *I* acted? Asking you to tattoo me, right there in front of Katie and Dean. They're going to hold that over my head for the next decade." He sighs, shrugging, working his shoulders with it.

I nod, because yeah, they're going to be annoying for the next little while, if not *forever*.

"Just don't get bored of me, okay, *meelaya?*"

"Never," I say, and think about what I said to Katie the other day: *never say never*, because it somehow ends up happening anyway. So I amend my statement in my own head.

"I won't. I just want to be yours, and I want you to be mine."

Russia nods, solemn and steady, and my heart thumps in the spaces between words. "I love you. I'm going to tell you as often as I can."

"As long as you keep calling me *meelaya*, then it works."

Russia grins now, bringing our hands up again, to press a few kisses on my knuckles, pressing his smile into them, too, so I can keep it there, like an invisible tattoo.

"*Meelaya*," he says, and my whole body shivers at the sound, my smile as big as a house. "What would you like to eat?"

"I want mozzarella sticks," I say, having thought about my consolation prize if Russia didn't show up to the restaurant. "And spinach dip with nachos."

Russia doesn't even bat an eye and keeps nodding, as if he wants me to continue.

We end up ordering a lot of food, the kind of food that requires three Styrofoam cases for the leftovers, and we end up walking to his place, Russia's foot getting better every day now, especially since the sidewalks and streets are no longer icy.

Spring's finally here, with summer around the corner, and the possibility feels *endless*.

We swing our hands in between us, and I feel like I could start skipping, start flying to the moon and back, skip among the starlight.

"What's got you so happy?" Russia asks, tugging my hand a little since I'm taking my time crossing the street, wanting everyone to look and see the both of us—together—*finally*.

"I don't know, it could be that I got my head out of my ass and confessed my undying love for you. Or it could be the delicious food I just ate, I don't know. Time will tell."

"Time will tell? Time will tell?!" Russia gasps, affronted, but it's playful, and there's a happy glint in his eyes, like he gets it, like he feels the exact same way.

I've never fangirled over a person before, let alone had this gigantic crush on a guy, *let alone* on a guy like Russia, who's usually not my style, not my vibe.

But life's done crazier things to me in the past—botched piercings, botched tattoos, and regrets of the *shoulda-woulda-coulda been* variety that I'll never get a chance to do again.

I'm glad that I didn't let this, this relationship, this love with Russia, slip through my fingers, be relegated to a past that I force myself not to think about ever again. Never ever again.

I never thought I would find him, the guy I was supposed to spend the rest of my life with, not having to change a part of myself to suit him. It's why, I think, I always added more change to my body—more ink, more piercings, cut and dyed my hair the way I wanted, a testament to change when all I really wanted was the person I would fall in love with to *stay*.

Never thought I'd get the chance.

Well, here I am, here *we* are.

Never say never.

TWENTY

I shuffle into the kitchen, eyes half closed, bumping into the kitchen island, reaching around blindly for the empty mug of coffee that Elena usually leaves out for me when she wakes up before I do (which happens five times a week), but my mug (the one that has a cute little fox on it, and says '*For fox sake!*') is not where it's supposed to be.

Confused enough that I squint my eyes open, too much sunlight streaming into the kitchen—that really shouldn't be happening 'cause our kitchen's set farther back, closest to our entrance door, and we don't get the morning light, just the afternoon.

And when I blink my eyes fully open, I realize I'm not in *my* kitchen, and yeah, *yeah.*

Except I'm alone in a place that is *not* my apartment.

Oh. Oh.

Huh.

I spin around on my back foot, squeaking against the floor, wearing a T-shirt that also isn't mine.

Yup, I slept over at Russia's last night, but he's nowhere to be seen.

I freeze, like a mouse frozen seconds before making the fatal decision to grab the cheese in the trap. The door is unlocked, revealing Russia holding a box of donuts aloft, like he was going to present me with some fancy and sparkly jewelry.

Nope, not yet.

"Uh, hi," I say, giving him a wave, blushing all the way down to my toes. Russia gives me a grin that *says* things. Ugh.

"Don't you look beautiful in the morning," he says, and I flap a hand at him.

"Please, not this early, you can't be cheesy this early in the morning. I need to eat breakfast first, okay?"

Russia laughs, dropping his keys in the catch-all bowl by the door, toeing off his boots and coming inside his apartment. He sets down the donuts on his kitchen counter, passing me by with nothing but a kiss on the cheek.

It's glorious, just glorious.

I watch Russia putter around the kitchen, making us breakfast (which consists of delicious coffee to eat *with* the donuts), and he pours me a glass of sparkling water—the very best kind of water, in my humble opinion.

I murmur my thanks, acutely aware of my bare legs, acutely aware that I should dash into his bedroom and try to find my underwear *and* some pants to pull on, even a pair of his boxers will do, but I'm feeling adventurous this morning, happy that we've found some common ground, a launchpad where we can both stand and head towards the next step.

The next step, and the next, and the next...

There are no real plans for the day—it's my day off, and Russia was just going to run some errands and be working from home because he can do that, unlike some of us.

"You're welcome to stay as long as you like, however long you like."

I snort, thinking of that one line in the animated version of *Mulan*, my favorite Disney movie of all time. "Yeah? How long would you like me to stay? Is forever an option?"

Russia smiles and there's nothing on his face that speaks to panic or worry, and I like it, I like it a lot.

This time is going to be different, I know so.

His blue eyes light up, his smile becomes playful. "Yeah, of course. However long you want."

I narrow my eyes at him, blowing steam off my mug of coffee, the smell of it going to my head, and I'm still trying to make a decision of which of the dozen donuts I'm going to eat first. Ah, shit, there's a *chocolatine* there with choco-hazelnut spread and the world's going to end if it doesn't get into my belly right *now*.

Russia laughs as I enthusiastically vacuum the adult breakfast loaded with carbs and sugar on top of glorious fried dough (the *best kind* of dough).

"Cute," he says, leaning forward to kiss my forehead. "I was going to make pancakes, but I don't know if you wake up feeling very hungry or not, so this was the next best thing."

I grin at him and give him a chocolatey kiss as a thank you.

Breakfast isn't even the best part of the day—there's cuddles on the couch, watching (but not *really* watching) *Home Alone* even though Christmas had passed us by, there's more food, Korean cuisine, which I've never tried before, but really like (an adventure for me instead of just eating pasta most of the time).

We even decide to take a long walk around the mountain, Russia getting chased by a few angry squirrels (who have zero problems with humans), looking for food.

We make plans for the next day, and the next, and the next.

And it's amazing.

I wouldn't have it any other way.

·♥·♥·♥·♥·♥·

The door to Russia's condo opens, and there's Russian (obviously) being spoken, a heavy bass of sound that's still kind of musical. I'm still learning, and I keep the litany of how to formally introduce myself to Russia—Tommy's—parents in my head on repeat: *hachoo pretstavitsa Sophie Kincaid, hachoo pretstavitsa Sophie Kincaid, hachoo pretstavitsa Sophie Kincaid!*

And I choke, of course, jumbling the syllables together as I greet his parents for the first time, wearing a cute polka-dotted dress for the occasion, my arms bare. Russia (Tommy, Tommy, *Tommy*) gave me a death glare when I tried to tell him I found this amazing foundation that could cover up my tattoos if he wanted me to, laying down the offer, but he wasn't picking it up.

I see his parents eye my arms, the part of my chest that's exposed by the square neckline, moving down to my red-painted toenails in my cute little sandals, making me almost as tall as Tommy for the occasion. The nail polish on my toes matches my lipstick, and my eyeshadow is neutral and understated since I'm going to be hitting them with all the color on my skin at first glance.

"Oh!" Tommy's dad, Georgiy, crows, his voice sounding a lot like his son's but grittier somehow. "I've got tattoos, too!"

And I feel so much relief I think I could pass out, right here and now.

Tommy's arm winds around my waist, anticipating the weakness in my knees, and holds me up as I get my bearings. The true test is if his mother, Galina, likes me.

Please like me, please?

Elena gave me a pep talk about meeting the parents, how it doesn't matter if they end up hating me, that if Russia wants to be with me, then he'll defy his parents in this, but that just seems like extra obstacles we're going to have to hurdle over, and I don't want that, not for him, not for me, not for *us*.

I hold my breath, waiting.

Galina looks like her son in the way that they both have those unsettling eyes, that intense blue that's their defining feature, and I feel her look *into* me, reading me, searching out the heart of me until she gives a brisk nod, and I clutch onto Tommy's hand that's circling my waist.

I passed the test; I know I passed the test!

"Tommy," she says in her heavier accent, the one she never shook off despite having lived in Canada for decades before moving back to St. Petersburg. She swings her gaze over to her son, and Tommy stands taller beside me, waiting for the final verdict.

I'm starting to get dizzy from the lack of oxygen, but you know, worth it.

"When's the wedding?"

I glance down at my left hand again where the engagement ring sits, and all the wedding preparations that will have to be done in the coming year as the new decade is going to be ushered in, all of us leaving the 2010s behind.

"We're getting married in May," I say, a little breathless, trying to catch my breath once and for all. May's technically just around the corner, a little more than six months away.

And nothing's going to stop me from marrying Tommy Ivanov in May of next year.

There's wedding discussions and plans that need to be made, and my parents meeting his parents in a more formal setting in person now that they're back from their home country instead of doing it over a video call with all four us in Charlevoix, squished onto a couch with shitty Wi-Fi to get a decent call in edgewise.

Tommy holds my hand the whole time, coaxes me through the whole evening while we eat, and I try to compete with his mom with the vodka shots but tap out three shots in.

"You can get married, *myshonak*," Galina says to Tommy. "Sophie can't best me at drinking." She places her shot glass down and gives me a radiant smile. "This is a very good thing." Tommy told me that his mom is old school, and a little tricky, so when she says that to me, I'm elated.

My heart starts up again, and my blush eats up the entire real estate of my face, and Tommy's laughing his head off and so are his parents, and while I feel a little woozy and that I need to have the heartiest meal right now to soak up all the alcohol I've consumed in such a short amount of time, I find myself smiling at everyone, at everything.

"You know what?" I whisper to Tommy when his parents start talking in Russian to each other, being all cute and shit.

"What?"

"I really, really love you. Like a lot. More than vodka. Is that okay?"

"Yeah, *meelaya*. That's more than okay." Tommy kisses my nose. "You still want to do this, still want to marry me? There's going to be a lot of religious stuff to do, too."

I shrug. "I don't mind. I really, really don't. I just want to get married to you, lock you down for the rest of our lives."

"You will, you just have to wait until May. Nothing's going to stop me from getting married to you in May. Nothing."

I smile, kiss his cheek, and get back to the conversation at hand.

I'm ready, for whatever the future brings.

TWENTY-ONE

"I think I'm going to pull the trigger and I'm going to cancel the wedding," I say, feeling like I'm about to cry. "I just...it doesn't make sense right now. Not at all, not when half the people I want to be there won't be able to show up."

Elena rubs my back consolingly, and I hang my head. Katie brings me a glass of water (I can tell it's her by her red nail polish that I still need to steal sooner rather than later).

"You do what you think is best," Katie says, handing off the sparkling water, voice muffled underneath her face mask. I lift my head to see her moving back, six feet away from me. Sera's sitting six feet away from me and Elena's sitting next to me because we're trying to finish packing up all my shit for Beckett to move in finally (instead of the other way around), and for me to move in with Russia, but everything's still up in the air.

I thought, foolishly, but I still thought about it, that lockdown in Montreal would be done after two weeks, even as the positive cases spiked and spiked and *spiked*.

Elena's been working from home, teaching her kids remotely, trying to figure out how to keep a bunch of young kids engaged as spring 2020 swoops in, but none of us can go out and enjoy the nicer weather (unless you're being careful with your social distancing walks).

But now we're all sitting outside of the building in the green space where we've set up chairs, and keeping our distance from one another, everyone bringing their own blankets if they get cold, all of us keeping our distance from Sera.

I want to bawl my eyes out.

If I let myself think about it, I could get worried that this is some kind of omen that Miss Rona decided to ruin the year in which I would be getting married, that I would finally be getting that honeymoon travelling Europe and then hopping to Moscow to see the small town where Russia grew up before his family moved to Montreal.

I was going to see a part of his life, experience a part of the world that I've never been to.

And now?

Now there's nothing to look forward to. Honestly, there are people *dying* and I'm sad that I'm not getting married. Shit. How selfish can I be?

"Thanks, guys, for helping me pack as much as you were able. Sera, I wish I could hug you, but accept my ghost-hug from afar."

Sera laughs, her eyes crinkling underneath her mask, her mouth and nose covered, but I can still tell that she's smiling at me. Which is nice to know. She groans when her glasses fog up, bringing her hands up to pinch the mask down over the bridge of her nose, adjusting her glasses, sighing again when they still fog up after the adjustment.

"Shit. How am I supposed to see? Damn. I'm sorry I couldn't help as much as the others," she says, even though she hefted most of the boxes and moved them down to storage for us, keeping her distance all the while.

"Sophie, it's not like you'll never get married, but just...be safe, all right? Right now, you're not allowed social gatherings of more than fifty people, and yeah, that could change, but I hope you guys can get some of your money back..." Katie says, breathing out a sigh through her mask.

"I can't believe this is happening. Honestly. What the hell?"

"Yeah, me neither." Sera adjusts her glasses again, arms flopping down at her sides when they continue to fog up, impairing her vision. "All right, guys, I have to go and see that Matty's actually doing his schoolwork and not driving his dad crazy."

There's a tightness to her voice, a stress, a worry, and I can't imagine what it's like to be her right now when I'm having such a shitty time being *me*.

We all trudge back inside our building, Katie waving goodbye to drive back home to *her* building, the rest of us taking two different elevators because Sera's got *two* people that she lives with who are considered high-risk and she isn't taking any chances.

With a wave goodbye, her elevator closes and hikes up to the tenth floor, while Elena and I wait to go up to our own place on the sixth, moving into our emptier apartment, wondering with all the stress-eating I'm doing if I'll need to do another grocery run for us and the MacLaine-Delos household, too.

I slump onto the couch and stare unseeing at our blank TV.

"Just because you're not getting married this year doesn't mean you won't ever get married, Sophie." Elena repeats what her cousin said.

"I know, I know. It just *sucks*."

"Of course it does, of course. I know you were looking forward to it, hell, *I* was looking forward to it, all of our friends were looking forward to it. It's okay to be upset or pissed off that you don't get to do something you were looking forward to."

"I feel like an asshole most of the time; like, people are getting sick, and getting intubated, and dying, and I'm here pissed off that I don't get to get married to my fiancé. What the shit? Even if lockdown is going to be coming to a close, it doesn't mean that we're going to be able to get married in a couple of months." I sigh, nodding to myself, coming to that final decision.

"Yeah, I'm gonna speak to Russia, and we're going to send out a mass email, call as many people as possible to cancel. It's not worth it. I want people to have fun, to have a good time, dance the night away. I don't want them to be afraid to come out or worried that they might get sick. No, I'm not doing it." I sigh, having made my decision but still getting sad over it.

"Come on, let's go. We'll use my car and bring all of this leftover stuff to Russia's. Make your fiancé kiss it better."

Russia does kiss some of it better, but we make the decision and start the ball rolling by cancelling as much as we can, trying to get as much money back as possible when all of the businesses in Montreal have been hurting.

Russia's working from home, and I'm...I'm looking for my next step because I don't know what's going to happen with my job.

The shop's been closed for the past six weeks, and if we do re-open (when we're allowed to, hopefully, please God), it's going to be very different, and people are going to think twice about coming to the shop—piercings and tattoos are definitely not considered to be *essential* services by any stretch of the imagination.

It's stressful, but I've got the government benefit helping out with my bills and my nest egg won't have to be touched unless something catastrophic happens.

Which, you know, I'm not gonna tempt fate here.

No one saw corona coming, *no one*.

And here she is, changing everyone and everything.

The world has ended as we know it, and we're still here.

"This the last of it?" Tommy asks, grabbing the box from me as soon as he opens the door after my weak ass knock that I had to re-do twice, refusing to let the box down and admit weakness.

I nod, slumping forward into his arms once he takes care of the last of my stuff, a shocked laugh escaping him as I wind my arms around him and squeeze.

"This sucks and I'm sad."

"Me, too, *meelaya*, me too."

"How did this happen, why did this happen?" I ask, keeping it rhetorical. I don't expect Tommy to delve into that kind of question today, if ever. It doesn't matter how or why as long as it's *here*.

"We're going to be fine, you'll see. The vaccine will be here faster than you know it, and the people we love will be protected and we can get married."

"Yeah." I nod against his chest, lean back and pucker my lips in a silent demand for a kiss. Russia leans down, delighted, like he's never going to stop expecting this from me, demands for kisses and cuddles, like he's not used to being asked for them, like he's not used to asking them for himself either.

"We're going to be fine," I say, struggling to believe it.

I'm one of the lucky ones, I know.

There's only eight (and a half) months of 2020 left, and I've just moved in with Russia and there's a lot more questions than answers right now, but that doesn't mean it's always going to be that way.

I have one of the most important questions answered already, but still, it doesn't hurt to ask one more time, just to make sure.

"You still want to get married when all of this is over?" I ask, and Russia holds me tighter to him, looking like he's about to roll his eyes but stops himself in time.

"This again? Yes, I do. Badly. Tomorrow, if we could go to civil court and get it done, if that would make you happy."

"Would it make you happy?"

"You make me happy, being with you makes me happy. I don't care what that looks like—big wedding or not."

I think about it, just think about it, wondering if I'd be happy with Elena by my side (the witness) for our union, and our parents coming down to City Hall to watch us get married (with a bunch of other couples, too, I would guess).

It feels a little empty to me, less like a celebration and more like a rush job, a tattoo that'll always have an unfinished portion for some reason or another.

"Okay, okay," I say, ducking my head, and pressing my forehead against his heart. "Let's just...wait for now. Please."

"Of course, anything you want."

"Okay, okay. I *still* can't wait to marry you, Tommy Ivanov," I say, pressing my mouth against his heart.

"I can't wait either. I love you, you know?"

I nod, hugging him more tightly to me, scared and worried, unsure of the future, but sure of one thing. "I know."

Fin
That's it for the Fangirl Chronicles!

Want an explicit epilogue between Sophie and Russia? Get it here.

What's next? Meet the Prewitt cousins who have one hell of a holiday season when the men they least expect come barreling into their lives.
Read on for a sneak peek of Get Cuffed.

Want to stay in the know? Sign up for my newsletter here to get your free books.

GET CUFFED

O *ctober...*

"Hey, Amber?" my assistant Liz's voice rises an octave, and I know I'm in trouble.

"Yeah?" I call around a mouthful of carrot sticks, wishing they were a stack of pancakes right now.

It's mid-afternoon, I haven't eaten all day, and I packed myself rabbit food this morning, trying to preemptively curtail how many calories I'm going to be ingesting for the upcoming holiday season from *now*, and it's only mid-October.

I'm preparing so I can be ready for my aunt's world-famous (not really the world, but definitely *my* world) pumpkin pie with vanilla whipped cream, and a sprinkling of cinnamon on top that already has me drooling just at the mere thought of it.

God, I would commit a crime for a slice of that pie—if I had the whole thing to myself and didn't have to fight to the death for it against my cousins, I'd topple governments.

"Mr. Kane is coming in, after all," Liz says, her shoulders hiking up to her ears, as if I'm going to hit her, reprimand her, because she re-booked (for the *fourth* time) Brody Kane.

The Brody Kane who's a class-A dick and an overall pain in my ass.

I'd gladly kill Brody Kane for a sniff of pie, a mere whiff of it baking in the oven.

I pull in a deep, deep breath through my nose, trying to be *calm* about all of this, when really, I had my day scheduled out, time-blocked to the minute, organized to every single task I had to do today, fingers flying across the keyboard to write up my reports on each one of my patients, and now I'm here.

The rest of the day is now *ruined* 'cause Mr. Pain in my Ass Brody Kane has decided to finally grace us all with his presence.

Liz hastily grabs my coffee mug, and I'd be worried about her sloshing the coffee around if there were any left over, keeping it out of reach so I don't do something nuts like fling it across the room.

The man infuriates me, God! If he was on fire and I had a glass of water, I'd drink that bitch down.

Shit.

Brody Kane and I, we have a history, true. The kind of history that friends and family know of, but not my assistant, Liz.

She just knows the bare minimum—that we can't really stand each other and that Brody *hates*, with every single cell in his entire being, that I am the one in charge, making him do exercises, testing his flexibility, mobility of his injured leg.

A history that I, for one, wish I could erase, just completely bleach from my brain. He's honestly just come back in my life to torture me—*obviously.*

What I've done to deserve this, I just don't know.

"Will you be okay?" Liz asks, and the way she asks ticks me off, too.

Because we both know I'm all talk and no bark, unless I'm really pushed to the brink, and anything Brody Kane says or does just isn't worth my time.

You say that now, but he's going to swear at you again when you make him work on his flexibility of his injured leg, and you know it. I'm a professional, no matter how many times I commit murder in my head.

It's going to be fine.

Fine, fine, fine.

It's not fine.

Brody Kane walks in a whole half hour late to his appointment, right when I'm eating my late-afternoon snack—a Cortland apple that I just picked over the weekend and had to convince myself to eat on the whole and regular before I stuck it in a pie.

Liz comes back to my office to let me know all about that asshole showing up even though I knew it was bound to happen, and I pick up my patient file, munching on my apple until I'm almost choking, wiping my face and sticky fingers before exiting my office and heading back towards the open-space area where we do most of our rehabilitation.

I want Brody Kane to not even notice my space, not to even look at it in case he contaminates it with his shit (and entitled) mood.

It's amazing that no one's lost it on him and brought him down a peg or two, honestly.

It's not gonna be me, that's for sure.

We have another twelve weeks of this, these stupid power plays—which brings us to just past Christmas (God, I've gotta put up with *this* until after Christmas?).

I can handle it, I'm a professional and I will not kill one of my patients, no matter how much his attitude is begging me to.

I chew on my last bite, pull myself to my full height, straighten my posture and get ready to rumble.

Brody Kane used to be pretty, back in the day. Soot-black eyelashes contrasting with his icy blue eyes, the kind that are clear and cold, the bronze skin, the kissable lips, the sharp jawline, it was all meant to devastate any high school girl and boy who took a single look at him and lost their collective shit. His cells, they recombined so beautifully, the way his muscle and flesh settled over his bones hit the DNA jackpot. But now?

Now?

Brody Kane has lost that roundness to his cheeks, the brightness in his blue eyes that I'd call innocence if I were looking for the right word. Those eyes are now steely when they look me over, sweeping me up and down, and there's a split-second almost-reaction where I want to cover myself.

I'm pretty sure he X-rayed me with those killer eyes of his and figured out the color of my underwear, like he knows about my body piercings, the tattoo curling around my thigh underneath my work-appropriate pants, down to the sneakers I'm wearing, knowing I'm going to have to demonstrate some things, and heels aren't really all that good for my balance to begin with.

I need all the balance I can get when I look at him, the inky black hair, the way it looks with those steely eyes, and then there's the rest of him, and if I let myself think about the rest of him, I'm going to swoon right here, or drop whatever I'm holding while my brain sits and buffers while I process *this* level of hotness.

Too bad he's such a dick though.

Too bad, too bad.

And I honestly wouldn't repeat that mistake again...

Nope, not me.

Not gonna happen.

It still happens though, feeling like I've gotten a brick to the back of the head at the mere sight of him, and he's not even wearing anything super nice—but maybe that's the clincher, he's just wearing a look that screams *boyfriend*, giving me the image of a cuddly boyfriend ready for me with open arms—until he opens his mouth.

"You're late," he says, glancing down at his expensive watch—the only reason why I know it's expensive is because I Googled something close to it. He looks down at my Louboutins (sneakers) and shrugs—like he can't get those seconds back that it took me to walk from my office to the rehab room. *Right.*

I don't say anything, ignoring the burn of indignation sitting at the back of my throat, wanting to spill out in harsh words. It's fine, I'll run on the treadmill after, pump some weights, whatever to get my mind off of him.

It's literally the third time we've seen each other, and I need alternative methods to cope with him as part of my day.

I nod, gesturing to the rolling chair (wheels locked, of course), for him to take a seat while I remain standing, and flip open his patient chart on my McGill clipboard and pretend to re-familiarize myself with his injuries.

"I thought you would have memorized that by now," Brody says, voice a little raspier from how I remember it, different and yet not.

I ignore him, running my tongue over my teeth, glancing down at my methodical notes. "I have a lot of patients, Mr. Kane," I say, off-handedly, flipping through the pages. "How's the level of pain?"

"Fucking awful," he says immediately, and I fight, I fight *hard* to not roll my eyes.

Not that I don't believe he's in pain. I wouldn't be able to do what I do if I couldn't tell when a person's in actual pain or not, if their body has reached their limit for the day. Hell, I didn't go to school for a million years and all those clinical hours to *not* be sensitive to someone else's pain thresholds—and that they're all different, depending on the day, time of day, and hell, what kind of food they've eaten.

I get it, I do.

It's just I can't really stand when someone's late—it's such gross disrespect for the person waiting for you, a middle finger up the nose that your time just isn't as important as theirs, and it definitely shows what kind of person you are if you're habitually late, without telling the other party why.

"We're going to try to do some front-loaded squats today..."

Brody looks like he wants to kill me, maintaining eye contact now for seconds too long, and I know enough to say that he's definitely not attracted to me anymore, so yeah, that prolonged stare? Summed up in one word—murderous.

"We're not doing any weights or anything, I just want to see if your flexibility has improved since the surgery."

"I don't know why you make me sit if I'm just going to be standing," he huffs, annoyed, voice clipped and sharp, like tiny stinging bees along my skin.

Sitting in a chair is basically a squat position, except you get to rest in that seated position.

I watch him stand up carefully, favoring his bad leg, getting himself upright before moving a few steps away from the locked-in-place chair. He makes a show of tying another knot at the waist of his sweatpants, and I resolutely keep my eyes pinned to his face.

It's not like I don't know what his body looks like, but when I knew him, his body was closer to that of a boy's, when we were together that very first time, and now? It's all *man*, and I hold the stare until my eyes begin to water, watching him blink first and only then do I do victory laps inside my head.

It's the small wins, sometimes. It all counts.

I'm sworn at a total of fifty times with no exaggeration involved. Fine, maybe just a little. And maybe those expletives weren't directed at *me*, per se, just in the general vicinity of my person, but it still pisses me off. He's got the dirtiest mouth of all my clients/patients, and I see everyone, male, female, intersex, cis or trans, from the ages of eighteen to eighty-nine years old (Mrs. Murphy is the absolute cutest and I want to be exactly like her when I grow up).

We finish our two-hour-long session with flexibility moves and slowly increase his range of motion before his frustration finally peaks and he gives up.

"Are we at the end?" I ask, making sure, wanting to verbally check with him and then carefully dissuade him from doing anything else. We're at the tipping point where the good kind of pain can change rather quickly to the bad kind of pain, and he's already made excellent progress (despite being a total dick) three weeks out from major knee surgery.

It's like looking at a stranger, the way he looks at me, teeth bared in a snarl, face a grimace of pain, his eyes squeezing shut to get that one more, elusive rep, before he collapses onto his back and just lets himself breathe.

I hate this part, I really do. I'm going to have to work on his hip flexors and we're going to have to get *close*, the kind of close that I never thought I'd be with him ever again, and yet, here we are.

I'm almost afraid to touch him, and steadily move my mind to that blank place where he's just another patient that I don't really know, and I have a job to do, to get him better so he can eventually get out of my hair and go do what he was doing in the first place before he came back to Montreal.

"Are we not going to talk about it?" Brody asks on a hiss as I come down to the padded flooring on my hands and knees, alongside his mat.

"I'm going to grab your left leg now," I say. "I'm going to support your knee and gently stretch out your hip flexors, if that's okay with you." I wait for him to give me his permission to touch him, my hands on my thighs, my knees on the floor as I watch him, doing the world's best impersonation of a starfish on the floor in front of me.

Brody nods to himself, shutting his eyes against the bright, bright lights. The days are getting darker more quickly now, and the artificial lighting makes everything worse. "We're not going to talk about it. Typical Amber."

I bite down, clenching my jaw hard. I ignore the flicker of pain in my chest, the little stab of hurt that I'm being reminded of a past we could have shared, that could have brought us into the future, together.

But we just weren't meant to be, and that's the way the cookie crumbles sometimes, and I'm not about to pick up the crumbs. I have some dignity.

What dignity? You're so lonely, you looked up how to get a platonic cuddler to help you fall asleep just last weekend.

And then Vick and Max came over and we had a cuddle pile and watched sad movies and bawled our eyes out. It was great, super cathartic and everything.

"Are you ready to begin?" I ask, prompting him to answer me, the kind of answer I requested.

Brody nods, then lets out a pained sigh when I place my hands on his left leg—the better one of the two, but unfortunately not his dominant leg——and get to work, slowly opening the hip flexors, working painstakingly slow to keep the injury from getting worse, concentrating on the feel of his leg and the socket I'm working on.

I can't afford to be distracted by his beauty, by the way that if I glance over at his face, those icy blue eyes are slits, and my brain hopscotches over to an old scene, an old favorite, where Brody and I gave our virginities to one another, on my eighteenth birthday.

I clear my throat and ask, "How's that? How does that feel on a scale of one to ten, ten being unbearable?"

"You're a lot quieter than you used to be," Brody comments, and the eye roll escapes me before I can clamp down on the urge. He snorts, and I glance down at him, his lips shaped into a grin, showing off that chipped incisor tooth that he never got fixed. I remember the feeling of it against my skin, little nibbles and bites and *whoa, horsey.*

"I'm working, Brody, and so should you be. Scale of one to ten?"

There's sweat at the back of my neck and his nostrils flare as if he can smell it. Weirdo.

"It's a seven moving up to an eight," he says, and I gently, carefully fully extend his left leg all the way down back onto the mat and then practically crawl over to the other side of his body so I can get at his right leg.

He swears again, a murmured *"fuck"* that I tune out as I position myself at his side, glancing down at his right leg now, and slowly put my hands on him to get to work.

"I want another PT," he groans, and we haven't even really started yet.

"What?" I nearly drop his leg before I can be mindful of it and place it gently back down onto the mat underneath his body. I frown, eyebrows pulled down low. "Are you making comments about how seriously I take my job? Really? *You?*"

Brody pretends to pat at his chest, but we both know he doesn't have a heart, not really, just a dank, old cave where things go to die, I'm sure of it.

"You're hurting me, princess, right here," he says, patting at his chest. It's a callback, to way back when, when I thought that shit was cute.

It's definitely not cute anymore. We're too old for that shit.

Princesses have to follow the rules, and an empress makes her own.

I raise an eyebrow. "Are you being a misogynist right now?" Like he'd admit it to my face, or anywhere, for that matter. "Are you doubting my capability as a PT, or is it 'cause I have a vagina and tits that offends you so much?" I shouldn't be talking like this, *I shouldn't be talking like this,* but there's just something about him that makes my skin itchy, all too tight over my bones and I can't *settle* and just take it.

We've come far in the world, but apparently not far enough.

If he makes a kitchen joke, I'm going to throttle him. I can do it, too, especially in his prone position. Liz can cover for me, and all I gotta do is call Vick and Max and they'll help me dispose of the body.

"Why the fuck are you looking at me like that?" he asks, rearing back as much as he can, scooting back a little, trying to put distance between us.

I guess I was broadcasting *that* particular thought too loudly.

Heh heh.

Take that, asshole.

"Amber, why the fuck are you looking at me like that. I didn't even say anything close to that!" His voice goes higher in pitch and for a split second, I think he's actually afraid of me right now.

I grin like a maniac, and Brody let's out a pained wheeze.

"Let's get you set up for your next appointment, yeah? Or would you like to be seen by another PT?" I say, getting up to my feet, holding a hand out to help him up, his palm slick against mine from all the sweating he's been doing, some of it from exertion, some of it from plain old frustration.

Brody gets to his feet after accepting my hand and my little grunt as I lean back to pull him to his feet, his sigh world-weary. "No, of course not. I didn't mean anything by it. Sorry."

If my eyeballs weren't stuck to the inside of my head right now, they'd have fallen out with how much they're bugging out.

Brody Kane? Apologizing? *To me?*

What kind of world are we living in? Has the apocalypse happened without my knowing it? Is there fire and brimstone outside?

Nope, just an October evening, the sky getting darker and darker until there's nothing left on the horizon.

"We'll get you set up with another appointment then. You can head out to reception and my assistant will let me know what you decide."

I watch him waffle, his beautiful face impassive as he blinks the sweat out of his eyes, his blue eyes practically glowing.

"I'll do that. Thank you."

I practically rear back from the force of my surprise, but keep my feet planted. I want to ask if he's gotten some bad news, if he's gotten sick, something—Brody Kane has been a pain in my ass ever since he got back into town.

I have the unique misfortune of my parents being best friends with *his* parents (seriously, they all went to high school together and the friendship never died, just got transferred to the kids), so I *always* knew what he was up to, how he was doing, his accomplishments.

He's been back in Montreal for something like six weeks, and there's been whispers down the grapevine about him relocating back home, professional lacrosse dreams crushed, winning the World Championships for Team Canada going up in smoke.

He moved out of province, but I was never really allowed to forget about him.

And now he's thanking me?

Yeah, right.

I nod instead, gathering his patient chart and exiting first, walking back to my office without looking back, without noticing anything else about him that crosses the patient-doctor line.

"I'll see you at dinner tonight?" Brody Kane *asks* it like a question, but it's more like a confirmation of my deepening suspicions throughout the day, the curdle in my belly, the dread weighing me down since eight a.m. this morning, my mom's phone call seemingly out of place and definitely suspicious.

Mom can't lie to save her life, and I *knew,* deep down in my lizard brain, that something like this was going to happen now that he's back—my parents (and his parents, probably) trying to be matchmakers.

I'd rather take a flying leap off the building's roof, break both my legs and spend the night in the hospital.

I don't dignify his answer with a response but keep walking and shut the door to my office firmly.

His laugh chases me all the way inside, and I can almost hear him as he heads towards reception.

Great, just great.

*You can pre-order Get Cuffed **here**.*

ABOUT THE AUTHOR

C.M. Kars lives in Montreal, Quebec, Canada where they speak French and say more than *voulez-vous coucher avec moi ce soir?* (I didn't just ask you that, I was just trying to make a point).

Never Say Never is the final book in *The Fangirl Chronicles* and she really hopes you like it a whole lot.

LEAVE A REVIEW: You know what to do now, right? Tell a friend! If you liked this book, please consider leaving a review **here**.

A whole tube of Colourpop's Roller Gloss in Pineapple Punch was used up in the creation of this novel.

If you would like to keep up with me/ask me questions, you can contact me at: cmk (at) authorcmkars (dot) com, find me on Facebook, or on Bookbub.

This concludes The Fangirl Chronicles, but like the title of this book, I never say never, so who knows? Maybe some day in the future I could add more to this series.

Did you miss Sera, Hunter, and Matty and the rest of the gang? I did, too. I'll have some news for you soon on upcoming projects, I promise. Sign up for the newsletter to stay in the know!